Ghostboy, Chameleon and the Duke of Graffiti

OLIVIA WILDENSTEIN

Chapter One

In retrospect, spray-painting an enormous white penis on Principal Matthews's Volvo woodie was not the idea of the century.

"What's gotten into you, Duke?" my mother yelled the second she burst into the principal's office.

I cringed. She hadn't taken the time to change out of her tennis clothes.

"I'm so angry! Your father's coming home early tonight to have a word with you."

Crap. My father never came home early.

My mother dropped into the free chair facing Principal Matthews's desk. There were so many coats of polish on it that I could see his clenched jaw without having to look up.

"Mr. Matthews, we'll take care of the damages. I'll have my husband's driver pick up your car this afternoon. If you could just give me the keys."

"That's kind of you, Mrs. Meyer," he said, "but I need to get home."

"I arranged for a rental. It'll be in the parking lot this afternoon."

His jaw loosened a little. That was a good sign. *Right?*

"You've thought of everything," he mused.

His eyes fixed me; they were very light, nearly see-through. I'd never looked at him that close, not even when he'd found me with the canister of white paint still poised in midair. I'd noticed his skin tone changing from pale to red though.

"Is there any way we could keep this off Duke's record?" Mom asked.

I suspected my principal wouldn't agree to it; the man was a stickler about rules and good behavior. He probably filed his taxes ahead of time.

"It would go against our institution's policy to falsify records. However…"

My mother leaned forward so abruptly I thought she might fall off her chair.

"If Duke puts in one hour of community service after school for a month, I'm willing to write that it was a misconstrued art project. Does that sound fair, Duke?"

I gaped at him. *A month!*

"Duke?" he repeated.

"He'll be free after school every day for however many hours you need him," Mom said.

I bit down on my lip. *Great. There goes my social life.* "But I have basketball practice on Tuesdays and Thurs—"

"You won't be playing for a while," Mom snapped.

"But the championship's mid-May."

"You should've thought about that sooner. And you can forget about playing on the weekends too," she added. "Actions have consequences. You're also grounded for the next four weeks at home."

I gasped but didn't argue for fear of her extending my sentence to my seventeenth birthday, or my eighteenth. "What sort of community service am I going to be doing?" I muttered.

"You'll be helping Mr. Darcy."

"Help him do what?" I snorted. "Clean the school?"

When he said, "Yes," Mom sat up much straighter.

A Meyer janitor—I doubted there'd ever been one in our family. I nearly smirked at the thought. Nearly, because the reality was that my buddies were going to have a field day with my new line of work. Plus spending time with the janitor wouldn't earn me popularity points at Francis Academy. Not that I had to earn any. My two best friends and I ran the sophomores. *Okay*, maybe we didn't run them, but we were the guys every girl wanted to date and every guy wanted to hang out with.

My mother squirmed in her seat. "Is there any other job you could offer Duke? Perhaps some accounting or—"

"No."

Her green eyes and newly Botoxed lips rounded into large Os. I could see the wheels spinning full speed in her head. What would she tell her friends? What would she tell my grandma? Actually, Grandma Preiss would probably get a kick out of my predicament. I rolled up the sleeves of my white shirt. Even with the fan blasting the office, it was hot, which was unusual for the month of March in Connecticut.

"You can start this afternoon." Mr. Matthews stood up, adjourning our meeting. "Mr. Darcy will be waiting for you in the teachers' lounge."

While my mother shook hands and pocketed the car keys, I headed for the door and drew it open. She flew past me, blond ponytail swishing furiously all the way down the stairs. I walked her out to the parking lot where her dark green Maserati was parked across two spaces.

"I'm sorry," I told her, as she flung her door wide.

"I should hope so. What got into you?" she exclaimed.

"It was just a stupid dare," I said.

"Who dared you?"

Since I couldn't tell her who'd dared me—because I'd taken an oath of secrecy—I said, "It doesn't matter."

She folded her arms. "It matters to me. Was it Owen? If it was, I'm going to have a word with his mother."

"It wasn't Owen," I said.

"Then who?"

"Let it go."

"Let it go? Someone made my son do something stupid, and you want me to let it go? I will absolutely *not* let it go! Give me a name."

"Why?"

"Because I think your friend is as responsible and should suffer the same *consequences*. I won't have my son be the only one picking up trash!"

"*Whoa...*Mom, relax. It'll be fine."

"Don't tell me to relax! I'm furious! So furious!"

I placed both my palms on her shoulders. "On the upside, it'll make a good essay topic for my college applications," I said, mainly to calm her down. I wasn't delusional. The next month would suck.

Mom sniffled.

"Don't cry."

A few tears plopped out, so I hugged her.

"I promise it won't happen again."

And it wouldn't, because I would never get a second chance to join the Alphas.

Chapter Two

On my way to the teachers' lounge at the end of the day, I began planning how to redeem myself to shorten my punishment. In my daze, I walked right past the rec room and had to double back.

The door was open. Instead of knocking, I cleared my throat. "Reporting for duty, Mr. Darcy."

As he made his way toward me, he tightened his brown ponytail. He resembled a hippy past his prime, which had earned him the nickname of Shagdar, a mixture of Shaggy and Darcy. Owen had come up with it last year. Not only had it spread, but it had also stuck.

"Nearly on time," he said.

I was one minute late.

"So what's the plan for today?"

"The plan for today, Mr. Meyer," Shagdar said, "is to scour the school grounds. The quad's filthy. Wrappers and soda cans everywhere."

I rubbed the back of my neck.

"I hope you don't find that beneath you." He cocked a bushy eyebrow. "The garbage pick and trash bags are in the closet next to the girls' bathroom. Ground floor."

I nodded and turned to go.

"You might want to change into something more comfortable," he called after me. "Wouldn't want to get grass stains on your uniform now."

"Can I wear my sports clothes?"

He nodded. "Hurry up. You're wasting time."

My plan all along. As I pushed through the doors of the locker room, I ran into Owen and Gabe, who were changing for basketball.

"Are you hiding from Shagdar?" Gabe asked, tying his sneaker laces.

I made a face. "You heard?"

"Yup. You're his bitch for the month," Owen said, guffawing.

I glared at my friend, and then past him, into his gym locker. His bag seemed to have exploded inside. That was Owen—messiest guy alive. I'd never seen the color of the carpet in his room—in spite of the squadron of housekeepers his parents employed—and I had spent many afternoons holed up in there, playing *Lands of the Fae.*

"I'm not hiding. I'm changing," I said, unbuttoning my shirt with the academy's eagle crest.

Gabe smiled, displaying what looked like an abnormal amount of pearly whites. "Did Shagdar lend you a pair of blue overalls?"

"Shut up," I said.

Owen grinned. He reminded me of the largemouth bass we caught last summer off the dock of his ridiculous mansion on Long Island Sound. "I still can't believe you got busted."

"Why?" I grumbled. "You two idiots were staring at Liane's rack instead of watching my back."

"She has a seriously nice rack," he said, running his freckled fingers through his orangey-blond hair. He was of Irish descent and had his ancestral countrymen's paleness, which contrasted sharply with Gabe's black skin.

"That's so not the point," I said as I rolled my pants off.

"So what's Mr. Darcy having you do?" Gabe asked, rising from the bench and stretching his legs.

"I have to clean the quad."

"Ouch."

The sound of the coach's whistle reverberated through the locker room.

"Gotta go," Owen said. "Have fun."

"Yeah right," I grunted.

As he slipped past me, he dropped his voice and whispered, "They're giving you a second chance."

"What?" I squeaked. I cleared my throat. "Why?"

Owen opened his mouth, shut it, and then opened it again, "Because you didn't talk." I had a feeling that wasn't the reason, but hey, I had a second chance. I didn't care how I'd gotten it.

Relief spread through me like dye in water, but it was instantly replaced by panic. What if I got caught next time as well? I would be expelled and my parents would cart me off to an all-boys' boarding school. My life would be over.

"Don't break a nail out there," Gabe said, winking as he left.

I really wanted to become a part of the Alphas, Francis Academy's exclusive, century-old club, which usually only recruited juniors and seniors. This year, they'd wanted Gabe because his father was running for governor of Connecticut; and they'd wanted Owen because his parents owned the largest, most expensive property in Greenwich, and because his older brother was already a member. They hadn't especially wanted me, but my friends had tapped me, and the Alphas had given me a chance. I'd blown it by getting caught. Stealth was the Alphas' motto.

In my blue gym shorts and white tee, I slunk out of the locker room toward the cluttered janitorial closet and rifled through it for my tools. The junior football team was training by the time I emerged on the field, which offered a nice distraction from plucking plastic wrappers and empty soda cans off the bleachers. I didn't play football because I wanted to avoid concussions and broken noses. Anyway, my height would've been wasted on that sport. Basketball was my calling.

A few of the guys waved to me during their water break and smirked at the sight of my *tools*. I just shrugged and bore my cross, reminding myself that I had a second chance, and that when I was inducted, no one would snicker. Not even Goth Girl perched on the top bleacher, whose black lips were tilted up in mockery. I held her gaze and waited stubbornly for her to break the connection. Just when I thought she wouldn't, she scowled and looked away.

Chapter Three

Liane, Francis Academy's head cheerleader, tossed her pink backpack on her desk and walked toward Gabe, Owen, and me. Unless our teachers forced us apart, the three of us were always packed together in the last row of every classroom. We'd sat together since we became friends back in middle school.

"Hi, boys," Liane said. Her voice was like a gust of air, weightless, as though she breathed after every word.

"Whassup?" Owen said. At times, he spoke like one of those dope dealers on Arcadia Street. Considering his family's wealth stretched back to the founding of Fairfield County, his speech habits were comical.

"My parents are going away this weekend and I'm throwing a pool party to celebrate. I was hoping you boys could make it," she said-breathed. I still wasn't certain how she got that much air between each word.

"Sweet," Owen told Liane's boobs.

She didn't seem to mind.

"We'll be there," Gabe said.

"Six o'clock on Saturday. The dress code is beachwear," she said and winked.

"Well, that sounds like fun," I said, as I fished my notebook and my copy of *Othello* out of my black messenger bag. "You'll have to send me some footage."

"Aren't you coming?" Owen asked, reverting back to normal English.

"Can't. I'm grounded, remember?" I said. "No basketball, no video games, no parties."

Maybe if I told my father why I got into trouble, he would take pity. Then again, rule number two of the Alphas was secrecy. No one outside the brotherhood could know the members' identities. If I broke rule number two, I wouldn't get my second chance. I would be out. I didn't want to be out. Especially not now that my best friends were in.

"Maybe you could sneak out. I'm sure Grandma P. would cover for you," Owen said.

"That's a thought." But if my parents found out, they'd check Grandma into a fancy retirement home. I liked having her around. "I'll see," I said, although I'd already made up my mind about not involving her.

Our scatter-brained, thirty-something English teacher, Miss Brown, erupted into the classroom, dropping a few books on her way to her big wooden desk. She heaved her satchel to the floor and returned to the path of mayhem, squatting to round up the toppled books.

"Everyone, take out a sheet of paper and a pen," she said, stacking everything haphazardly on her desk.

I would never admit this to any living being, but her class was my favorite, partly because I loved English and writing, and partly because her assignments were original and fun.

Turning to the blackboard, she grabbed a piece of white chalk and scraped: "Being a rock star is difficult, especially during an alien invasion…"

"Now, I want you all to begin with this prompt, but use Shakespeare's writing style."

A collective groan erupted around the classroom. I didn't

groan but I made sure to chew on my lip to mask my eagerness. Miss Brown rubbed her hands together, and a cloud of white dust materialized from her palms. Flecks landed on her black skintight sweater, which gave me an idea for the scene I was about to write.

Gabe accompanied me that afternoon as I changed into a pair of cargo shorts and a tee. He wasn't hanging out with me out of the goodness of his heart. He was waiting to see our college counselor. Not that I needed company. I had earphones and my cell was packed with music.

He sat on the bench next to me, reading out an article about his dad's campaign. "The journalist calls him 'the entrepreneur who wants to give back,'" he said. "My dad's a capitalist, not a fucking communist. God, journalists are shit. Don't they check their facts?"

"Generosity, not cupidity, will get your dad elected."

"*Cupi-what?* You and your SAT words."

"Shoot me. I like nice words."

"What does it even mean?"

"It means being greedy," I said.

Gabe grunted. "Whatever. Anyway, I think people have a right to know what sort of politician they're voting for. If they elect my father thinking he's going to give handouts, they'll be royally pissed."

"You don't even like politics."

"I might not like them, but until I can move out of Connecticut, I'll be mixed up in them."

"Unless you emancipate yourself, you'll always be tied up in them," I added, tying my sneaker laces.

"Dude, your feet are huge," he said, changing the subject.

"You know what big feet mean?" I said, giving him a sly grin.

He cracked a smile. "Get over yourself."

As we walked back out into the deserted school hallways lined with steel-blue lockers, I asked him, "When's my second chance?"

Gabe's eyes widened. "Keep your voice down."

"When is it?"

"In a month."

"What will I have to do?"

"Don't know."

"Can you find out for me?"

"I'll try once I'm inducted."

His initiation ceremony would be held soon. He would receive the gold-and-ruby cuff links and the burgundy velvet blazer. I'd never coveted clothing and jewels until I heard of the Alphas. Now, I dreamed of the day they would be bestowed upon me.

"*Ugh.* It's time. Gotta go," he said, checking his bulky chrome-and-rubber wristwatch—his parents' present for his sixteenth birthday.

My parents' birthday present to me had been autographed first editions of my favorite fantasy series, *The Pursuit of Kings*. I wouldn't have minded a nice watch, but the books were cool.

"See you tomorrow," he said, sauntering up the large wooden staircase.

I collected my tools from Mr. Darcy's closet and headed out to the field. There was no game, but it wasn't deserted. Weird Goth Girl was there, perched on the top bleacher like a vulture searching for its next victim. Well, I wouldn't be Cora Matthews's victim. *Yes,* Matthews, as in Principal Matthews, as in his daughter. That was her ticket into our private establishment. The board, composed of former students and a bunch of parents, would never have welcomed a girl like her, a girl who painted her face white and black, and sported piercings all over her eyebrows. Rumor was she'd sliced her tongue lengthwise to resemble a viper. I didn't know if that was true, but even without the forked tongue, Cora was one odd girl.

As I climbed up the bleachers, I tried to picture her without makeup and facial jewelry, but it was like attempting to decipher a car's paint job from a black-and-white picture. The only thing remotely attractive about her was her long, shiny black hair. As I swept the back row, I glanced at her. She was reading a book, so I thought it was safe to study her. Dumb assumption.

She caught me staring and her mouth moved. I frowned. Surely, she wasn't addressing me. Still, I popped out one of my earphones.

"What are you looking at?" she snapped.

I plugged my earphone back in and lumbered down to the next row and then the next, pretending she hadn't just spoken to me and I hadn't just stopped to listen like an idiot. I could feel her dark gaze still on me.

This time, I took out my earphones and asked, "You see something you like?"

Those large, haunting eyes of hers turned back to her yellowed copy of *Wuthering Heights*. "I'm not into pretty boys."

Good. I wasn't into weird girls.

Chapter Four

It had been raining all morning, so no one hung outside for lunch. The whole student body was packed inside the black marble cafeteria, which had been a ballroom when our school had been a private home in the early eighteen hundreds. To this day, it remained one of the only spaces not decorated with linoleum and eggshell paint, which made the plywood tables and steel chairs stick out like eyesores.

"Maybe you're off for the day," Gabe said, slurping down a carton of chocolate milk.

My heart thumped at the thought, even though I was convinced Mr. Darcy would find me something to clean indoors. Maybe I would be on mopping duty, or maybe I would have to rearrange his closet of novelties. I wrinkled my nose. At least when I cleared the quad of garbage, I got fresh air. The air inside the school was stale.

"You're awfully quiet," he said.

Was I? "What if he has me clean the urinals?"

He placed both forearms on the table. "Shagdar wouldn't. You'll probably have to wash the windows or something."

"I haven't done that since I was eleven," I said.

"You cleaned a window at eleven?"

"Remember that day we stuck chewing gum against the one in my room?"

He smiled. "Yeah, I remember."

"Well, after you two bozos left, Mom saw the gum and made me scrub it off."

"Fun times."

"Yeah," I grunted. "A real blast. Took me over an hour."

"Seriously? At that speed, Shagdar will ask Principal Matthews to double your sentence."

"Don't give him any ideas," I said, looking around the packed cafeteria. "Where's Owen?"

"Talking to the coach about scheduling more training before the championship. You'll make some games, right?"

"I have to." I needed to find a way to sneak basketball in without my parents noticing. I tried to come up with one but became distracted when a freshman girl tripped over some junior's outstretched feet and sent a slice of pizza flying straight into Liane's chest. "Classic," I said, chuckling.

Face as red as her fresh tomato stain, Liane jumped out of her seat and cursed out the poor girl.

Gabe was grinning. "Maybe I should tell her to run."

Just as he said that, the girl fled the cafeteria, tears streaming down her cheeks.

"She figured it out," I said.

"Yo, Liane. You want me to lick your top clean?" someone yelled.

Liane glowered and trotted out of the cafeteria, flanked by her friends.

"Most entertaining lunch I've had in a while," I said, gathering up my stuff.

By the time I made it out, the girls were filing into the bathroom. All of them. I always wondered if they had couches and magazines in there. Otherwise, it had to be boring as hell.

I made my way to the teachers' lounge, where I found our janitor having lunch with Miss Brown. They seemed odd together. Miss Brown was pretty—in a chaotic way; Mr. Darcy looked greasy and undernourished. I stayed in the doorway and knocked on the open door. The custodian glanced up.

"Um, do I have to clean this afternoon?" I asked.

"Yes," he said. "And you'll even have a partner."

"Who?"

"Just be here at three thirty."

"Okay," I said, and left, wondering who landed in the principal's bad books.

I thought it was Owen, but he said no. I asked the other usual suspects, but none of them were in trouble.

When I walked up to the teachers' lounge that afternoon, I froze and gaped at my partner. Cora was leaning next to the entrance, one black boot planted on the wall, red shoelaces undone.

"*You* got detention?" I asked.

She glared at me.

"Doesn't being the principal's daughter afford some privileges?"

"You obviously don't know my father."

"What did you do?"

"I had a disagreement in the locker room."

I smirked. "I'm sorry I missed it. What about?"

One of Cora's eyes closed a little. "Oh, you know, girl stuff." She smiled sweetly at me, but it was one of those phony smiles. I could tell because my dad was a pro at them. He usually addressed his widest grins to the people he liked the least.

"Did someone suggest makeup remover?" I asked.

The smile snapped right off her face. "Screw you, Meyer," she said just as Shagdar arrived.

He fixed the two of us with a narrowed gaze. His eyes were already freakishly close together. If he tapered them anymore, they would collide against the bridge of his thin nose. "Cora, is Duke giving you trouble?"

"I'm fine," she muttered.

"You sure?"

"Yes!" she said.

Shagdar didn't ask her a third time. Instead, he gave us our assignment, which was…*drumroll*…window washing. Gabe was psychic.

"I call the second floor," she said. "I'll grab the supplies from the closet up there." She ripped past me and dashed up the stairs.

The air wobbled with her scent. It reminded me of the roses my mother grew on the trellises nailed to our house's brick walls —wild and flowery. I frowned. I'd expected her to smell cold and sterile, like antiseptic or metal.

"Cora!" Shagdar called out, but she was already gone. He watched the stairs for a second before turning back to me, a stricken expression suspended on his face. He was probably sad she was so messed up. "What are *you* still doing here? First floor. Now. The supply closet's at the end of the hallway."

As I trod up the stairs, I wondered if I would run into her again. I kind of wanted to, if just to solve her. When I got to the first floor landing though, I thought better of pursuing my macabre fascination and jogged to the supply closet.

I thought about the enigma that was Cora Matthews all day on Friday. I didn't see her around school, and she was no longer grounded that afternoon. It was just me and my pick.

During Shabbat dinner that night, I asked my parents if I could swing by Gabe's house the next evening. In truth, I was planning on stopping by Liane's party. At the beginning of the week, I'd been okay with the whole no social-life-for-a-month situation, but that was Tuesday. If I didn't leave my house soon, I would die of boredom.

"No," my mother said, between bites of salad.

She wiped the dressing off her plumped lips. I wasn't sure

why she used Botox or why Dad let her. Mom was pretty. She'd been a model back in the day.

"I need to study for a political science exam, and I was thinking I could ask Mr. Turner—"

"I thought Gabe's father was in New York this weekend for a fundraiser. Isn't that what Myra told you at the club, honey?" Dad asked Mom.

I tried to appear stunned at the news. Granted, it was the first I'd heard of it, but still, I'd lied and would be caught if I didn't at least feign innocence.

My mother nodded, fixing me with her green eyes as though trying to see through me—she usually managed.

"Why don't you have him come over here? Especially if he's alone all weekend," Dad said in his deep, booming voice.

"But, Michael," Mom exclaimed, "that defeats the purpose of Duke's punishment."

"Oh, right," he said.

"Give Duke a break," Grandma said, placing her hand on top of mine. Her skin felt like parchment, soft and paper thin. "He's a good kid."

"Thanks, Grams," I murmured.

She smiled, her creased face contorting. Unlike my mother, she was staunchly opposed to plastic surgery.

"He drew a...a..." My mother's cheeks flamed, which would have made me chuckle had I not suspected I would be grounded for life. "He vandalized private property."

"Did you happen to snap a picture?" Grandma asked me.

"Mother!"

"What? *I* thought it was funny," she said.

"Then maybe you should've paid for the car's paint job. Five hundred dollars!" Dad's voice crackled like a gramophone.

I'd read somewhere that deep voices inspired respect and confidence, and conferred leadership. When mine broke at thirteen, I'd hoped to develop the same baritone as my dad, but it never happened. My voice wasn't high-pitched, but it wasn't deep. Even Cora's was deeper, raspier.

"He said he was sorry," Grandma said. "And should I remind you both that you did some pretty naughty things in your time. Remember when I caught you—"

"Mom, please." My mother cupped her wineglass and took a long gulp. "This conversation is about Duke, not about Michael and me." After another sip, she set down her wine glass and sighed. "How about you ask Gabe to come over h—"

Dad placed his elbows on the white tablecloth and said, "No."

The point was to go to a party, not hang out with Gabe at my house anyway. I toyed with my napkin ring—a coiled gold branch.

"I'm sorry, Duke, but what you did was horrendous," Dad said.

I didn't think drawing a cartoonish-looking wang qualified as horrendous. Pointing this out wouldn't help my case though.

"I don't want you to run with the wrong crowd," Mom added. "This is why we pay a fortune to put you in this school. So you can meet good people. So you can become a good person."

I wondered if I should tell her that money didn't make people good; it made people rich. I shoved some brisket inside my mouth and swallowed, propelling my frustration down along with the meat.

"He's not some hooligan, sweetie. He's a kid," Grams said.

Dad sighed. It resonated in his sizable ribcage. "Rules are rules, and you broke one. End of story."

He was wrong.

Not about the rule-part; about the end part. This story was just beginning. The plot: Duke Meyer aka Cool Kid is on his way to becoming Duke Who? Maybe I'd even become friends with Goth Girl.

Yuck. I wobbled my head to get rid of that dismal thought.

Chapter Five

"I swear, if you mention Liane's name and the word 'tits' in the same sentence again, I'm going to cut off your ball sack," I told Owen on Monday during lunch.

We were sitting on the bleachers, showered by the blindingly hot April sun, talking about the pool party I didn't get to go to.

"What crawled up your ass?" he asked me.

"He's just pissed he didn't see them," Gabe said, picking at his lasagna.

Was I? Was that why I was being a dick? "Are you guys officially hooking up?"

"Officially hooking up? Where do you come up with that shit?" Owen gave me his largemouth bass smile. "You bet your pretty ass we're dating."

"Dating?" Gabe mused. "Is that what you call groping and slobbering all over each other?"

Owen smacked him.

"What about you, Gabe?" I asked.

There was a gleam in his light brown eyes. "I'm a politician's son. I have to act respectably." He winked. "I looked but I didn't touch."

"Who was the object of your *respectable* attention?" I asked him.

His gaze locked on the cheerleaders who were lounging on a bench a few rows below us. Of course.

"Which one?" I asked.

Liane stood up and headed our way.

"Cassie," he said just before Liane made it to us. "Hi, L."

"Hi, boys." She swooped down onto Owen's lap and rubbed her face against his.

I had to look away before my lunch made a second appearance.

I'd hooked up many times at parties, drunk on beer and music, but that was the extent of my experience. Kind of lame. Maybe I should date. Maybe if I had a girlfriend, she would stick with me during my community service. I thought about that, mostly to avoid listening to my buddy strategizing about how to bang Liane during their next date.

It had started to rain sometime after lunch. By the end of my classes, the school grounds were soaked with mud, so I was on indoor duty again. Shagdar had me buff the cafeteria's marble floor. Gabe stuck around. He even helped stack the chairs on the tables while I moved around the room. He seemed preoccupied. Every time I would ask him about it, he would shrug. At some point, I stopped asking. He would tell me what was bothering him eventually.

On Tuesday, the weather was decent, downcast but not raining. Gray skies were depressing, but at least I would be outdoors. As I changed into my *work* clothes, Owen barreled into the locker room.

"It's happening!" he said.

"What? The zombie apocalypse?" I asked.

"No, asswipe." He dropped his voice to a loud whisper. "It's Gabe's initiation this afternoon."

Jealousy reared its petty little head as I stuffed my feet into my sneakers. "What's the plan?"

"Can't tell you."

"Oh, come on. Give me something to think about while I'm out there picking up *your* trash," I said.

Owen shook his head. "No can do, buddy."

My heart thumped a few times. "Are you going to New York again?"

For his initiation, they'd flown all the members of the Alphas to the city by helicopter for a private rooftop party with a bunch of swimsuit models.

Owen mimed zipping his lips. "You'll get all the gory deats tomorrow. I gotta head out. Don't pull a muscle with your nifty nabber."

I flipped him the finger. With music blasting in my eardrums, I set out toward the football field. When I spotted Cora up in the bleachers, I doubled back toward the crowded front quad.

A girl from my art class—I think her name was Annabelle or Anna Beth—came up to me with an armful of empty juice bottles. I pointed to the trash bag. She threw everything inside.

"Hey, Duke," she said.

I took out my earphones. "Hi?" I hadn't meant it to come out as a question.

Her long blond hair swung around her shoulders. The tips were bright pink, as though they'd fallen into one of the paint buckets. "It's really humid today," she said and ran her fingers across her collarbone.

My gaze followed her hand, which hovered over her bouncy cleavage and the ginormous cross dangling right above it. I suddenly remembered Gabe saying he'd taken Anna-whatever out for ice cream and all she'd talked about was Jesus.

"Do you need help?" she asked.

"I've got things covered," I said, looking at her face again.

The way her brow furrowed made me think she was disappointed. Maybe she wasn't *that* religious. Maybe she just hadn't had anything else to discuss with him.

"You're welcome to stick around though," I said. And she did. "So Gabe tells me you're very involved in the church."

"Dad's the pastor, which makes me involved by proxy."

"Are you religious?"

"Average."

"Define average."

"I go to church every Sunday, observe Lent and the rest of the religious holidays, but I'm open minded about other faiths, and I don't believe in confessionals."

Was this her way of telling me she wasn't married to God? "Because you don't sin?"

She winked at me. "Oh, I sin. I just don't tell God because I don't think it's any of his business."

"What sins are you guilty of?" I asked, stopping and leaning against the garbage pick. I was sort of hoping that her sins would start with, *One day, in band camp...*

Her cheeks reddened. "I read my older sister's diary once."

"What else?"

"I lied to our gym coach about a sprained ankle to cut volleyball."

"And?"

She grimaced. "That's it."

There went hoping…

I jerked upright and unstuck the pick from the ground. For some reason, Annabelle/Beth followed me.

"What?" she asked.

"What do you mean *what?*"

"You just shut me out."

"Because I need to get a move on. I have the whole football field to clean after here."

She seemed confused. "I should go home anyway. I need to practice the flute for choir."

I had to smile at that. "You play the flute?"

She nodded and her manga-inspired hair brushed against her breasts. "Do you play?"

"No."

"Any instrument?"

I shook my head. "I tried, but I'm musically challenged."

"I can teach you," she said.

"There's no hope for me. But I'd like to hear *you* play, maybe after school, underneath the bleachers or something."

A crushing blush seized her. "I don't think that's a good idea."

"Playing for me?" I asked, pretending that's what I was alluding to.

She went nearly purple. "I didn't think you would be like the rest of them."

"The rest of them?"

"I thought you would be nice, but I guess I was wrong." She flicked her hair back. "Have fun with your *pick*."

I chuckled and mused that the female psyche worked in mysterious ways.

Chapter Six

The following morning, when I didn't see either Gabe or Owen in first period, I had the sinking feeling they were still skydiving over the Grand Canyon or bungee jumping in Japan. By the end of the day, I still had no messages or phone calls. I shoved my arms and head into my orange Beatles T-shirt, yanked on a pair of gray board shorts, grabbed my tools, and made my way out to the football field. Halfway across it, I realized I'd forgotten my phone. *Whatever.* I could go without music for one hour.

I was so concentrated on the grass that I failed to notice the black figure. I hesitated for a millisecond before moving forward and climbing the metal stairs. Since when did I let myself be intimidated by a girl? Especially Cora. Still, I skipped her row to avoid confrontation.

"Do I smell?" she asked.

I flicked my gaze to hers. How was I supposed to respond to that? *Yeah, you do. Like roses.* I was most definitely not saying that. "Didn't want to bother you."

She sat up and plopped her book down next to her. It was *Heart of Darkness.* She must've finished *Wuthering Heights.*

I nodded toward the book. "What do you think of it?"

"It's shit," she said.

I frowned. "No, it's not."

"Yeah, it is. There's so much raging testosterone, and it's extremely dark."

"I thought you would like dark stories."

She smirked. "You've thought about what type of stories I like?"

I lost my ability to string words together. When I saw her blackened eyes squeeze shut a little and her head cock to the side, my composure came soaring back. "I don't give a crap what sort of bizarre shit you're into. I doubt anyone in school does," I said. "You're not the kind of person people care about."

Her cocky expression tumbled right off her pasty-white face. I'd gone too far with the last part and now felt like a massive jerk. Cora stuck her bare feet into her black combat boots and busied herself with the red laces.

"I didn't mean it like that," I said.

"Whatever." Her raspy voice had definitely dropped an octave.

I extended my fingers and grazed her shoulder.

She recoiled. "Get your hands off me, Meyer."

And I did.

My fingers tingled as though her skin had burnt mine. Maybe she was a witch. I could totally picture her as part of a cult. It would explain the freaky makeup.

She stood up, grabbed her library copy of *Heart of Darkness*, and stuffed it inside her backpack. I tried to read her expression, but her hair fell like a black velvet curtain around her face.

As she trampled down the stairs, I had another thought. "Do you wear all that makeup because of your mom?"

She didn't turn around, but I heard her say, "What makeup?" before racing across the field in her plaid skirt and white shirt, as though she couldn't get away from me fast enough.

When I got home, I chucked my bag on the floor, kicked off my shoes, and lumbered into the kitchen for a snack. I found Grandma sitting at the marble island, sipping a glass of wine, made up and dressed in a cream pantsuit. Her light gray hair—which was more purple than gray—formed a cotton-candy halo around her face. I didn't ask if she was going anywhere, because she was always classy, even if she spent her day lounging around the house.

I yanked open a cupboard door, grabbed a bag of pretzels, and then slammed it shut.

"You're in a mood," she said.

"Bad day," I grumbled.

"Tell me about it?"

"There's nothing to tell," I said, filling a bowl with pretzels. "Isn't it a bit early for alcohol?"

"It's wine. Wine doesn't count as alcohol."

"Then why can't I ever drink some?" I asked.

"Because it hampers growth."

"All the more reason I should."

"A man should be tall. Your grandfather was very tall." She lifted her glass of wine and took a sip. "You look so much like him, with those green eyes and dark hair of yours."

"I wish I'd known him." Grandpa had died the year before I was born. That same year, Grandma had moved in with us. She'd helped my mother take care of me. Neither believed children should be raised by nannies.

She put her glass down and toyed with her wedding band. I'd never seen her without it. "You know, I didn't love him at first."

I grabbed some pretzels and stuffed them in my mouth. "Really? Why?"

"He didn't bother courting me. He just said he wanted to marry me, and I told him 'over my dead body,' and then he explained to my father how solvent and serious a man he was, and my father decided that, considering I was in my late twenties, I needed to marry. Six months later, I was Mrs. Preiss."

"I didn't know it was an arranged marriage."

"I'd rather everyone think he seduced me with roses and sonnets."

"Why?" I asked her, sliding onto the barstool next to her.

"Because no one would understand how I could love a man who never once brought home a bouquet."

"He must've brought you something."

"He did. Stability. *And* he was an amazing father. They don't make fathers like him anymore."

"Why did you only have Mom then?"

"She was a handful." She smiled even though I felt it was a cover-up.

"Why did Mom stop after me?"

"Your dad wanted only one child," she said. "Now, can we please discuss something else, or I'll have to switch to alcohol."

I shoved my shaggy bangs out of my eyes. I needed to have them cut, but hated going to the hairdresser's. "Grams, why would a girl make herself look ugly?"

"Are we talking about a specific girl, or is this hypothetical?"

"Hypothetical," I lied.

"Maybe she doesn't do it on purpose."

"She definitely does it on purpose."

One of her penciled-in eyebrows lifted. "So this is a specific girl?"

I shrugged.

"Maybe *she* thinks she's pretty," Grandma said.

"That's impossible."

"Duke, if you don't give me more details, I'm going to say things you won't agree with. How does she make herself look ugly?"

"She uses too much makeup."

"How much are we talking?"

"*Girl with the Dragon Tattoo* much," I said.

"Well, in the book, she does it because she was abused. Maybe this girl was too."

"No. I mean, I don't think so."

"Maybe she's just rebellious then."

"Maybe," I said.

"Or it's associated with grief. Did she lose someone she was close to?"

"Her mom. Apparently, she left them, but it was years ago."

"Doesn't make the pain less painful," Grams said. "Time does not heal all wounds, honey. Wisdom does…or so I heard. What would I know about being wise?"

My grandmother was the wisest woman I'd ever met, made wiser by her pretense to the contrary.

"Look at that. It's five thirty. Time for my dirty martini," she said, "and time for your homework."

I kissed her wrinkled forehead before I left. She'd once told me each wrinkle was the imprint of Grandpa's caresses, of her parents' loving touch, of each hand that had ever stroked her face. I hoped I'd added my fair share of wrinkles.

Chapter Seven

Twenty-one more days. That's what I contemplated as I drove toward Francis Academy on Friday in my navy Jeep. And out of those twenty-one, six were weekends, which meant I only had fifteen effective days of community service left. *Woo-hoo.*

When I spotted Gabe's black Prius, souped-up with spinners and a bass system that made it vibrate, I parked next to it. I jumped out of the car and jogged toward school. The first person I noticed was Annabelle, or Beth. I still hadn't gotten her name straight, not that it mattered. She disappeared, pink hair and all, into the girls' bathroom the second she saw me.

I bit back a smile as I walked to English and dropped into my seat. "So? How was it?" I asked Gabe.

"Awesome."

"As awesome as Owen's?" I asked.

"*Hell* yeah."

Miss Brown came in, long, curly hair arranged randomly around her face.

"What did you do?" I asked.

"Tell you later," he said when Miss Brown began her lecture.

"Where's Owen?" I whispered.

"Probably sleeping it off."

I kept quiet after that, partly because I was interested in Miss Brown's lecture and partly because I found Gabe's side-stepping frustrating.

English whizzed by, unlike the rest of my classes that morning. When lunchtime rolled around, Gabe stopped me on my way to the cafeteria. "Come," he said.

I frowned but went along with him. "Where are we going?"

"Locker room."

"O-kay…Why?"

"You'll see."

And I did. Six of the guys on the basketball team were changing into their sports clothes.

"I got the coach to let us use the court," he said.

I wasn't a hugger, but I seriously considered hugging him.

"Just get changed. We only have forty-five minutes," he said.

After we were done pounding the court, we took quick showers and jogged to the cafeteria to see what was left of the lunch buffet.

When we walked out with our sandwiches, I said, "Now spill."

"We flew to Mexico on Pablo's private jet."

"No way!"

Pablo was a senior at Francis Academy. His father owned most of the telecoms in Southern and Central America. He was new money—unlike Owen—and behaved like new money—like Owen.

"Think *Girls Gone Wild* meets *Lands of the Fae* with paintball guns," Gabe added.

"Seriously?" I said, way too loudly.

He nodded.

"I can't believe I missed that!" I bit a huge chunk out of my tuna fish sandwich and wiped my mouth with the napkin balled in my left hand. "What did you tell your parents?"

He smiled, displaying way too many teeth. "That I went to a telecom convention with Pablo's dad."

I snorted. "They bought that?"

"Pablo's parents are financing Dad's campaign," Gabe said, as though that was reason enough—and it probably was. "It doesn't matter if they actually believed it. Dad's thrilled I'm hanging with Pablo. You know his motto: *Make friends in convenient places.*"

Just then, his phone buzzed. He slid his finger against the screen and stuck the phone to his ear.

"Hi, Sleeping Beauty," he said, stopping in front of our classroom.

Students were beginning to file in.

Gabe's eyes widened and a roomy grin spread across his jaw. "No shit…All night? Dude, that sucks…No, I'm fine…I'll stop by on my way home. Should I bring Liane? Maybe she can nurse your colon back to health." He chuckled. "Chill. I won't tell her about your explosive diarrhea." Still chortling, he hung up. "Owen exported some amoebas."

I smirked.

"He's in the hospital on an IV for dehydration," he said. "Come with me after school—You're still on trash duty, aren't you?"

"Yup."

"Want some company?"

"I'm good," I said.

On my way home that afternoon, I phoned Owen to see how he was doing. "You missed a good game," I said.

He groaned.

"What time will you get out?" I asked.

"Seven."

"I'm on my way then." I swung the car around while dialing my mother for permission. I couldn't risk my exile being extended.

I hated hospitals. They made me think of dying and smelled

like tears. Both my dad's parents died of cancer and both died at that hospital. I wasn't as close to them as I was with Grandma P., but still, they were family. Watching them turn into specters of themselves had been awful.

The elevator in the lobby pinged and drew me out of my gloomy thoughts. I was about to step in when my gaze met Cora's. She marched out past me, scowling. I turned to watch her leave.

The elevator was closing. I wedged my palm between the doors, forced them open, and stepped inside. On my way up, I tried to stop thinking about Cora, but her perfume clung to the elevator as thick as smog. By the time I'd arrived on the second floor, my lungs were full of damn thorny roses.

Chapter Eight

I was becoming used to playing janitor *extraordinaire*. The hardest part about my punishment was not playing ball whenever I wanted. Especially when I caught some of my friends' games.

On Saturday, the weather was amazing, ideal for scarfing down barbecued ribs by Owen's ginormous outside pool. We had a pool too, but it was on the small side, and swimming, especially alone, was not my favorite activity. On the upside, I'd never gotten so much homework done, nor had I seen so much TV with Grams. Mom and Dad spent their weekend at the country club, lunching and playing tennis—although I wasn't even sure about the tennis. They went to chew the fat with their friends. Considering the number of friends they had, there was a lot of fat to chew.

On Sunday, while skimming the Internet, I ended up on an article about diversity and avatars, and the newest trend around goth avatars. I closed down the window and was about to power off my computer when I typed the word *goth* in my search engine and clicked on a website dedicated to this weird painted-and-pierced species. I'd always assumed they worshipped Satan, but instead I learned they worshipped tolerance. I also read that many were same-sex-oriented. Was that Cora's case? She'd said she wasn't into pretty boys.

Maybe she just wasn't into boys.

Owen was back on Monday, looking splotchy and red from too much sun. He was making out with Liane by her locker. I tried to avoid the sight of their tongues colliding as I walked past them.

Classes passed uneventfully. The weather was now in the high seventies, so we took our lunches to the football field to watch the team train, and the cheer squad flounce around their pom-poms and short skirts in the inert air.

"Liane wants to go to the movies Friday night to watch that scary flick about zombies returning to earth. She's bringin' Cassie for Gabe," Owen said, turning his aviator-shaded eyes toward me, "and she was thinkin' Joss for you."

"Joss? She's a man," I blurted out.

"She's not a man," Gabe said.

"Oh, come on. She's nearly as tall as me. And she has extremely wide shoulders. Freakishly large," I said.

"Good point." Owen toed off his beige loafers and propped his very white, freckled feet atop the bench in front of us. "What about Amanda, then? I'm sure she'd be into you."

Amanda was another cheerleader. She was half-Korean and half-American with a small nose, brown hair, large eyes, and tanned skin. I watched her perform a cartwheel on the field that ended in a split. I was about to say *why not*, when I remembered I was grounded.

"I need to check with my parents to see if they'll preemptively lift the embargo on my social life," I said.

"Embargo?" Owen snorted.

"What?" I said. "I don't make fun of your simple language."

He laughed. "Simple language," he repeated with a small

head shake. "Good one." After a beat, he said, "Dude, four weeks is *looonng*. Maximum I ever got was forty-eight hours."

Gabe snickered. "What did you do to deserve such *rough* punishment?"

"Remember when I uploaded a picture of a turd to my brother's Facebook profile?"

"It's burned in my retina," I said, still grossed out. "Can't believe Eddy never got you back for that."

"Oh, he did. He took a dump in the trunk of my brand-new ride."

I chortled while Gabe doubled over, tears streaming down his cheeks.

"And you never told us?" he said, trying to rake in some breaths. "Your brother's a fucking genius!"

Even Owen cracked a smile. "I'll admit I got my ass handed to me," he said, his attention on Liane, who was heading toward us.

"What did you think of our routine?" she asked, swinging onto Owen's lap.

"I was distracted by that tiny skirt of yours," he said, before kissing her.

That sobered me right up. "I think I'm getting heatstroke."

I rose and started walking away when Liane called out, "Hey, Duke? Did Owen tell you about Friday night?"

I twisted around. "He did. Thanks for the invite, but I don't think I'll be able to make it."

"That's too bad," she said.

And I agreed with her. It was too bad. Why couldn't my parents be more like Owen's?

When I set out with my tools that afternoon, the football team wasn't practicing so I started on the field. Perched alone on the top bleacher was Cora—as usual. Instead of making a U-turn, I deliberately went toward her.

I rolled my earphones into my shorts pocket. "I saw you at

the hospital," I said, trying to catch my breath from my quick ascent.

She stayed quiet, eyes trained on yet another new book.

"Are you sick?" I asked.

"I thought I wasn't the kind of person people cared about."

I sat down. Not next to her, but on the bench across the aisle. "I'm sorry I said that."

"Why?" she asked, looking up. "It's the truth. And no, I'm not sick."

I frowned. "Then what were you doing in the hospital?"

"Stealing blood bags."

"Seriously?"

"Of course not." She narrowed her black gaze. "Have you always been this gullible?"

I shifted my attention back to the field below. "Why do you push everyone away?"

"Because I don't like people."

"You can't dislike everyone."

"Yes, I can, and I do. The values of people in our school are rotten and superficial."

"Not everyone," I said.

"Name one person who's not obsessed with having the biggest house, the hottest body, the largest bank account."

"Me."

She snorted. Her hair shone nearly blue underneath the bright sun. I wondered if it was soft.

"That's easy to say when you have the big house and the trust fund. You might have other interests, but you're still like the rest of them."

"And you're not because you're poor? Is that it?" Heat blistered my tone. "Is that why you cover yourself with that gunk? To make sure everyone knows you're different?"

Her lips warped into a smile. "You got me. Now can you please leave me alone?" She went back to contemplating her book.

"You know, if you stopped trying to be so different, maybe you'd fit in."

She snapped it shut. "Why would I want to fit in, Meyer?"

"Because you don't look happy. Maybe, if you put yourself out there, you would be."

She cocked a thin black eyebrow. The silver rings strung though it sparkled. "Do you think I'm unhappy because I don't have friends?"

"Everyone needs friends."

"Oh, Dukey," she said, making her voice sound all airy, "do you want to be my friend?"

"Don't call me that."

"Isn't that what your *friends* call you?"

I stood up and grabbed the trash sack and garbage pick. "Coming from you, it sounds insulting."

"Good. It was meant that way." Her voice was so low it sounded like a far-away roll of thunder during a heat wave.

"I honestly thought there was a heart underneath all that war paint," I said before starting back toward the football field, away from her cynicism.

"There is!" she called out. "But a heart's just an organ— useful to pump blood, useless to propel emotions."

Scientifically, she was correct, yet I didn't agree with her. I couldn't. My heart was beating much too fast, and it wasn't because my freaking organs were lacking blood.

Chapter Nine

On Tuesday, my afternoon chore was prepping the gym for the parent-teacher meeting. I didn't worry too much about what my teachers would tell my parents. I was a good student, and I got a lot of crap about it from Owen, whose grades were barely passable. He didn't need good grades though; I did.

Unless I became an Alpha.

"I've seen slugs move faster than you," Shagdar said, unfolding a chair.

And I've seen homeless people with cleaner hair. His limp brown ponytail flopped as he worked the room. I snapped open yet another table's legs and set it upright.

Leaning over it, I asked, "You know Principal Matthews pretty well, don't you?"

His narrowed gaze contracted toward his nose. "I do."

"What happened to his wife?"

"That's none of your business, Duke."

"But Cora has serious issues and I was wondering…" I looked down at the chipped wood and ran my nail underneath the veneer. It peeled off. "I read somewhere that people became goth to hide bad stuff. She's not being abused or anything?"

"Abused?" His voice rose. "That's a horrible thing to assume. Don't you go spreading such a rumor. Colin is a stand-up guy and a great father. And cut Cora some slack. She hasn't had it easy."

"It was just a question," I mumbled.

"Well, there are some questions better left unasked. Or at least ask *her*. If she wants to confide in you, she will. If she doesn't, leave her alone."

Wow…Protective much? "Yeah. Whatever," I said and returned to flipping open tables and chairs for the next forty minutes.

When I got home, Grandma P. was sipping a nearly empty martini glass while my mother shrugged into a beige blazer.

"I'm running late for the meeting," she said, grazing my cheek with a kiss.

I swiped off her sticky lip gloss.

"What am I going to hear?" she asked, tousling her curled hair in front of the foyer's large mirror.

"What you always hear. That the school's lucky to have someone as well rounded as me."

"And whose knowledge of the human anatomy is impeccable," Grandma P. added with a wink.

"You drink too much, Mom."

"It makes living with you bearable, honey."

"Your application for the nursing home is all ready. Just tell me when," my mother said.

I grinned at my two favorite women, whose beloved activity was verbal jousting.

Grandma wound her frail arm around my waist. "What would poor Duke do if I ended up in a nursing home?"

"And who would make you dirty martinis?" I added.

"Exactly." Grams handed me her empty glass. "Use black olives. The green ones taste sour."

"Comin' right up."

Mom took off for my school while I was in the kitchen. I nearly tripped over a huge metal vase—surely one of her new acquisitions. Some people collected tchotchkes; my mother collected vases. Her favorites were the glass-blown ones, the ones that were so outrageously colorful or oddly shaped that being receptacles of flowers was downright degrading. It made buying her presents easy.

When I returned, Grams swiped her drink from my fingers and offered up her arm. "I saw that the new episode of *Pursuit of Kings* came out. Shall we?"

I took her arm and walked to the windowless media room. We sat down on the oversized brown suede couch and turned on the huge TV.

"So, did you discover why she uses so much makeup?" Grandma asked just as battleships started catapulting fire onto Emerald Rock.

"Huh?"

"The girl you told me about…You know, the one who looks like—"

"I don't want to talk about her," I said.

"Did something happen?"

"Nothing happened."

From her silence, I assumed she'd let the subject go. I was wrong.

"You'd tell me if something happened, right?"

"Yeah, Grams." *Not*, I added in my brain.

Anyway, nothing would happen. Cora's heart didn't beat for others.

When I stepped out of home ec on Wednesday, I thought I was dreaming. Only in my dreams did Cora ever wear anything other than her plaid skirt and white button-down shirt with the school crest. It was beyond weird that she'd made appearances in my subconscious, and the only explanation I'd come up with was that I was a teenage guy with raging hormones, and Cora was a girl, and boys with raging hormones dreamed of girls.

It was totally normal.

I was normal.

Gabe, who was standing beside me in the door to the classroom, gawked at Cora as she trudged past us, shoulders rolled back and head held high. "I never realized she had such a tight ass."

I'd been having the same thought. And from the expressions of the guys around us, we weren't the only ones. I'd never bothered looking below her ghost-like face, but now, all I could see was her incredible body barely contained by the bands of black leather.

"Why isn't she in her uniform?" I asked.

"Beats me. Maybe she was out all night in some freak club and didn't have time to change," Gabe said.

"That's a shit theory."

"Why are your claws out?"

"My claws are not out," I said. "Whatever."

I could feel him watching me as I walked to the locker rooms to change for track. I hated running. Hated it. I thought it was the biggest waste of energy that existed in this world, but today, I pounded the dirt with pleasure. Adrenaline spiked through my bloodstream and oxygen filled my lungs. I'd never run so hard in my entire life, aside from that one time I'd run after the UPS truck that had forgotten to deliver my PlayStation.

After a quick shower, I hit the cafeteria for some food, grabbed a lunch tray, and headed out to the quad. I found Owen and Gabe on the bleachers with Liane and two other cheerleaders.

"Hi, lover boy," Gabe said as I dropped down next to him on the bench.

I cut my eyes to his, hopefully conveying my choice thoughts on this new nickname.

"Hey, Duke?" Liane tilted her head to the side to look at me through her large, pink-framed sunglasses. She was lying on the bench above, legs draped over Owen's lap. "Did you manage to get a free pass for this weekend?"

"After the parent-teacher meeting, I'm sure my rents will agree to anything," I said.

"Mine ripped me a new one," Owen said.

"Like every semester," Gabe said. "You should study."

"I do study." He dragged his index finger along Liane's bare leg. "Just not subjects they teach in school."

Liane caught his wrist midthigh. Owen chuckled and lifted his hand away, pulling it through his brassy hair.

"How do you put up with Mr. Romantic over here?" Gabe asked Liane.

She smiled. "He has his moments."

Gabe took in her expression with…*displeasure*? I looked from Liane to him, and it hit me that he might have feelings for Owen's girl. That didn't bode well. Just as I had that thought, Cassie touched his arm and whispered something in his ear. When he murmured something back, Amanda rose and came to sit by me.

"Don't you feel like a fifth wheel? I feel like a fifth wheel," she said. Her shiny brown hair was up in a bun atop her head. "I'm not sure I can stomach going to the movies with those four. Say you'll go."

"I have to check," I said.

"Should we grab dinner after the movie?" Liane asked. "We could go to Teddy's on the pier if the weather's nice."

Owen leaned over to plant a kiss on her. "Anything you want, babe."

Gabe's attention flicked from their locked lips to his half-eaten tray at record speed. "You girls know what happened to Goth Chick?" he asked, to change the subject.

I shoveled lasagna inside my mouth to stop myself from telling him to shut up about her.

"Yeah," Amanda said.

I nearly choked on the food.

"Some girls switched her clothes in the locker room after volleyball," she said, smirking. "It was, like, retribution for something. Anyway, leather's probably more her style than plaid skirts."

"It was just a silly prank. They gave her back her clothes," Cassie added. "You have to admit, the girl's a freak and most probably wears only leather when she's out of school."

"She has one hell of a body," Owen said.

Liane punched him playfully.

I didn't want to discuss her body, or the cruel prank. "I need to check what Shagdar's having me do this afternoon," I said, standing up abruptly.

I grabbed my tray and walked back into school. After flinging it on the cafeteria racks, I hurtled down the basement steps toward the chemistry lab. I had another twenty minutes before class started, but it beat hanging aimlessly by myself in any other part of the school.

I wasn't expecting anyone else to be there, but sitting at one of the long tables, picking at something in a plastic container, was Cora. She was wearing her white blouse again and, I assumed, her plaid skirt. I walked to the table next to hers.

She latched on to the container's lid and popped it back in place. Her nails were painted navy blue like my car.

"What they did to you wasn't cool," I said.

"Did you come down here to comfort me? Because if that's the case—"

"I had no idea you were down here. Trust me, if I'd known, I would've stayed away."

Cora got up and started packing her stuff. "I was leaving anyway."

"You don't have to."

"I know that, Meyer. The thing is, I want to."

"Why are you always running away from me?" I asked. "Do I scare you?"

She snorted. "Scare me? You? Give me some credit."

"Then why?"

She cocked her head to the side, and her long, silky black hair tumbled past her left breast. I jolted my attention to a Bunsen burner.

"Why are you always trying to talk to me? Do weird girls turn you on? Is that it? Am I some deranged fantasy of yours?"

I wanted to tell her not to flatter herself and a bunch of other things. Instead, I said, "What if you were?"

Her neck snapped straight and her expression blanked. I'd startled Cora Matthews. "Then I would tell you that I'm not worth it. I'm damaged."

"I'm good at fixing things."

Her jaw clenched. "I'm damaged, Meyer, not broken. I don't need to be fixed," she said, eyes blacker than ever.

And on that parting note, she left me sitting alone in the classroom, feeling confused and annoyed. It dawned on me then that what I'd told her was true, that she was some strange fantasy of mine, but not because she looked different. What I fantasized about was solving her.

Chapter Ten

Gabe offered to stay with me that afternoon. I wanted to turn him down, worried about the conversation he wanted to have. But then I realized that hiding from the people who knew me the best was not my style, not even if their judgment stung.

Nervous, I went into the locker room with him. He toyed with his phone while I changed into shorts and a black T-shirt with *The Police* printed in white. It was only after I'd retrieved my janitorial instruments that Gabe broached the subject of Cora.

"What's the deal with Goth Girl, Duke?"

"Don't call her that."

"Why? That's what she is," he said.

"She has a name."

"What's the deal with *Cora*?"

"There's no deal," I said.

He stopped walking; I continued.

"We've been friends long enough for me to realize that there is a deal! I'm not going to judge you."

I stopped and turned around. "Why would you judge me?"

"Because that chick's weird," he said, trotting toward me.

"You'll be happy to know she doesn't give a crap about me," I said.

Gabe fiddled with his shirt collar. "Just tell me something. Why her? You could have any other girl in school. Why Cora?"

"Why Liane?" I shot back.

His posture stiffened. "What are you talking about?" His vocal pitch had risen.

"Oh, come on. It's so obvious."

I thought he would shake his head and deny it. Instead, he asked, "Is it?"

I nodded.

"Do you think Owen knows?" he asked.

"He's the least intuitive person in the world, so definitely not."

Gabe still didn't relax. "I'm trying to turn it off. Focus on Cassie. Maybe if I hook up with her, I'll stop wanting what I can't have."

"I don't think it works that way."

He rubbed his palm against his close-cropped black hair. "She's Owen's girl, Dukey. You don't go fish in your friend's pond."

"We suck at picking girls."

"Tell me about it."

I went to find my mother as soon as I got home. She was curled up on one of the lounge chairs near the pool, flipping through a glossy magazine and sipping iced tea, while my grandmother did water aerobics.

"Can I go to the movies with the guys on Friday?"

"Hello to you too, honey," she said, setting down her magazine.

I plopped down on the lounge chair beside her and knotted my fingers in my lap.

"You're still grounded, Duke," she said, but there was a hint of hesitation in her voice.

"Weren't you just telling me how pleased the teachers were with him?" Grandma asked.

My mother sighed. "Let me check with your dad."

When Grandma asked Mom why she had to consult my father about every decision taken in our household, I rose and left.

My father was not in a good mood that night. He barely spoke to anyone during dinner. As Mom served dessert, she asked him about my outing. He asked her if it had been four weeks, and she shook her head. So he said no.

Grandma shot my mother a look that made her jumpy. I was relatively certain it had to do with the conversation they'd had by the pool, the one I'd evaded.

My mother took a breath and squeezed her eyes shut for the briefest second. Would she stand up to my father? That would be a first…

"Michael, Duke has been extremely well behaved, and you heard his teachers yesterday. I think we should let him go out."

"Rules are rules," Dad said.

"I know, but it's been over two weeks. And he's still doing community service in school and—"

"My point exactly. *Over two weeks* is not four."

"But it's just the movies," Mom said.

My grandmother tipped back in her chair and crossed her arms, attention ping-ponging from daughter to son-in-law.

"He'll be back as soon as it's over. Right, Duke?" Mom asked.

"Right."

Dad sighed and it resonated inside the wood-paneled dining room. "Fine. But letting you off the hook one night doesn't mean you're absolved. Understood?"

"Yes," I said.

Grams grinned and attacked the apple crumble on her plate

with her spoon while Mom fidgeted with her glass of wine. She'd done it, and yet she seemed nervous. Dad reached out and covered her jittery hand with his. He smiled at her, and with that smile, her entire body relaxed. It was as though my father had some secret power over my mother. He could rid her of anxiety with a simple stroke of his fingers. I looked down at my own fingers and thought that, if superpowers existed, controlling emotions would be neat.

I could touch Cora and make her better, happier. I seriously had to stop obsessing over her. I thought about Amanda and about sharing a bucket of popcorn with her and about touching *her* hand and about kissing her. Those thoughts made doing the dishes fly by. They also made my raging hormones rage louder.

That was a good sign, right?

Chapter Eleven

My alarm jolted me out of a dream that had felt so real. My body was slick with sweat and hard all over. I groaned and stuck my pillow over my head. Why couldn't it have been Amanda's naked body I'd fantasized about? Why did it have to be Cora's? I jumped into the shower and sloughed away the remaining traces of my thoughts.

In my uniform, I went to the kitchen to gobble down a heaping bowl of cereal. Mom was already there, reading the newspaper and nursing a mug of coffee. Grandma was next to her, buttering up a thin slice of raisin bread.

"I need a haircut. I was thinking of going after school," I said.

She looked up from the paper. "Don't cut it too short, all right?"

I snorted. I was sixteen and my mother was still telling me how to cut my hair. "Damn, there goes my buzz cut," I joked.

"I always found men with buzz cuts extremely sexy," Grandma said.

Mom and I both gaped at her.

"What? I'm old, but not dead."

My mother set down her mug. "But buzz cuts, Mom? Really?"

"Men who have buzz cuts usually have a lot of muscle and interesting tattoos and—"

Mom covered her ears. "Duke, leave while you still can," she said, the corners of her mouth tipped up.

Grandma P. shook her head and her fluffy purplish hair shivered. I dropped kisses on both women's cheeks and trotted out to my car. The sky was deep gray and the air was muggy, a sign that it was going to pour any second. I hoped I would make it to school before the storm hit. Just as I parked, a lightning bolt slashed the sky, lighting it up like the Fourth of July. I counted seven seconds to the roll of thunder that came next. Divided by five, the storm was one and a-half miles away.

I strode quickly into the school and up to my homeroom. As I took a seat, the clouds were cleaved open by another bolt. The amount of rain that poured out was spectacular. Soon, the curtain of water was so dense that it blurred the elm trees lining the school property. I spent most of class gazing out of the window, listening to the relentless drops. It felt cleansing and appeasing, as though the rush of water was dislodging the remnants of my sticky dreams.

At the end of class, I told the guys about my parents' consent.

"Are you out of the doghouse for good?" Gabe asked as we walked to English.

"No," I said.

"That's too bad."

"Can you come over and hang with me on Saturday?" I asked him.

"Can't. There's a meeting. My first one," he said.

"About what?"

"Dunno yet. But you know the club rules: *Initiation before information*. I took an oath."

"Not in front of a Supreme Court justice."

"They're way scarier than the Supreme Court."

"Remind me why I want in?" I asked as we turned the corner and entered our buzzing classroom.

"Because they'll make Harvard come true. They run the country, Dukey."

Anticipation lifted the small hairs on the back of my neck before seeping through my body and raising my pulse. Rolls of thunder cracked like whips outside, mirroring the hectic thumping of my heart.

As I drove back home from the hairdressers underneath the still-pounding rain, I was surfing on a wave of Zen that felt too good to be true. Even working alongside Shagdar in the chemistry lab, rearranging cabinets and cleaning test tubes had proved therapeutic. There had to be a beach or a cliff against which my wave was going to crash. It was only natural. No wave coursed the ocean endlessly. Sure enough, my beach came in the form of the bus stop on Perryridge Road and the dark figure standing next to it.

I pulled up to the curb and rolled down my window. "Get in."

Cora glanced at me. "I'm good."

"No, you're not good. You're soaking wet. Don't be stupid. Get in."

"It's illegal."

"What is?"

Her mascara had trailed down her white cheeks as though she'd cried. "Minors driving around other minors," she said, hugging her backpack against her chest. "You could get in trouble."

I was momentarily taken aback that she abided by rules—and that she cared I could get in trouble—but then I regained my sound senses. "For God's sakes, Cora, *get in.*"

And, to my great surprise, she did.

"You're obnoxiously persistent," she said.

"I know. It's one of my best traits." My lips curved as the aroma of roses filled the car. "Being offensively annoying is my second greatest quality. Now where to, Flashdance?"

She snorted. "Really?"

"Awesome shower scene."

As I pulled back on the road, I felt her black eyes on me. For once, they didn't feel like they were drilling a hole inside of me. Maybe it was the way they sparkled with amusement. Well, I hoped it was amusement and not derision.

"Where do you live?" I asked.

"You can just drop me off at Loughlin Park."

"Do you live in the park?" I asked, turning right at the light.

She didn't answer. She just clutched her black backpack tight against her chest.

"You can put your bag down. I don't care if my car mat gets wet," I said.

"Glad to know."

For all that, she didn't put it on the floor.

"Are you carrying illegal substances or something?" I asked her.

She grimaced. "Let it go, Meyer."

I screwed up my forehead to figure out what she had in the backpack. As my gaze slid over her shirt, my jaw went slack. Rain and white cotton were a deadly combination.

"Brake!" she yelled.

"Huh?"

All at once, I stepped on the brake and looked away from the black lines of Cora's bra plastered against her see-through shirt. I missed the bumper in front by an inch. Possibly less.

"Don't make me regret accepting a ride," she muttered.

Heat snaked through my body at dizzying speed. I kept my eyes glued to my windshield—to avoid a collision *and* to cool down.

"What were you doing on Perryridge?" I asked her, not trusting myself to even peep at her.

"Just walking," she said.

"Did you not see it was raining?"

"I don't melt." There was a smirk in her deep voice.

I slowed down as the light turned red. "You might not melt, but you'll get si—" I spun toward her. The hospital was on Perryridge! "You were at the hospital, weren't you?"

The red glare of the glowing taillights ahead made her cheeks seem less pale and tinged her wavy black hair burgundy.

"Sure you're not sick?" I asked.

"Are you done trying to figure me out?"

"I wasn't…" I let the lie trail off.

"Look, I don't want to talk about it."

She reached for the door handle. I locked the car. It was a creepy move. She would totally think I was all kinds of deranged, so I unlocked the car.

"Don't leave. I'll shut up," I said.

Her fingers hovered over the handle, but they didn't settle. They were slender and golden. I felt the sudden urge to know if the rest of her was as golden.

"I'll stay if you stop staring at my body like you want to eat it," she said.

Oh, God! Oh, shit, God. God of shit. I swallowed and pulled my gaze back to the street, and then attempted to tape back together what was left of my ego. "Are you into girls? Is that it?"

"I don't see how that's any of your business."

"You are, aren't you?" I asked, whipping around. My pulse jackknifed in my throat. I'd solved her! Well, not everything. I still didn't know why she visited the hospital. Her eyes ground into mine, but I was no longer startled by their intensity. I expected it. I welcomed it. It was part of what made her so intriguing in the first place.

"I'm not sick," she said, her voice low.

Well, there went my theory. "So you just really don't like me."

"I have a boyfriend."

"You do?"

I ran Francis Academy's entire male population in my head. I'd never seen her hanging out with anyone and thus decided she was lying.

The park was up ahead, so I slowed down. I didn't want to arrive too fast because she would leave and I would be left in the dark—again.

"He's not in school," she added as though reading my thoughts.

Of course not. She was lying, but I played along. "Is he also weird like you?"

She glowered, and rightfully so. I'd just called her a weirdo. I was a horrible person. One second I wanted to pull her backpack away from her chest and snap her seat belt off, and the next I wanted to shove her into a category of people who existed on the frayed edge of society.

"Here's fine," she said.

"Cora, just let me drop you off at your house."

A weighted sigh seeped out of her. "Fine."

"You're going to have to give me an address."

"Maplewood Drive. At the end of it."

We didn't talk the rest of the way. I knew we'd arrived when I caught sight of her father's restored Volvo woodie.

"Thanks," she said as she opened the door and slipped out.

I tipped my head and conjured up a smile I wasn't feeling. "Sure."

She seemed to draw her backpack closer to her body, not to conceal her chest as much as to keep herself steady, as though it were a buoy that would keep her afloat.

"You're getting drenched," I said when she still hadn't moved.

"I'm already drenched." Her voice sounded like thunder. It was thunder. It struck my heart. Damn, sexy voice.

She bit the inside of her cheek; it dimpled. For the slightest second, I hoped she would confess that her boyfriend was a fabrication, but then I stopped hoping. I seriously needed to stay away from Cora…for my sanity.

I raked my hand through my still-longish bangs. "You'll get rid of me quicker if you shut that door."

And just like that, her uncertainty vanished and she closed the car door. She didn't slam it, but she very well could've. The inaudible pop sounded a hell of a lot like my pipe dream bursting.

Chapter Twelve

I fantasized about Cora again that night, but not in a good way. In my dream, she was terrified of me and kept backing away. Granted, she was naked, besides the backpack, which she used as a shield. It was just large enough to cover the most secretive parts of her body, or perhaps she was just small enough to fit behind it.

When I woke up in the middle of the night, the bed sheets were wrapped tightly around my legs as though I'd been wrestling them in my sleep. Feeling hot, I kicked them off. Still boiling, I threw off my T-shirt and lay there in my boxers, watching the blades of my ceiling fan spin until rays of sun trickled over the horizon. When I finally got up to scavenge for some food, the house was quiet. Even my mother, usually an early riser, hadn't come down to the kitchen for her morning coffee.

Thinking about coffee made me crave a cup. I rarely drank it; I rarely drank anything warm. I found little pleasure in singeing my palate and tongue. Considering I'd slept a grand total of four hours, I needed caffeine, and drinking an energy drink at the crack of dawn was out of the question, so I spooned ground coffee into the percolator, filled the water tank, and turned it on. Then I opened the fridge, took out some cold cuts, dill pickles, and mayo, grabbed a few slices of bread from the breadbasket, and made myself a sandwich.

I went to sit on one of the bar stools tucked underneath the island and scarfed down my concoction. The coffee machine beeped just as Grandma arrived, her hair in rollers. She walked toward the fridge to pull out the butter and strawberry jam while I got up to pour myself a cup of coffee.

She eyed the beverage. "Bad night?" she asked, taking a plate out of the cupboard.

"Yeah."

"Me too. My bedroom felt like a Turkish bath. You should've seen my hair this morning. I looked like I'd stuck my finger in an outlet."

I chuckled. That was the way it looked all the time. The Jew-fro was the one trait I hadn't inherited from my mother's side of the family—I got the Meyer's silky hair gene. I took a gulp of coffee and scorched off a layer of my throat. I dug the carton of milk out of the fridge and poured a lot of it in my coffee. My beverage was now room temperature and somewhat palatable. I returned to my seat at the kitchen island.

"What movie are you going to see tonight?" Grandma asked, putting her plate next to mine and sitting.

"The new dystopian one where the entire planet is wiped out except for an underground prison."

"*Ooh*…I want to see that."

"I'll go back with you if it's any good."

"Or I can just come with you tonight," she said. "Owen and Gabe won't mind my company."

Some of my coffee went down the wrong hole. I gagged and then coughed.

"What is it, honey? Am I not cool enough to hang with your *peeps*?"

"My peeps?" I asked, grinning. "You've been brushing up on your urban slang, I see."

"How else am I supposed to understand your friends?" she said with a wink. "And, sweetheart, I was just teasing you about *crashing* your *part-ay*."

"Good. I would've felt bad sticking you in the row for the hearing impaired."

"What?" she asked.

"It was just a joke, Grams."

She drew in her eyebrows. "What?"

I was about to repeat myself when I caught the glimmer in her eyes.

She winked. "Gotcha."

"Wow…I'm really not awake yet." I downed my beverage while studying the slate gray sky. At least it wasn't raining anymore. Not that I'd minded the rain. What I'd minded was my impromptu meeting with Cora brought upon *by* the rain.

"Everything all right, honey? Ever since you came home last night, you've seemed…thoughtful."

"All's good," I said.

"You can talk to me if you want."

"I know, but I need to shower before school. Don't want to be late."

I took an extra long shower, which meant I had to rush through my morning routine of pulling on my uniform, brushing my teeth, and gelling my hair. I drove slowly toward Francis Academy, because the rain had filled the roads with puddles of brown water that splashed the sidewalks as my wheels cruised through them.

When I got there, the hallways were buzzing. Granted, it was Friday. Everyone loved Fridays. Someone slapped my back as I walked toward my locker. I glanced sideways and found Owen beaming, his mop of orange hair uncombed but gelled nonetheless.

"What?" I asked.

"Tonight's the night you're getting laid, and all thanks to me, bro," he said.

"What are you talking about?"

"Well," he began, wiggling his eyebrows. "Liane told me that Amanda was hot as shit for you. Tope, huh?"

"My parents expect me home, *alone*, straight after the movie."

"Maybe your dad would change his mind if he realized how much good it would do his son."

"I'm not sure what part of that is more mental, me telling my father, or you telling me I need to get laid."

"He's a guy and you're a virgin," Owen said. "All fathers want that for their sons. Remember when my dad got me a hooker for my birthday last year?"

"Everyone remembers," I said. "That's all you could talk about for the longest time."

I hadn't envied him, because one, I thought hookers were dirty, and two, I would've died of embarrassment if my father had bought me sex. Plus it would never have flown past my mother.

Owen's parents were different though. They'd stayed married because divorces were unacceptable to both their families, but they weren't *together* together. His father had had several extramarital affairs, which everyone knew about, including his wife.

"Maybe you can sit in the back or something," he suggested.

The reminder of my virginity made my temper flare. "Just shut up already."

Owen's face became somber. "I thought you'd be stoked."

"Well, I'm not losing it in a movie theater with a bunch of people watching."

"Fine. Whatever. It's your dick, not mine."

"Yeah. It is."

"I'm late for history. I'll catch you later." He turned and walked off.

When we did catch up—we had English just before lunch—I'd calmed down and he'd shrugged and that was the end of that.

I saw Amanda during lunch. She sat with us at our table—*yes*, we had our table. When you weren't a dork or ugly or quirky, you got to pick a table in the middle of the cafeteria, and no one could hijack your spot. Everyone else migrated around the center tables but never settled. Francis Academy was built on cliques even though it boasted equality and fairness. At twelve years old, I'd already understood that equality was just an appealing theory.

My gaze drifted around the room. I'd rarely surveyed the people sitting in the *fringe*—as we called it. I spotted Cora at one of those tables, sitting alone, nose buried in a battered book. I couldn't make out the title from the distance.

"Did you, like, hear my question?" Amanda asked.

I veered my attention back to her. Her green-brown eyes were wide and expectant.

"No, I'm sorry. What did you say?"

"What sorts of books do you read?"

"You mean, outside of the ones for school?" I asked.

She nodded and her short brown hair bobbed. It was very shiny.

"Mostly fantasy. Anything by Tolkien or Dalson."

"I, like, love *Pursuit of Kings*," she said.

The fact that she'd used the word *like* in the middle of a sentence was off-putting to the secret nerd within. "Did you read the books?" I asked.

"Uh-huh. All seven of them."

"Really?" I angled my body toward hers. "What's your favorite storyline?"

"Magnolina's. And yours?"

"Her brother, Drampton's."

"I, like, *love* him!"

And for the next thirty minutes, Amanda and I bonded over

imaginary characters and their fictional dilemmas. During that time, I hadn't even looked back at Cora's table. When I finally did, she was gone.

Maybe I'd finally found the solution to forgetting Cora.

Amanda.

Chapter Thirteen

The theater was packed. Finding spots together was a feat, so we split up, sitting two by two. Obviously, I was paired with Amanda. As we squeezed past a row of people and dropped into our seats, I felt as if I was on an actual date. It made me insanely nervous. I leaned back, trying to settle my nerves, all the while managing choppy small talk.

When the lights dimmed, I relaxed. Several previews came on, but I could not, for the life of me, concentrate on any of them. All I could think about was whether I should reach out and hold her hand now, or wait for a frightening part in the movie, or just wait for her to hold mine, or not hold her hand at all and just kiss her. Or not kiss her. Maybe she didn't want me to kiss her. Maybe Liane had lied to Owen about her being interested in me. Maybe—

She leaned over and whispered, "I don't like scary movies."

Instead of saying something smooth, I shot out, "You can hold my hand." It was so freaking lame. Did desperation smell? If it did, I reeked of it. I chewed on the inside of my mouth trying to come up with a line that could do some damage control, but I got sidetracked by the feel of her fingers sliding through mine. I blinked at her.

She tilted forward, and for the briefest second I thought that the moment had come to pucker up and go for it. I started to lean in when she swerved her lips toward my ear. I jolted my attention to the screen so that I didn't look like I'd been about to plant one on her.

"I was hoping you'd say that," she murmured.

She likes me. The certainty of it hit me like a sledgehammer. I stopped overthinking, spun my face toward hers, and met her lips head on. My mind went blank as I tightened my hold on her fingers and probed her mouth open with my tongue. She tasted sweet, like gummy bears.

She deepened the kiss. Someone grunted behind us. Whatever. I wasn't forcing them to watch. When we finally came up for air, I turned to glare at the person. After that, and during the several other make-out sessions that ensued, I didn't hear him make any more noise.

When the movie ended, we got up and walked out of the Cineplex, bodies parallel but not touching. Hand-holding was for couples. We weren't a couple. I glanced at her as we waited for the others to emerge.

Maybe we could be a couple.

"I hope you weren't too scared when all the prisoners ripped each other up," I said.

She smiled. "I don't remember that scene."

The others arrived at that point. Owen had his arm slung around Liane, whereas Gabe and Cassie were walking awkwardly side by side. As soon as they reached us, Cassie hurried toward Amanda.

"Did you like it?" Liane asked Amanda.

"Not cool to refer to my boy here as *it*," Owen said, giving me a giant wink.

I chuckled.

"I was talking about the movie, silly," Liane said, her voice even lighter and breathier than usual.

Amanda peeked at me. "It was nice."

Liane smirked. "You obviously didn't watch it because it was *not* nice. It was disgusting."

Amanda's grin dimpled her cheeks. I hadn't noticed she had dimples. I liked girls with dimples. Cora had some at the base of her spine. I'd seen them that day she wore the leather getup. I was sort of surprised I remembered them.

"I'm starved," Cassie said. "Liane, you driving with us?"

"Yeah." She ducked away from Owen. "Do you still have to go home, Duke?"

I nodded and Amanda's smile dissolved. I sort of wanted to kiss her again, but not in front of everyone.

"Are you, like, grounded for the whole weekend?" she asked.

I cringed. "Yeah. Ten more days before I'm a free man again."

"Good," she said.

"Sorry to interrupt but my stomach has started consuming itself. Can we please go?" Cassie said.

The girls all waved.

"See you in a second, baby," Owen said.

Liane looped her arm through Amanda's, and together, they walked toward Cassie's silver convertible.

"So?" he asked.

I shrugged. "It was fine."

"Fine? Just fine?"

I was not about to discuss how it felt to kiss Amanda with my buddies.

"You okay, Gabe?" I asked, diverting Owen's attention.

He hadn't said a word since he'd come out of the theater, hands stuffed inside his jean pockets. "Let's just get this dinner over with."

"That bad?" I asked.

"That bad."

"Lucky for you, there are plenty more *does* in Francis Academy," Owen said, play-punching Gabe's shoulder.

"Yeah, lucky me," he mumbled, trudging toward Owen's car.

Owen lifted an eyebrow. "What's eating him?"

"Don't know," I said, even though I did: the only *doe* Gabe wanted was Owen's. "He's probably stressed about his father's election."

"Shit. I had no clue. We haven't talked much since I started seeing Liane."

"Maybe it's not even that. Maybe he's just having a bad day. I wouldn't worry."

He grunted. "Me? Worry? Dukey, did Amanda's sweet lips fry your brain?"

I chuckled and shook my head. "G'night, Owen," I called out, jogging to my car to drive my lonely ass home.

Chapter Fourteen

I thought of Amanda all day Saturday, or more specifically, of her lips. I remembered enjoying the moment, but we were in the dark, surrounded by people we didn't know. What would happen on Monday, in the light of day, surrounded by people we knew?

I couldn't see myself pitching her against my locker, which led me to wonder if it was *her* specifically or if I would feel this way about any girl. I closed my eyes and tried to imagine myself making out with someone else. That someone else turned out to be Cora. The idea of making out with her made my lids snap up and my pulse skyrocket, so I traipsed down to the gym in our basement to clear my mind.

After a grueling half hour, I declared my mind clutter-free and went to put away the free weights when a sudden pain ripped through my right side. I lost my balance and stubbed my toe on my mom's elliptical, cruising head first into the weight rack. It took me a second to sit up. Sweat dripped past my eyebrow and into my eyes. I swiped it away. Dizzy, I clutched the machine and heaved myself upright. More sweat dribbled down. Digging my fingers into my side, I grabbed a towel and patted my face. I was about to chuck it into the hamper when I caught sight of a large red stain. Hunched over, I walked toward the mirrored wall and thrust my damp hair up. I'd sliced my forehead open on the metal edge. I could barely feel it, though. The pain in my side superseded all other sensations in my body. Clutching the railing, I hobbled up the stairs.

Mom was in the kitchen, standing over a chopping board, dicing broccoli.

I leaned against the wall, lifted the towel, and pressed my hair up. "Mom?" I croaked.

She shrieked and then clapped her hand over her mouth. Dad came barreling into the kitchen, the newspaper dangling from his fingers.

"What?" he asked, rushing to her side. "Honey, are you okay?"

Mom bobbed her head up and down and pointed to me. Dad turned sideways.

"How on earth did you do that?" he asked, crossing the kitchen toward me.

"I hit my head, but—" A new wave of pain fired through my waist.

"It looks deep," he said. "What do you think, Estee?"

Mom approached, paler than the white marble countertop. She stared unblinkingly at my forehead, but then her lids closed and her knees went soft. Dad released his newspaper and grabbed her just before she hit the floor.

I grunted as the pain increased. I grabbed a breath and held on to it tightly. Strangely, it squelched some of the discomfort. When I could talk, I mumbled, "My side…hurts." I sucked in a new breath.

Mom's eyes snapped open and color returned to her cheeks. "Where? Right or left?"

"Right."

"Appendicitis. Stitches. Hospital. Go," she said, hyperventilating.

I placed the towel back against my head.

"I'll drive," Dad said, helping Mom into the living room. "Rachel!" he called out.

My grandmother clambered down the stairs, rollers askew in her lavender-gray hair. "What did I miss?" she exclaimed, out of breath. "Good lord, what happened?"

She ran toward my mother who was slumped on the couch, the back of her hand resting limply against her forehead.

"She fainted," Dad explained. "Just stay with her while I take Duke to the ER."

"ER?" she asked.

"Duke. Forehead. Appendix. Blood," Mom whispered.

Grandma ogled my face.

"Chicken. Oven," Mom whispered. "Burn."

As she looked back down at her daughter, Grams chuckled. "You two go ahead while I play charades with this one."

Dad latched on to my arm, helped me out of the house and into the car. I reclined my seat to the maximum and focused on breathing. One hundred and forty breaths later, we swerved into the hospital parking lot. Dad rolled into a spot, turned the car off, and pounced out of the driver's side. He ran to my side, clicked my seat belt off, and lifted me as though I were a rag doll —which wasn't too far from how I felt.

Thankful for his support, I limped into the ER. He deposited me in a chair before going to the receptionist's desk and returning with a bunch of forms. I was glad I didn't have to fill them out because I couldn't even read them. The words seemed distorted, as though I were staring at them through a fish-eye lens. The whole waiting room seemed skewed, which didn't help with the searing pain in my forehead. I ended up closing my eyes.

To pass the time, Dad told me about when he'd had his appendix taken out in the middle of a sailing competition. When his story ended, he stood up and marched over to the front desk. He had very heavy footsteps. They were surely echoing through the entire hospital because they were resonating inside my skull.

"What does it take to get some medical attention around here? A severed limb?" he shouted at the receptionist.

"Sir, please, keep your voice down," she said.

"My son's forehead is sliced open and he has a burst appendix!"

"We are aware of your son's condition. The nurse is on her way."

"This is unacceptable!" Dad growled just as an orderly appeared with a wheelchair.

"Duke Meyer?" she called out.

Still huffing out complaints, Dad led her to me. She was a big woman with a big Southern accent and big blond hair. Dad grabbed my arm and helped me into the chair before trailing my Hummer-like nurse into the elevator and down a sterile white hallway. She wheeled me into a hospital room and began asking me about allergies, blood type, what I'd eaten last and when. As she drew blood, she asked Dad to sign the consent forms. Then she handed me a pastel-yellow robe and told me to strip and go to the bathroom.

When she went to find the surgeon, I scanned the room. A blue partition was drawn, which made me realize I had a roommate. From the muted cartoonish voice of *Mike the Ranger*, I established it was a kid, probably a boy. I didn't think girls liked cartoons about an almighty forest ranger who could transform into a mountain lion to save people.

A stab of pain jolted me from my thoughts. Dad placed the clipboard beside me and helped me tug off my sports clothes. I donned the robe before sliding my boxers off. Dad balled everything up and waited, silent and anxious.

"It's going to be fine. It doesn't even hurt that much," I lied.

He raked his hand through his thick salt-and-pepper hair, and was about to say something when a man in a long white coat came in.

"Hi, Duke, I'm Dr. Monroe. I'll be operating on you today." He scanned the clipboard the nurse gave him. "I see you have no allergies. Oh…And I read here I'll be sewing up your forehead too. Double whammy!" he said, with a bark of laughter.

I didn't find it very funny. Neither did the nurse or my father.

When Dr. Monroe realized his joke had fallen off its mark, he grew serious and explained the laparoscopic procedure. "If your appendix didn't burst, which we'll know after the lab results come back, you should be on your feet by tomorrow and in school by Tuesday."

"Not in any rush," I mumbled.

"Okay then," he said. "Shall we see what's going on inside that body of yours?"

I lowered myself into the wheelchair again. Cold sweat snaked down my neck and made me shiver. My father started following us, but the nurse blocked his path.

"I'm sorry, sir, but there ain't no visitors allowed beyond this point," she said.

In the haze of pain clouding my brain, I managed to say, "Dad, go be with Mom."

He gawped at me as though the top of my head had blown off. "I'm not going anywhere."

"Please, Dad. You'll go crazy waiting here."

"If you'd like, I'll arrange for someone to call as soon as the operation's over, Mr. Meyer," the doctor said.

Dad stayed silent, but I could sense his distress. It seemed to vibrate against the shiny vinyl floor.

"Your son's in good hands," the doctor said. "I'll have him out in no time."

The nurse wheeled me past a set of double doors, leaving my father standing alone in the white hallway. As they prepped me for the procedure, I stopped wondering if he'd stayed. I became dedicated to halting the trembling that had erupted in my body from the mixture of cold and pain.

The nurse laid me out on the operating table and slipped a catheter underneath my skin. I winced as some chilled fluid entered my veins, bringing with it a welcome, silent darkness.

Chapter Fifteen

When I opened my eyes, I was in the recovery room. My head, my mouth, and my throat felt as though they'd been scoured with a Brillo pad. I blinked in and out of consciousness while a nurse checked my forehead and the bandage below my waist. Fluorescent tubes buzzed overhead. They made me think of an upside-down highway.

The nurse parked my stretcher next to my bed and encouraged me to stand, which I did, staggering. Both my side and my forehead throbbed, but the pain was significantly duller. I sat on the hospital bed and then lay down.

Hummer-nurse attached my IV drip to a new pole. "Press on that call button next to the headrest if you need me. But don't be callin' unless you feelin' green like the underside of a turnip."

She left with the stretcher and closed the door. The room was quiet and dim, which meant it was probably late. I wondered if my parents were somewhere in the hospital. Just as I had that thought, Dad, Mom, and Grandma burst into my room. They rushed to my side like a tidal wave, asking me a trillion questions. *How are you feeling? Did they sew up your forehead? Are you in any pain?* I had no idea who said what, still lost in the fog of the anesthesia. A new wave of fatigue poured over me, and my eyelids began drooping. The hushed voices continued, but the sentences were gurgled.

Something soft touched my cheek. In my comatose state, I imagined it was Cora's palm. I pushed my cheek into it and mumbled, "You came."

"Of course I came, sweetie."

Not Cora's voice. I tried to drag my lids up, but it was like trying to hoist venetian blinds with a broken string. I gave up and gave in to sleep.

A bright light pressed against my clasped lids. Aliens were drifting down from their spaceship to take me home. I was being abducted.

"No," I mumbled. "I'm not coming with you."

"Huh?" was the alien's response. It creased its triangular forehead. "You don't have to. You can stay right here."

The alien had a childish voice. Bizarre, considering the number of wrinkles on its purple skin.

"I have no interest in your planet," I said again.

"My *planet*?"

My eyelids flipped up and I jerked backward from the flashlight shining in my face. The movement awakened the incision on my right side, making the whole area ache.

"Hi," said the childish alien voice.

"Turn that thing off," I muttered.

The handheld flashlight snapped off, but my bedside lamp switched on, revealing a small and very human boy.

"Oh, sorry. I didn't mean to wake you," he said.

"Yes, you did," I said grumpily.

"Okay, maybe I did." He shifted on his feet. His head was leveled with mine, yet he was standing. "I'm Jaime. You've been out for a long time."

I rolled my eyes toward the ceiling. "It's called sleeping. That's what people do at night."

"I can't sleep," he said.

"I can see that."

"What's your name?" he asked.

I was tempted to ignore him, but he seemed too young to be alone in a hospital at night. "Duke. Duke Meyer."

"No way!" he whispered, seemingly in awe. "I'm sharing my room with the Duke of Graffiti? The guy who spray-painted the woodie on the woodie?"

"Do you even know what a woodie is?"

"Duh!"

Maybe he wasn't as young as I thought he was.

"How did you hear about the…incident?" I asked.

"Greenwich is small."

The story must've spread from my classmates to the rest of their families, and thus to our entire town.

"You're, like, my hero," he said.

"Hero, huh? I vandalized someone's car. Not very heroic."

"I know. Still thought it was cool, though."

"Glad I made your day then," I said. "Are you here by yourself?"

"No. You're here too. You weren't abducted by aliens."

I cocked a brow and a jolt of pain radiated through my forehead. "Ouch."

"I never had appendicitis," Jaime said, toying with the strings that kept his Batman pajama bottoms up. "Does it hurt?"

I nodded.

"There's some pain medication on your table. You wannit?" he asked.

"Hell yeah."

I shot out my palm and he dropped two tablets into it. I swallowed them and then chased them with the cup of water he gave me.

"Are you sure they were pain meds?" I asked, suddenly more awake.

"They could have been peanut M&Ms. Did they taste chocolaty?"

I snorted.

"Don't worry," he said. "They were pain meds. I'm used to taking them."

"Really? Why?" I asked.

"For pain. Duh."

"You're a smart aleck, aren't you?"

He grinned and thick black lashes blinked down over blue eyes that seemed to take up a third of his face. "So where did the aliens want to take you?" he asked, going to sit on his bed. I could see it now that he'd drawn the divider open.

"On their spaceship," I said.

"I would totally go."

"You'd go with a bunch of creepy, triangular-headed dudes on a spacecraft destined for God-knows-where? Get out...You would never set foot on that thing. You'd probably run home crying to your mommy."

"My mom's dead, *and* I don't cry."

"Oh. Sorry, I...umm...didn't mean to—"

"That's fine." He shrugged his narrow shoulders. "She died when I was born, so I never knew her."

"How old are you?"

"Eight. What happened to your forehead?" he asked.

"Sliced it open."

"How?"

"I fell against a metal weight rack," I said.

He giggled and I noticed he was missing two teeth.

"What?" I asked.

"You should make up a cooler story. Like you were cut with a knife while defending a woman and her baby in Montgomery Park."

"*Okay...*" I didn't want to shoot the kid's idea down, but I wasn't going to brag about some fabricated feat.

"You're not gonna do it, are you?"

"What?" I asked. "Lie?"

He scrunched his brow in disappointment, and gaped down at his bare feet that swung without touching the floor.

"How about I tell people I was juggling ninja stars, and one slipped and carved out my forehead?"

He looked back up at me. "Cool. But not as cool as my story. How about you got caught by government spies, and they tortured you because they thought you were harboring a Colombian drug lord in your basement?"

"*Umm...*You have a very active imagination, don't you?"

"I read a lot."

"At eight?"

He was rolling a piece of the rumpled bed sheet between his thumb and index. "It takes my mind off things."

I grunted. "What sort of things do you have going on at eight?"

"Just because I'm young doesn't mean I have no life."

"That's not what I meant, Jaime."

A long silence set in. Rubber soles squeaked just outside our door. I wondered if someone was coming to check on us, but the footsteps continued and then petered out.

"Why are you in the hospital?" I asked.

"I don't want to talk about it," he mumbled.

My gaze darted to the small pile of comics on his nightstand.

"Do you like comic books?" he asked, following my line of sight. His voice had perked up again.

"Yeah."

"Do you want to borrow one?"

"Sure. It's not like I can sleep anymore," I added under my breath.

He didn't say he was sorry. Probably because he wasn't. He slid off his bed and carried over a few books. I selected a *Superman*, which looked as though it had basked in the sun for a decade.

Jaime peered at the cover. "Lois Lane's going to activate a de-aging machine and turn herself into a baby, but Clark Kent will give her the antidote. He puts it in a baby bottle to teach her a lesson."

"I wouldn't want to watch a thriller with you," I said.

"Sorry."

"It's all right. I'll just find something else to read." I took another book from the pile he'd placed on my tray. It was an equally vintage-looking comic strip. The colored ink had turned sepia, like the family photographs on my grandmother's nightstand.

"I think that's the one where Archie marries Veronica," he said.

I frowned.

"Show me the last page?" he asked.

I flipped to the last page and held it out so only he could see it.

"Yup. I was right."

I sighed. "I guess I won't be reading that one either."

"Just because you know the ending doesn't mean you shouldn't read it," he said as the door of our bedroom flew open.

"Well, slap my head and call me silly! You boys havin' a party without me?" Hummer-nurse winked at Jaime but shooed him off my mattress. "It's the middle of the night, hun. Off to sleep or I'll get in trouble with your daddy."

"Okay," he grumbled. She tucked him underneath the covers and then replaced my empty IV bag with a fresh one. "What time did you take those pills I left ya?"

"About ten minutes ago."

She checked my blood pressure and bandages and then

clicked off my nightlight. "You'll be outta here before the day's out. Healthy as an ox. You need anythin' else?"

"I wouldn't mind another glass of water," I said.

"Comin' right up. And you, hun?" she asked Jaime.

"Same thing."

"I'll be back before you can spell Yolanda," she said.

"Thanks, Yolanda," Jaime said.

"Anythin' for you, sweet pea." She stood still for a second, staring at him.

When she left, Jaime whispered, "Yolanda'll give you some candy if you get on her good side."

I squelched my first thought, which was, *how do you know that?* Obviously, he'd spent a lot of time in this hospital. Even though I was curious, I didn't try to coax it out of him. Maybe Yolanda would tell me. "How do you get on her good side?"

"Talk to her about her cats," he whispered. "She loves cats."

Just as he said that, she trundled back into the room and put a glass of water on both our trays. "Nighty night, boys," she said, before leaving and closing our door.

"Hey, Duke," Jaime said, his voice low.

"Yeah?"

"Could you tell me a story?" he asked.

I chewed on my lip, trying to come up with something that would entertain an eight-year-old. I decided on the alien abduction tale, but this time they were taking Jaime back to their planet, which was salmon colored because fire raged underneath the white rocks, and the air was devoid of gravity, so you could fly around. As I wove a more complex plot about kidnapping specific humans to bring new skill sets to their planet, I realized that I wouldn't have minded being abducted by aliens after all.

Chapter Sixteen

Dazed, I stared at the empty bed next to mine. It was made, the sheets pulled tight. The comic books were gone. It had looked that way since I woke up. When Yolanda brought me breakfast, I asked where Jaime had gone. She told me home. Then I asked what he had, and she told me to mind my own business. And then I asked about her cats, trying to weasel myself into her good graces, and she skewered me with a look of pure horror and left the room muttering something about a mule chewing on bumblebees.

"I'm here!" Mom exclaimed, snapping me out of my daze. She rushed over to me.

Grandma P. came in after her, wheezing. "I can taste metal. That's it…I'm going to have a heart attack."

"You're in the right place," Mom said. "Better have it now rather than in the car."

Mom looked different. I squinted and tried to make out what was off.

"I know, I know…I look dreadful. I didn't sleep *and* I forgot to put on makeup before leaving the house." She fished a pair of big sunglasses out of her handbag and put them on. "Lean on me."

"I don't need to," I said.

"Duke Meyer, you've just been operated on. You are not walking out of here without my help."

So I placed my palm on her arm and pretended to need her.

The second we got home, Grandma and Mom took their jobs as my nurses very seriously, feeding me pills and bowls of chicken-noodle soup, clocking in so many hours at my side that I didn't have a minute to myself. I was almost thankful that Dr. Monroe had only prescribed two days of rest.

By Monday night, I was feeling so restless that when Dad suggested we all go to the country club for dinner, I jumped at the opportunity. I shrugged into my dinner jacket, which was required in the dining room, combed my hair over the Band-Aid on my forehead, and trundled down the stairs, nearly forgetting that I'd been operated on forty-eight hours ago.

We piled into my mother's car—Mom and Grandma in the back, and Dad and I in the front. Even though the drive took a total of seven minutes, it felt longer. Long legs and cramped seats were not a good match. When we arrived, I pried my body out of the car and stretched it out like the bellows of an accordion.

We left the Maserati with the valet and climbed up the stairs to a glowing room filled with white tablecloths and piano music. Since my parents knew everyone, we stopped at every table.

"Hey, Duke," came a breathy voice. Liane.

"Hi," I said, as my parents stopped by her table to greet her mother and father.

"Heard you had appendicitis. I had it four years ago."

"Yeah." I shifted from one foot to the other.

This was probably one of the first conversations we'd had without Owen present. Liane smiled. I smiled, and then I went back to shifting.

"Well, I better get my Grandma to her seat before she collapses," I said.

Grandma pursed her wrinkly mouth. "Collapse? How old do you think I am?" she asked, trying to sound vexed.

I took her arm and led her away.

"Oh, I get it," she said.

"You get what?"

"You went to the movies with that girl."

"Maybe."

"This is the first time you've seen her since you kissed, isn't it?" she asked.

"Kissed?" I said way too loudly. "Liane and I are just friends." *Okay, not truly friends.* "She's dating Owen," I clarified.

"Who's dating Owen?" my mother asked as a waiter pulled up her chair. She placed her purse on the table.

"Liane," Grandma said.

"Oh." Mom twisted around to examine Liane.

"Could you be more subtle?" I grumbled.

She turned back toward me. "She's a very attractive girl."

She waited for a reaction. I didn't give her one.

"Her father's a smart man," she continued. "Started a fund that now makes several hundred million."

"Good for him," I said, taking the seat between my grand-mother and mother.

"So who did you kiss?" Grandma asked.

"I didn't kiss anyone." I was growing warmer, so I picked up the menu and tried to hide behind it.

"What are you two talking about?" Mom asked.

"Nothing," I said, hoping she would let it go, but she was my mother *and* Jewish. She would never let it go.

She plucked the menu from my fingers. "Do you have a girl-friend, Duke?"

"No," I huffed, thankful that my dad was still greeting people. "I do not have a girlfriend."

"Why not?" Mom asked.

"Because there's no girl I want to date," I said. Couldn't they just leave me alone?

"I find it hard to believe no one has caught your eye," Mom said. "Or shown interest in you. I mean, look at you. You're so handsome."

"Thanks, Mom. Can we please change the subject now?" I tried to take my menu back, but she held on tight.

"You would introduce us, right?" Grandma asked.

"To whom?" I asked.

"To your future girlfriend," she said.

"Yeah, sure." *Over my dead body.*

Dad was winding his way back to us. When he sat down, he asked, "What are the specials?"

I'd never been so thrilled to speak about food.

Right before dessert, Liane came over to our table. "Hey, Duke, I have a problem with our English assignment. Could we talk a sec?"

Both my parents surveyed me. Dad quickly lost interest, but Mom didn't—she probably wasn't convinced by my explanation of whose girlfriend Liane was.

"I'll be right back," I said and trailed Liane out of the dining room and onto the wrap-around balcony overlooking the dark tennis courts.

"I made a mistake and I'm not sure how to fix it."

"Do you have your homework with you?"

"Not on my homework, silly," she said, laughing nervously.

"This isn't about homework?"

She shook her head and her straight blond hair rippled.

"Is this about Owen, because if it is, I don't like to talk about—"

"Just hear me out."

I chewed on my lower lip, already uncomfortable.

"I don't really…*click* with him," she said.

I frowned.

"He's very, *umm*, childish. I don't think I've ever had a serious conversation with him." Her fingers toyed with the long metal and pearl necklace looped around her neck. "On Friday, I started talking with Gabe, and I, *uhh...*" Her voice trailed off, but I knew where she was going.

"You can't do that to Owen," I said. "Or to Gabe."

"But he likes me." She let go of her necklace. "I can tell."

"Maybe. But you can't dump Owen to go out with him."

"What can I do then?"

"Why are you asking me?"

"Because. You're their friend."

I sighed. "Break up with Owen. And then, *maybe*, in a few weeks, you can entertain the idea of hooking up with Gabe. Shit, Liane, you should've picked better the first time around!"

She stared down at her feet, which made me feel bad for having raised my voice.

"Look, just wait awhile. Like maybe until the summer, or until Owen lands a new girlfriend."

"Okay," she breathed.

"And don't be too brutal when you break up with him. He likes you a lot."

She sighed. "I know. Speaking of which, Amanda really, *really* likes you. She's been asking nonstop about how you're doing, and if she should come by your house with cupcakes."

*Amanda...*I hadn't thought much about her since my appendicitis.

"Do you like her?" Liane asked.

"I don't know."

"Well, if you don't want to end up like me, you better make up your mind," she said.

"Thanks for the advice."

"No. Thank *you* for listening."

Liane hugged me and all thoughts of Amanda whooshed out of my mind.

"Sure," I said. "Anytime."

After I returned to the table, I contemplated what I should do about Amanda. My mother and grandmother desperately tried to decipher my mood and thoughts since I wouldn't even throw them a bone as to what had gone down on the balcony. Question marks were popping out of their heads as though they were characters in a comic strip. My dad didn't care. He was much too busy discussing whiskeys with the maître d'.

When dessert arrived, I'd decided to ask Amanda out. Maybe I could meet her under the bleachers. But what if Cora was there?

Agh…What was my problem with that girl?

That made up my mind. I would go out with Amanda because she'd help me forget about Cora. And all would be well again in Duke Meyer's life.

Chapter Seventeen

It usually took me ten minutes to get ready for school. On Tuesday morning, it took me fifteen. I didn't primp or anything; I just spent more time styling my hair to cover my bandage. When I checked my watch, I saw I was running very late.

I nearly forgot about breakfast in my haste, but Grandma and Mom were both up and had fixed me a heaping plate of pancakes, fresh orange juice, and my cocktail of pain meds. I inhaled everything in a matter of minutes and rushed out to my car.

The heat was sweltering, and it wasn't even eight o'clock. I blasted cool air to keep my shirt from sticking to my skin. After I parked in front of Francis Academy, I didn't get out of the car straight away. I strategized and breathed. When I felt ready—or as ready as I would ever be—I jumped out of the car and strode into school.

As I spun my lock, I surreptitiously searched for Amanda. I didn't see her and had no idea about her schedule.

"Hey," Gabe said.

I jumped.

"Can't believe you're already back in school, man. You should've milked your bed rest."

"I know, but Mom and Grandma were glued to my backside," I said. "I had to get out of there."

He screwed up his face. "Did they take your appendix out through your forehead?"

"What?"

"What's up with the Band-Aid?" he asked, pointing to my head.

"I was juggling knives before my appendix burst."

"Why would you juggle knives? What's wrong with you?" he asked.

The humor was lost on Gabe. When I told him the truth, he smirked.

"By the way, how was the meeting?" I asked.

"Wouldn't you like to know?" he said. "Soon, my friend, soon."

"How soon?"

As I dug through my locker, a folded note fell at my feet. I picked it up, ran my finger over the large, elegantly curled *A*.

"Apparently very soon," he said. "What does it say?"

I flipped it open. *Ernesto's, Sunday April 27, at 1:00 p.m. Jacket and tie required. Password: ants,* was written in cursive on the cream-colored paper. I nearly dropped the note. My second chance.

"Will you be there?" I asked, suddenly anxious.

"Yeah, I'll be there. And so will Owen."

My heart drummed inside my chest as I shut my locker. "What do you think they'll have me do this time?"

Gabe started down the hall, and I trailed after him.

"Haven't heard anything," he said.

"I hope it won't be illegal again," I mumbled, mostly to myself. "Shoot. I can't go on Sunday. I'm still grounded."

"Well, you need to get ungrounded. You don't make these people wait."

"Yeah. I *know*."

"I have an idea. Sunday, we have that school hike in the Poconos. Maybe you can tell your parents you signed up and are dying to go."

"Are you kidding? I just had my appendix taken out. I can't ask to go hiking. Plus I hate hiking," I said. "I'll think of something."

As my mind hurtled through half-a-dozen excuses, I ran smack into someone. Muttering something about watching where I was going, Cora knelt down to collect her notebook and the scattered papers. I got on my knees, wincing—bending at my waist tugged on the puncture wounds.

"I'll catch you in class," Gabe said and left.

I gave Cora the papers I'd gathered. She took them from me and tucked them back inside her notebook without looking up. She didn't say anything, but I caught her wiping her eyes. When she pushed herself up, I rose too. I tried to snag her attention, but she kept her gaze averted.

"You okay?" I asked, reaching out to touch her. I chickened out in the end, and boomeranged my arm back to my side.

"Yeah. I'm awesome, Meyer," she snapped.

"Don't bite my head off. I was just asking. And you're obviously not fine."

Silence.

"Is it your boyfriend?" I still had trouble believing she had one.

She swiped the back of her hand against her cheek and dislodged some of the white foundation. Streaks of golden skin appeared. "Something like that," she murmured croakily, before dashing out through the school doors, leaving the scent of wild roses in the air of the empty hallway.

Dazed and very confused, I hurried to art class before Mr. Walker marked me down as late. I checked the blackboard for the assignment—portraits—and went to pick up a piece of charcoal and tubes of paint from the supply shelves before settling in front of an easel. I scraped the charcoal against the large sheet of white paper and swirled dabs of gray and black paint along the curved lines.

Twenty minutes into the task, Mr. Walker stopped by to see what I was working on. "Interesting, Duke," he said, scratching his goatee. "I love the luster in the irises and the thickness of your brushstrokes."

Cora's haunting black eyes stared back at me. "Thanks."

"So much emotion. Are you going to build a face around them?" he asked.

I frowned. "I did."

"They seem to be floating."

"Well, they're not," I said.

I felt him glance at me.

"Art *is* subjective," he admonished, and then strolled over to the next person.

I went to wash my brush in the sink and strip my fingers of the clingy black powder.

When class was over, I ran into Amanda.

She tipped her head up and smiled. "Hi."

"Hey. Are you free for lunch?"

She nodded and her loose brown hair meshed with her long gold earrings.

"Meet me by the football field?" I asked.

Color touched her tanned cheeks as she nodded again, and we parted ways.

I had the urge to pump my fist in the air, but that was moronic, so I settled on a satisfied smile. It gave Gabe pause when he saw me slide into the seat next to him in math.

What up? he scribbled in the margins of my textbook.

I got myself a lunch date, I wrote underneath.

Cora?

I shook my head no and shot him a look.

Amanda?

I nodded.

What happened to Cora?

I shrugged.

Good. The girl's a train wreck.

I glowered, but then I blinked away my glare when his thick brows cocked up. Gabe didn't write anything else in the margins of my book.

As soon as the bell rang, he asked, "Where's Owen?"

I hadn't even noticed he was absent. "Maybe he's sick," I said. Liane must have broken up with him. Since I didn't want to deliver the news, I suggested he call him.

"Yeah. I'll do that during lunch since you're ditching me," he said.

"Now I feel bad."

"Chill, Dukey. I was just kidding. I can survive without you and Owen."

As we made our way out of the classroom, I pondered if having a girlfriend would ruin my friendships.

Chapter Eighteen

Pulse hammering through my body, I watched Amanda cross the football field toward me. She had really nice legs. Granted, she was on the cheer squad, but not every cheerleader was fit. And she had a cute face. I corrected my brain. She had a great face.

"Hey," she said when she spotted me standing under the bleachers.

"You came."

She grinned. "Yes, I came."

"So I was think—"

She pressed herself up on her toes and kissed me, and subsequently, I stopped thinking. I reached one hand behind her waist, tucked the other behind her neck, and kissed her back, feeling kind of drunk and jittery, like a child on a Lucky Charms high. Her hands rested against my chest. Through the white cotton, I felt their warmth. I remembered how soft they'd felt when I'd held them during the movies.

I deepened the kiss. How had I not considered Amanda before? She was perfect girlfriend material and superhot. I'd made the right decision. She pulled me closer and then she pressed me away, and her mouth released mine. I opened my eyes and looked into hers.

"So what were you thinking about?" she asked. Her lips, still damp from our kiss, were curved into a smile.

"What?"

"You were about to say something when I, like, interrupted you."

"I have no clue." And I truly didn't. "And you're welcome to interrupt me like that anytime."

Her fingers tugged on my shirt. "You asked for it."

Not in so many words, but *yes, please, make out with me to your heart's desire, Amanda.*

I floated in and out of my afternoon classes. I was on such a high that the **B-** I got in home ec didn't even irk me. After my last class, I went up to the principal's office to give him the surgeon's note barring me from overly exerting myself for the next few days. He took it from me but didn't read it.

"You're feeling well, though? Coming to school is not too tiring?" he asked. "I remember when I had my appendix taken out. They butchered my right side. Apparently, the procedure's much less invasive today."

Had the surgeon mentioned my appendectomy on the note? I couldn't remember, nor could I decipher it from across the desk.

"Just so we're clear though, I'll postpone your punishment until your doctor gives you the green light, but you'll have to make up the lost time, okay?"

"Okay," I replied a bit glumly. There went hoping it would be cancelled altogether.

After I left his office, I called Owen to find out how he was doing. He told me he hadn't come to school because of a spontaneous stomach flu, but he did throw in that his relationship with Liane was over. He'd been about to break up with her anyway. I didn't believe that for a second but let it slide. Owen had a hefty dose of confidence and would forget about Liane quicker than Drampton decapitated his detractors in *Pursuit of Kings*. Right before hanging up, he threw in that Sunday would rock the shit out of me, or something along those lines. Which reminded me that I needed to get my parents' consent.

As though they'd sniffed Amanda on me, Mom and Grandma bombarded me with questions as soon as I got home. I feigned exhaustion to be spared. It wasn't a total lie. Walking around the school hallways and sitting in stiff wooden chairs had taken its toll on me.

Later, at dinnertime, as I sat next to my grandmother, the dopy grin I'd been sporting all day must've made an appearance because my father asked me what was wrong. Dad wasn't very intuitive when it came to human emotions; in business though, he could spot problems and opportunities from a distance.

"Owen and Liane broke up," I said to get everyone off my back.

"Already?" Mom said.

"Who's Liane?" Dad asked.

"You know, that pretty blond who came to speak to Duke during dinner at the club yesterday," Mom explained.

Dad frowned, speared some carrots, and buried them inside his mouth.

"Derek's daughter. The fund manager," Mom continued.

"Oh," he said.

The skin around his eyes was smudged purple. Dad didn't sleep much, but the marked circles and his mood, which wavered between grim and annoyed, told me he was stressed.

"Everything all right at the office?" I asked him.

His fork clattered against his plate. Mom jumped at the noise. Grandma stopped eating.

"No," Dad admitted. "We got a complaint about one of our drugs. A guy's blaming us for causing tumors in his kid."

"Is he suing?" I asked.

"On what grounds?" he grunted. "For all anyone knows, his kid's cancer has nothing to do with our drug." He grabbed his fork again and impaled a large piece of potato.

"What do *you* think?" I asked.

My father's broad shoulders hiked up. "I have a team of people paid to think so I don't have to."

"That doesn't answer my question," I said.

"Our environment causes cancer!"

"Then why are you so angry?" I asked, keeping my voice even.

"Because I'm tired, and I don't want to talk shop at home!" Dad roared.

"Don't take it out on me," I snapped back.

I was about to stand up when Mom clapped her hand over mine to keep me in place. "Let's discuss something else."

"Can I be excused?"

"Duke—" Mom started.

"I have a lot of homework," I said.

I rose and left, my good mood soured by my father's bad one. Although I climbed the stairs calmly, when I got to my room, I slammed the door shut and vaulted onto my queen-sized bed. I stuck my earphones in and blasted some vintage Bon Jovi. My reprieve was short lived, though. The door opened and Dad filled the entire space. I took out my earphones and sat up. It would've been suicidal to ignore him.

"I'm sorry for taking my stress out on you," he said.

I wondered if my mother had made him come up and apologize. He trudged in and wheeled my desk chair next to the bed. It was covered with my American flag comforter. He didn't bother tossing it off; he just sat.

"It's just...I keep thinking...What if it *was* our drug that caused the boy's tumors? What if more people come out of the woodwork with similar illnesses?"

"Can the kid be saved?"

Dad rubbed his thick gray hair and leaned back in the chair, which creaked under his weight. "According to his father's letter, he's terminal. I usually don't even see the letters of complaints, but considering—" He stopped short. "But I did. And all day, I kept thinking, what if it were you dying?"

"I'm sure it's just a coincidence."

"Maybe." Dad got back on his feet. "Anyway, I don't want you to worry about this. I'm sorry I went off on you. Come back downstairs. Your mom will be heartbroken if you don't try her chocolate soufflé."

Together, we returned to the dining room. Dad wasn't angry anymore. He was just sullen. He even revoked my month-long punishment. At least now I didn't need to beg to leave the house on Sunday.

After dinner, Grandma served a round of whiskey. Alcohol wouldn't rid my dad of the macabre weight resting on his shoulders, but it would help mitigate his guilt. We all moved into the living room to deliberate on life. It was one of those conversations that put the trivial things into perspective, and that led my mother to heavy weeping. Granted, Mom cried over everything, but a child dying rendered her inconsolable.

It didn't leave me indifferent, but I lived by the principle that things or people I didn't know didn't affect me. Maybe that made me selfish, but it definitely kept me sane.

Chapter Nineteen

Owen was outrageously cheerful on Wednesday morning. He didn't mention Liane and I didn't either. When I told him I was free of punishment at home, his cheerfulness increased tenfold. He planned for me to come over and catch up on some video games after school. I agreed, even though I sort of wanted to hang out with my new girlfriend.

Amanda and I sat together at lunch, picking at our food between make-out sessions and college discussions. Where I wanted to go to Harvard and double major in business and comp lit, she wanted to teach English to refugees in Africa.

"Would your parents let you go?" I asked her. If I told my mother I was moving to a war zone, she would shred my passport while reminding me how much more good I could do with a college degree.

"The second I turn eighteen, they don't have much say in what I do," Amanda said.

"Are you close to them?"

She shrugged. "Not especially. They're divorced, you know."

I didn't know.

"I'm stuck living here with Mom, when I'd much rather move to LA to live with Dad," she said.

"That sucks."

"Yep."

I could tell from the sudden shift in her mood that speaking of her parents was a downer, so I switched topics. "Have you ever been to Korea?"

"No."

"Do you want to go?"

"Maybe someday, but I don't, like, know anyone there. All my family's in the States," she said, crumpling the piece of apple cake on her tray. She patted her fingers against her plaid skirt to dislodge the crumbs.

My gaze wandered down to the short hem of her skirt that offered an unbeatable view of her chiseled legs. Without a doubt, a man had designed Francis Academy's uniform. I thanked him.

"What about you? Any foreign origins?" she asked.

"Nope. I'm as American as they come."

"What are your parents like?" she asked.

"Dad's the CEO of a pharmaceutical company. He works a lot, but he makes it a point to be home for dinner whatever happens at the office. Mom spends her days worrying about me or hanging out in the country club. And then there's Grandma. She also lives with us. It's sort of like having a second mother."

"You're an only child?"

I nodded. "And you?"

"Same," she said. "It's funny getting to know someone after, you know…hooking up with them."

I nodded. I didn't know much about relationships, but I wondered if it was better to know a person before dating them, or if dating a stranger could work out. Just because it hadn't for Owen didn't mean that it wouldn't for me, right?

I drove to Owen's after school and fried a hefty dose of brain cells discussing Fae combos, sentinels, and a possible replacement for Liane since he was already on the hunt for a rebound. The sacrifice of brain matter was worth it, though; Owen was psyched by the time I left his house.

Mom had surpassed herself at dinner that night. She'd made Beef Wellington from scratch with my grandmother. Dad was in a much better mood. I didn't ask him about work. Instead, we spoke about Gabe's father's rise in the election polls and Owen's mother's descent into alcoholism. Mom had spotted her intoxicated three afternoons in a row at the club, and she was worried.

"There's so much drama in this world," Mom said, sipping her red wine.

"In your world, honey," my father corrected her.

She made a face. "It's your world too."

"You're my world," he said, and I swear, I threw up a bit in my mouth.

"Did you know everything about each other before you started dating?" I blurted out.

They both gaped at me. I'd never asked much about their relationship before, so I understood their surprise.

"I knew everything there was to know about your mom, including her favorite flavor of chewing gum. And her mother's too, I might add." He winked at Grandma.

Mom's green eyes twinkled. I wasn't sure if it was because of my dad's declaration or my novel interest. "Why do you ask, honey?"

"No reason," I said, taking my empty dessert plate to the kitchen to evade cross-examination.

As I went upstairs to start on my homework, my grandmother whispered something about being certain I had a new girlfriend while I went upstairs to start on my homework. An hour in, there was a knock on my door.

"Come in," I said.

Dad entered, his gaze tracing the uneven gray lines of my rug. "Umm…Duke, I had something I wanted to give you."

"What?"

Little beads of sweat trickled down his sideburns. I frowned. I'd rarely seen Dad so nervous.

"Here." He extended an orange shoe box.

"You bought me loafers?" I asked, taking it from him. "That's really—" My voice died as I opened the box and gawked at its contents. I replaced the lid at lighting speed and put it down on my desk.

"Yeah…*umm*…it's not shoes," Dad said.

"I got that." I was now tracing the lines in my rug in time with my father.

"I put this together because I thought that…that you might have an easier time understanding with magazines. I'm more of a visual person myself and—"

"Thanks!" I exclaimed, desperate to put an end to this tortuous sex talk.

"Okay," Dad breathed out. "We're good?"

"We're good."

"Your mom put some condoms in there. Wasn't sure which sort was better, so she put in a variety." Dad shot this out so quickly I didn't have time to die of embarrassment.

I would never, ever be able to sit at a meal with either of them without imagining them discussing what type of condom they should buy me. The minute Dad left my bedroom, I dropped my head against the table and banged it slowly. Maybe if I banged it enough, I would have a concussion and all would be forgotten.

Chapter Twenty

"What do you think you're doing?" I asked Gabe the second he settled down next to me in home ec.

"I'm sitting down."

"You know very well what I mean," I hissed as Mrs. Gill came in.

He gave me a sly smile. "I was just talking to her."

"You shouldn't *talk* to her, or hang out with her, or—"

The smile vanished. "Chillax, man. It was harmless."

"If Owen even suspects something—"

"There's nothing for him to suspect."

"Well, keep it that way." *Ugh.* I sounded like my mom.

"I will. Until he has a new girl. Then Liane's game." As Mrs. Gill scraped the words *macronutrients vs. micro-nutrients* on the blackboard with a piece of chalk, Gabe added, "He has his eye on that junior on the swim team."

"He told me," I said, keeping my voice low.

"He wants to ask her out. Encourage him."

"You still have to wait."

He shrugged.

"I'm serious," I hissed.

"Mr. Meyer, since you seem so keen on speaking, would you please disclose the elemental composition of lipids?"

Crap. I flicked my gaze to my open textbook and speed-read the text. No elemental composition popped out. I bit down on my lip and gaped up at Mrs. Gill, who shook her head. Her jowls wobbled like a turkey's wattle. She was obviously indulging in too many lipids, whatever their composition.

"Miss Marcy?" Mrs. Gill called next.

Cassie spoke up, "Carbon, hydrogen, and oxygen."

"Thank you for paying attention to my lectures. May I suggest you do the same, Mr. Meyer? I would hate to see your grade point average dwindle because of my class."

I jerked my head in assent.

"Good. Now, who can tell me the composition of carbohydrates?" Mrs. Gill asked.

Several people raised their hands. I wasn't one of them, but I listened, intent on not giving my stout, middle-aged teacher any more ammunition against me. After my earlier B-, I couldn't afford another bad grade in home ec or any other subject for that matter. I didn't want to risk my parents grounding me again.

As soon as the bell rang, I sprang out of my seat and headed toward the locker rooms.

"Never seen you so excited to come watch me run," Gabe said, pushing through the door. "Wouldn't have to do with a certain chick?"

"Shut up."

"No, *you* shut up." He batted his short eyelashes, making his voice all syrupy. "Oh, Dukey."

I slugged his shoulder.

Gabe snickered as he unbuttoned his shirt and stuffed it inside his locker. "So how's Amanda?" His voice was back to normal, but he was still fluttering his nonexistent lashes.

"She's fine," I said.

"Just fine?"

"I don't kiss and tell."

"Come on, give your brother something. Especially since it's your fault I'm not getting any."

"How's it my fault?" I asked.

"You're my freaking conscience."

"And that's a bad thing?"

"It's an annoying thing."

As Gabe pulled on his gym shorts, I scanned the locker room. "Where's Owen?"

"He got detention. They suspended him from gym," he explained before baiting me about Amanda.

I tried to keep quiet about her, but he pestered me so much that I told him she was an awesome kisser and had a great body. That seemed to satisfy him. When I walked out of the locker room, I spotted her standing next to the coach in her sports uniform. The girl's shorts were short, shorter than their plaid skirts, which looked awful on some. Amanda wasn't part of the awful group. Her sculpted legs stood out in the sea of emaciated and chunky ones. She beamed at me as I walked toward the gathering.

Gabe rammed his elbow into my ribs, arms folded against his chest. "Put her out of her misery, man. Go."

"Shut it," I muttered through gritted teeth.

"Chicken," he teased.

"The coach is standing right there. I'm not going to go plant one on her in front of everyone."

"I would if she were my girl."

"Let's discuss that once you have a girl," I said, just as Liane approached Amanda.

She whispered something in her ear that made Amanda's cheeks turn pink. Then she grinned my way...or Gabe's way. Her blue gaze surfed right past me to my bulky, beaming sidekick.

"Be careful," I whispered.

"Yes, irritating conscience." Like a ventriloquist, his lips didn't move.

The coach split everyone into groups of six for a relay race. Gabe and Amanda were on the same team. As we filed out to the track field, I dug my black wayfarers out of my shirt pocket and put them on.

I found a spot to sit somewhere along the track.

"How're you feeling?" Liane asked. She was standing a few feet away.

"Good."

"Thanks for listening the other day."

"Sure."

"How's Owen?" she asked.

"Fine."

She smirked. "Good to hear I don't make a lasting impression on men."

"That's not what I meant," I said, as Gabe trotted up to the space next to Liane.

She shrugged. "I know. It was just a joke."

"Ready to be beaten, blondie?" Gabe said.

"In your dreams," she responded with a chuckle.

As she bent over to stretch her legs, I glanced down the track at Amanda who was talking to Joss, the man-girl Liane had suggested I date. The coach blew his whistle and everyone fell silent. Then he blew it again, and the first runners were off.

He jogged toward me. "A word, Duke."

"Yes?" I stood up and rubbed my hands together to dislodge the dirt.

"When can you start training again?"

"I think next week. I'm seeing the doctor on Saturday. I'll ask him."

"The championship's in two weeks," he said. "And I'm worried about—"

"I'll be at the next practice. *And* I can train during lunch."

"Okay. But scouts and professionals will be there. I need us to win. You understand, right?"

I frowned. "What are you trying to say, Coach?"

He was watching the runners. "If by any chance you're not well enough to play, I don't want it to affect the team."

"I'll be well enough."

"Okay. Report to me on Monday."

"I will," I said and watched as he jogged up the field toward the finish line.

"Watch out, Duke!" Joss called out.

I jerked out of her way. I hadn't realized I was standing on the running track.

"Sorry!" she yelled as she zipped past me like a roadrunner. She extended the baton, and Liane took it from her.

"Don't choke on the dust I kick up, Gabe," Liane teased right before her fluorescent-pink sneakers dashed down the track toward the last of her teammates.

Gabe was still chuckling when Amanda passed him the baton and he flew down the track.

"God, I hate running," Amanda said, to me or to Joss, I wasn't sure.

She jabbed her fingers into her waist and breathed heavily. Her lips were red, redder than usual. They made me forget about the coach and his warning. I felt the urge to kiss them, but bit the inside of my cheek instead.

"Plus, it wasn't a fair race," she added. "Joss's legs are, like, twice the length of mine."

"No, they're not," Joss said.

"I take it you don't like losing," I said, watching Amanda.

"I don't like losing to Liane *and* Joss. Those two have egos the size of Walmart."

"We do not," Joss said.

Amanda laughed. The coach blew his whistle to signal the end of the relay. I approached Amanda, who hung back, waiting for me. I was about to grab her hand when she rose up on her tiptoes and snuck a kiss on my mouth. It was way too brief, and I would have remedied that had I not heard some whooping and clapping a short distance away—Gabe and Liane. I shook my head at them, all the while smiling.

Then I concentrated on Amanda again. Even though her neck and cheeks were splotchy red from the attention, I dipped down and lengthened the much too rapid kiss. Our coupledom became official by lunch period, and by the end of the day, all of Francis Academy knew we were dating.

Chapter Twenty-One

"Can we hang out this afternoon?" I asked Amanda after lunch on Friday.

She sidled against my locker and sighed. "Can't. I promised our neighbor to babysit her twins."

"That blows," I said, gazing down into her hazel eyes. They seemed more green than brown in the rays of sunshine that fell across them.

"The weekend's coming up. We could maybe, like, see each other then."

I was getting used to her offbeat placement of the preposition. "Sure. Saturday?"

"Dad's coming into town tomorrow, and we're spending the whole day in the city. He doesn't come very often."

"I wouldn't have suggested ditching him," I said defensively.

"I know. Is it awful that I'd rather spend time with you than him?"

"Not to me, but you might not want to mention that to your father."

"How about we chill at my house on Sunday? Mom's coming back late, and Dad's on the red-eye back to Cali."

My bright orange shoe box popped into my mind at the

mention of her empty house. I was about to whip out a *hell, yeah* when my own weekend plans dawned on me.

"*Crap*," I said. "I have a thing on Sunday."

"A thing?"

I shrugged. "I'm hanging with the guys."

"All day?"

I had no idea so I nodded.

"That's too bad," she said.

No, it wasn't too bad. It sucked. Big time!

"My mom's rarely around on weekends," she said. "So I'll be free next Saturday *and* Sunday." Green and gold specks churned mischievously in her irises.

I was way too riled up, and self-conscious about being riled up, to utter intelligible words, so I kept quiet.

Amanda grinned, aware of my stiffening. She pushed up on her heeled sandals and teased my lips open. "Lunch tomorrow?" she asked.

"Yes," I breathed. It came out all wheezy. I coughed to clear my tight throat.

"Bye, Duke."

"Bye, Amanda," I said, watching her disappear into the classroom and feeling as if I should visit the showers in the locker room before math.

The second bell rang. I would have to cool down without the help of icy water. I slapped my locker door shut, grabbed my messenger bag, and dashed up the large wooden staircase to the first floor.

Later that day, I ran into Miss Brown and Mr. Darcy standing in the parking lot, talking. Her face was drawn, and her messy curls made her look as though she'd been caught in a windstorm. The second they saw me, they jumped like two kids caught passing notes during an exam.

"Hey, Duke," he said. "Am I seeing you on Monday?"

I beeped my car open. "I think so."

He gave me a snappy nod, then rotated back to Miss Brown, "Are you going to see Colin tonight?"

Simultaneously, she folded her arms and glanced at me. Her worried brown eyes seemed wider, wilder.

"Just keep me posted if there's anything I can do," the custodian continued, seemingly unaware of her discomfort.

Miss Brown nodded and he left, jogging back into the school. She didn't follow him back inside. She didn't move at all. She just remained poised next to my car.

As I got in, she said, "I wanted to suggest you submit that piece you wrote about your grandmother to a competition, Duke. It was so touching. I mean, just your title, 'Falling without Flowers,' is brilliant."

"Thanks, Miss Brown, but—"

"I'm serious." She freed her arms from their tight knot. "Will you do it?"

"I'll think about it," I said, pulling open the car door.

"Please do. I've been raving about your talent in the teachers' lounge."

I wrinkled my nose at the idea of being discussed in the rec room. "I'll ask my grandmother. It's her story."

"Of course."

I hopped into my car. "Have a nice weekend, Miss Brown."

"You too, Duke."

As I drove away, I found myself wondering if the custodian fancied Miss Brown, but then why was she on her way to meet with a dude named Colin?

My phone rang. I slid my finger against the screen. "Hi, babe," I answered, trying out the nickname. I always thought calling a chick *babe* sounded cool. Now that I'd said it out loud, I was having second thoughts.

"Hi," Amanda said.

She sounded as though she was smiling. I wondered if it was

because I'd called her *babe*. And then I wondered why I was wondering about stuff like that.

"The twins are doing their homework, and I was doing mine, and I thought of you," she said.

I smiled smugly. Amanda was thinking of me. It momentarily made me forget that I was driving, and I merged without checking my blind spot. My heart somersaulted into my throat as the driver I cut off hit his brakes. I slammed my foot on the gas pedal while he pounded on his horn, his tires squealing to a stop. Miraculously, we avoided a collision.

"Am I bothering you?" Amanda asked. Her voice had lost a few degrees of assurance.

"No!" I said when my heart had returned to its appropriate cavity. I put the phone on speaker and stuck it in the cup holder to avoid another moment of inattention. "So what are you studying?"

She sighed. "Biology. I'm terrible at it."

"I could give you some private tutoring next weekend."

This time, *she* was quiet for too long.

My forehead furrowed. "Amanda?" I hoped she hadn't hung up on my wayward ass.

"I was just taking this call into another room."

"So you don't shock the twins with our conversation?" I asked, leaning back.

"No, so I don't bother them while they work."

Was she serious? She probably thought I was totally depraved now. I slapped my forehead, which made my scar smart.

"And so I don't shock them with our conversation," she added in a low voice, and I swear she was laughing.

Chapter Twenty-Two

I spent a big chunk of Saturday watching Gabe and Owen run around the Modleys' indoor court. I wanted to play but contented myself with spinning a ball on my finger.

"Dude, you're throwing like a girl!" Owen yelled over the loud rap music vibrating in the huge space. "Actually, I've seen chicks make better layups than your sorry ass."

"I barely slept last night. Dad dragged me to this fundraising dinner in Hartford. It just wouldn't end," Gabe said, stealing the ball.

He dribbled and flung it into the basket. It hit the rim, circled once, twice, three times before falling out with a pathetic thump.

Owen retrieved it. "You better get back on your game before the championship. We need an all-star team."

I stopped spinning the ball and thought about the coach's warning.

"Don't you have a doctor's appointment?" Owen asked.

"Yeah," I said, standing.

I bounced the ball twice, and then tossed it toward the basket. My body felt stiff, and my arm movement, restricted. The ball landed out of bounds.

Owen cocked an eyebrow, but he didn't comment on my terrible shot. Instead, he flicked his wrist and glanced down at his gold Rolex. "It's only four." He let his arm fall back. "If the doc okays some b'balling, come back and practice with us."

I doubted he would. "I'll call you." On my way out, I scrutinized my sullen reflection in the shiny varnish the estate caretaker applied each year to all the wooden surfaces of the Modley mansion.

I drove straight to Greenwich Memorial, took the elevator to the third floor, and followed the receptionist's direction to my surgeon's office in the pediatric unit. I sat down in the empty waiting room, next to a truck-shaped bookcase filled to the brim with books. I selected one at random and started flipping through it.

"If it isn't the Duke of Graffiti."

I frowned when I spotted Jaime standing in the doorway. I shut the book. "The nurse hated cats."

He grinned. "I know. The neighbor's cat ate her parakeet. Actually, it ate two of them."

"Then why did you tell me she loved cats?"

"I thought it would be funny."

"Well, it wasn't. She was about to slap me," I said.

His small shoulders curled forward. "Sorry."

I was going to tell him that he should be when it struck me he was back in the hospital. "What are *you* doing here?"

He shrugged. "They had to take some blood." He lifted his T-shirt sleeve and displayed his forearm plastered with a Batman Band-Aid.

"Why?"

"To run some tests."

"What do you have?" I asked him.

He shifted from one bright blue sneaker to the other. "Nothing contagious."

"That's not why—"

"There you are," a voice said somewhere behind the little boy.

I was startled, because I recognized whom it belonged to. Seconds later, Principal Matthews materialized next to Jaime. When our gazes met, he froze.

"H-Hi…" he stammered.

I just stared like an idiot. "You have a son?"

His eyes slid down to Jaime, and then back to me. They were the same blue as Jaime's, except colder, flintier. He placed his hand on the boy's shoulder.

"Yes," he said, finding his composure quicker than I. "Are you getting your stitches out?"

"Yeah. The ones in my forehead." I tugged my floppy hair up to point out my scar. Given that I couldn't ask him why he'd never told me he had a son, I said, "I juggled some ninja stars. It was stupid."

Jaime cracked a large grin. I had to bite my lip to keep from mirroring it.

"Ninja stars?" my principal asked, eyes widening. "You might not want to play with sharp objects in the future."

"I learned my lesson."

A nurse appeared next to them and crouched to Jaime's height, her orange rubber shoes squeaking. "I need to borrow you for a second, little man," she said gently.

Mr. Matthews's fingers dug into his son's shoulder. I could see the fabric bunch around his nails. "I thought we were done for the day."

"We are. This is about that lollipop we discussed earlier," she said with a wink. "If that's okay, of course."

Jaime craned his neck to look up at his dad. "Can I?"

"Anything you want, kiddo," he said.

Still grinning, he followed the nurse, but then he doubled back. "I thought about what abilities I could give the aliens. If you ever want to hear them," he added quickly.

"Sure thing," I said, after which he dashed away for his promised candy.

Principal Matthews furrowed his brow. "Aliens?"

"It was just a story we made up the other night in the hospital," I explained. It hit me that he must've known I'd met his son. I wondered if Cora knew also.

"Don't give him false hope."

"What?" I asked, cheeks warming.

"Don't promise you'll meet him again if you're not going to," he said, rephrasing the comment I'd understood the first time around.

"I would never do that."

He didn't say anything and neither did I. We lingered in awkward silence. He was looking my way, but not at me. His gaze stuck on the truck bookcase next to my chair. I wasn't sure if he was reading the titles or inspecting the case itself.

"Is…is Jaime all right?" I asked.

"Not really," he said in a quiet voice. "I suggest you don't mention to Cora that you met him. She's very protective."

So Cora didn't know. I nodded just as Jaime popped back in the doorway.

"I got sour apple and caramel," he said, licking a flat green lollipop. "And I got one for you too, Duke."

He walked toward me, holding out the second green lollipop, oblivious to the stiffening of his father's posture. "You like sour apple, right?" he asked.

"It's my favorite."

"Mine too."

"You sure you don't want to hold on to it then?" I asked him.

"Dad will flip if I eat two."

"I won't *flip*," he said.

Jaime smiled.

"We should go," Mr. Matthews said. "I have to start on dinner."

"But it's the middle of the afternoon," Jaime protested.

"Cooking takes a lot of time."

Jaime started retreating toward his father when he spun around. "You want to come over for dinner?"

I bit my lip. "I don't think I can make it tonight. Some other time?"

The light in his eyes blunted. "Sure. Bye." He vanished down the hospital hallway.

"I'm sorry about that." Principal Matthews's mouth opened and closed a few more times, but nothing came out. Finally, he said, "See you on Monday." And then he shuffled out of the doorway and down the hall after his son.

Had it not been for the green lollipop I was holding, I would've wondered if our encounter was real.

"Duke Meyer, Dr. Monroe is ready for you," the nurse with the orange shoes said.

I rose and followed her down the narrow corridor toward an open door. "What does he have? Jaime Matthews?"

She glanced over her shoulder at me but kept walking. "I'm not authorized to disclose medical records." Her voice held none of the earlier tenderness.

I lowered my gaze to her rubber shoes and listened to the squashing sound they made against the wide ceramic tiles. A bunch of scenarios played out in my mind: a heart murmur, a chronic disease, cancer...I tightened my hold on the lollipop, crinkling the wrapper beneath my fingers as though I could squeeze the truth out of it, but it was just a piece of candy covered in plastic, not some crystal ball.

Chapter Twenty-Three

I stood outside my front door, wired and jumpy from the cup of cold, sugary coffee I'd inhaled half an hour ago. I'd slept poorly, in other words, not at all, and yet, felt more awake than ever, ready for my big meeting.

Gabe's shiny black car screeched into our driveway, windows down. "Ready?" he yelled.

I nodded like one of those bobble-headed figurines people stuck on their dashboards.

"Owen's waiting for us," he said. "Get in."

I jogged to the other side and dove into the passenger seat, smoothing down my black trousers. I'd ironed them and steamed my jacket and tie. My mother and grandmother were convinced I had a date, which was good—I hadn't needed to lie. A few minutes later, we pulled up in front of a red awning that read Ernesto's. My stomach grumbled as I got out of the car. I should've eaten before leaving. I needed to be attentive and alert, not starved.

"Password?" the bouncer asked.

"Ants," Gabe responded before I could. He looked at both of us before shifting sideways and letting us through.

Ernesto's was a fancy hole-in-the-wall that used to be a

brothel. I'd come once before, for my grandmother's birthday. It was decorated in bottle-green velvets, mirrors, and dark wood. A dozen suit-clad men were already sitting around tables. I spotted Owen and walked over to him. A place card with my name on it had been propped on the plate in front of his. I sat and scanned the room.

The last time—before my first hazing—I'd met a lawyer, a Mr. Davies, in his office. It had just been him and me. He'd given me a task, explained the rules, and then dismissed me. I'd been so excited to tell the guys—and buy a can of spray paint—that I couldn't get out of his building fast enough.

The lawyer was talking to a man who appeared to be twice his age. As though feeling my gaze on them, they lifted their eyes to mine. Mr. Davies nodded while the other scrutinized me. When he smirked, I looked away.

"Does everyone know about the first time?" I asked Gabe, my voice low.

"Yeah. But don't worry about it."

"Shit," I mumbled.

He shrugged. "You got a second chance. Focus on that."

Someone tapped his fork against a glass.

"The Wolf's here," Owen whispered.

I snapped my gaze to the man standing up. The second I recognized him, my jaw dropped and I blinked, totally awestruck.

"*He's* the Wolf?"

"Yup."

"Did he fly all the way from Silicon Valley for the meeting?" I whispered.

"I think he had some business in New York promoting the new 3-D tablet," Gabe murmured back.

Wow, was the only word that came to mind.

"Hello, gentlemen," he said, staring around the room through his wire-rimmed round glasses. "It's such a pleasure to be among you today. It's been too long."

"Here, here." Glasses were raised.

I twisted around, grabbed mine, and lifted it high. Then I took a small sip before placing it back next to my plate.

"Apparently, we have two orders of business today," he said.

A hush fell over the room.

"Firstly, I don't know if you've all heard, but there's a new law Mayor Turner has brought to my attention about creating a lump-sum taxation in Connecticut."

Gabe squared his shoulders, tense from the sudden scrutiny.

"He's going to mention it in his campaign as we inch closer to Election Day," the Wolf continued. "It would be a show of good faith if you could shoulder his initiative. Bobby offered to host a party at his house. Langdon proposed to write up a nice little article in the *Connecticut Times*. If anyone else can think of a way to further Mayor Turner's incentive, please let me know before we dismiss."

Buzzing murmurs erupted around the room. The Wolf clanged on his glass again, ruby cuff links glinting in the dim lighting. I checked my friends' shirt cuffs, and sure enough, both had hooked them in.

"Duke Meyer. Stand please," the Wolf said.

I grew warm as everyone's attention converged on me.

"Even though this is out of character for the Alphas, the majority has voted to give Mr. Meyer a second chance." The leader of the prestigious pack examined me. "I hope you know how lucky you are, boy. I've been head of this organization for close to six years, and I've never heard of second chances."

I nodded. Or at least I think I did. I was too busy liquefying. My shirt was sticking to my back and my hair was damp.

"Also, it's the first time we invite an initiate to a meeting before he's sworn in. No pressure," he said, the sides of his mouth curving.

People chuckled. I desperately wanted to wipe my brow, but didn't dare move.

"Duke Meyer," he said solemnly. "You must dump three hundred goldfish in Francis Academy's pool."

"I can do that," I found myself saying out loud.

The Wolf gave me a taunting, crooked smile. "I'm certain that you can, Duke, but there's a hang-up. Just to make it more challenging. You'll have to do it right before a swim meet."

I would get caught. And expelled this time!

Unless goldfish could survive in chlorinated water for several hours…I could dump them in the middle of the night. But were there cameras in the pool house? And where would I find three hundred goldfish?

The Wolf walked over to me. He was much shorter than he looked in magazines; the top of his head came up to my shoulder. "Are you aware of how you got a second chance?"

"No," I said.

The Wolf's gaze slid to my right, over Gabe, and then beyond him to Owen.

"You have good friends," he said. "They put their membership on the line for yours."

"Huh?" I asked.

"You fail, they're out."

I shot my friends a look. They both shrugged.

"My boy won't fail," Owen said.

Gabe gave me a thumbs-up.

The blood drained from my face when I grasped what was now at stake. This wasn't just about me.

"Good luck, Duke," the Wolf said.

I would need more than luck to succeed! I would need a freaking divine intervention.

Chapter Twenty-Four

On Monday morning, I hobbled down Francis Academy's hallway, barely greeting anyone. I had trouble concentrating on anything besides goldfish. I'd read they could survive in a pool for a few hours, but then other blogs spoke of minutes, and I didn't know which to trust.

As I came out of the locker room at the end of the day, I spotted Cora treading into the school's two-story library. I froze. She reminded me of Jaime, and I hadn't thought about him since Saturday.

Mr. Darcy popped out of the library while I was still gawking. "Were you looking for me, Duke?"

"Um. Yeah. Reporting for duty," I said. I was very ready to be done with my community service.

He tightened his greasy ponytail. "Since I only have you until Friday, could you help me Hoover some of the classrooms?"

I wasn't sure why he was asking. It wasn't as though I had a choice.

"Actually, start in Principal Matthews's office. The vacuum's in the closet next to the girls' bathroom."

I was about to leave when a thought hit me. I turned back

toward Shagdar. "If you need help cleaning the swimming pool, I'm your man. I clean the one at home all the time." A big fat lie. "Just thought I'd put it out there. You know…if you're looking for things for me to do."

He nodded and his ponytail wobbled. "Well noted. Now go. Tick tock."

I spun on my heels.

"And, Duke? No touching anything."

"Of course," I said.

"After you're done there, just keep going on the third floor until your hour's up."

"Okay."

Relieved, I hopped up the stairs. I wouldn't have to break into the pool building if Shagdar gave me access. Voices flitted out of a classroom on the third floor, so I hurried to the closet, pulled out the vacuum, and barricaded myself inside the principal's empty office. Nabbing garbage wasn't the grandest job, but it was a hell of a lot more manly than operating a Hoover. The only thing missing was a frilly apron.

I plugged in the vacuum and began the ultimate, most boring activity in the entire world. I tried to listen to music, but the motor was too loud. I kept my earphones in anyway to dim the noise. As I guided the head of the vacuum underneath the desk, I knocked over the principal's metal nameplate. I bent over to grab it. Rising, I read it: Colin Matthews.

Colin. Miss Brown and Shagdar had been discussing a Colin before the weekend. *And the plot thickens…*Miss Brown was fraternizing with our principal outside school. Definitely a better choice than Mr. Darcy. At least my principal didn't have bad hippy hair or wear blue overalls. It also explained why she'd been jumpy when our janitor asked her if she was seeing Colin after school. Miss Brown surely didn't want students to uncover her extracurricular activities. Bored, I tried imagining them as a couple and decided that they fit together as well as a broken hinge. I couldn't think of a single thing they had in common.

She was kooky and crazy haired whereas he was serious and well groomed; she was sprightly whereas he looked like he'd existed during the Great Depression.

I mentally slapped myself for thinking such an awful thing about our principal. He'd lost his wife and his son was sick— even though I still didn't know with what, but I had the sinking feeling that it wasn't good.

A hand touched my arm and I jumped. The vacuum toppled over and started sucking the air.

I bent over to switch it off. "Creep up on people much?" I asked, trying to even out my pulse.

Cora slipped her fingers into the pockets of her black leather jacket. The zipper seemed like it was about to rip. For a second, she reminded me of Catwoman—well, a zombiesque version of her. "Heard you met my brother."

"I did."

"Stay away from him."

I was about to tell her I had no intention of stalking him, but changed my mind. I folded my arms over my chest. "Why?"

"Because I'm asking you to."

"He's really nice, Cora."

"Yeah, and he's young and impressionable."

"What makes you think I'm going to go looking for him anyway?"

She dragged her black gaze over my face. "To get closer to me."

"Closer to you?" I exclaimed. "Do you hear how insane that sounds? I have a girlfriend, in case you didn't notice."

Her nose twitched. "Everyone noticed. Great choice. A cheerleader. Still think you're so different than the rest of them, Meyer?"

"Unbelievable." I shook my head. "What did I ever do to you?"

She turned away, and her wavy hair swung against the black leather, tossing the scent of wild roses around the room.

"I need to get back to work," I said.

Her jaw set tightly.

"Why didn't you deny the rumors about your mother leaving?" I dared to ask.

She spun back. "Because she did leave."

"Not willingly."

"It's no one's business."

"But—"

"Just keep it to yourself," she snapped, before retracing her path to the closed office door.

"Cora?"

She kept her back to me. "What?" There was an edge to her voice.

"What's wrong with Jaime?"

I thought I heard her say, "Everything," but I must've imagined it because she said, "If I tell you, will you leave him alone?"

"Why is that so important to you?"

She sighed. "Because it is."

"Why?"

She twirled around. "Because he's fragile! Because he's my brother! Because I don't know how much more time I have with him! Because everything's going to shit again! Because the cancer—!" She stopped talking.

I hadn't realized it, but I'd walked right up to her and rested my palm on her cheek. Her skin was cold and velvety. She raised her face to mine, eyes as round and panicked as a deer's. I should've dropped my hand and stepped back, but I didn't want to.

She blinked away the doe eyes. "Stop it, Meyer! Stop trying to be some superhero." She tore my fingers off her cheek.

There was no ripping noise, but I felt like she'd left a piece of herself with me. As the door slammed shut, I looked down at my palm. It was paler, whiter—alabaster like Cora's cheek. I should've wiped the makeup off against my shorts. Instead, I made a fist to preserve this strange piece of her.

Chapter Twenty-Five

When I got home from school, I ran into Grandma and my mother in the kitchen. They sat huddled at the island over cups of steaming tea. As soon as I came in, they went quiet. I walked over to the fridge and pulled it open to find a snack. I could feel their gazes prodding me. I shut the fridge and turned around.

"What?" I asked.

Both their eyes widened; both their fingers clasped their white mugs tighter.

I placed my palms on the marble countertop. "What's going on?"

"Nothing." Mom sprang up like a jack-in-the-box. "Well, look at the time. I have a hair appointment in a few minutes, and I'm not even dressed."

I took in her tennis skirt and white polo shirt, wondering what she meant by not dressed. She seemed fine to me. Without another word, she vanished from the kitchen.

"Is something wrong, Grandma?"

She tilted her head to the side, eyebrows knit. I gestured to her tea.

"Oh, that." She made a face. "Your mom's making me drink

this. Apparently, it's good for my liver." She took a sip and wrinkled her nose. "That's probably the only thing it's good for." She took another sip, and then pushed it away. "My liver's requesting something else. I think there's some sparkling wine left over from the other night. Pour me a glass, will you?"

"Okay," I said, taking a glass from the cabinet and filling it. I slid it toward her.

"I wanted to ask you if you ever found out what happened to that girl with all the makeup."

I pushed away from the countertop and reflexively turned my palm up. It was no longer white. I'd washed away Cora and the dust the vacuum had kicked up. "I did."

"And?"

I lifted my gaze to hers. "I'm not supposed to talk about it."

"Oh, come on, honey. It's just me. Who would I even tell?"

"Mom, Dad—"

"I promise I won't."

I hesitated. "Her brother's very sick."

A few seconds passed before she asked, "How sick?"

"Bad sick. Cancer sick."

She rubbed her palms over her freckled arms as though warding off a chill. After a beat, she asked, "Did she tell you?"

I nodded and leaned my elbows on the cool marble. I didn't mention it had been involuntary. "Can I ask your opinion about something?"

"Shoot."

"Two things actually."

"Yes?"

"My English teacher asked me to submit that story I wrote about you and Grandpa to some competition. Would you be okay with that?"

"You don't have to ask for my permission. It's your work."

"It's your story," I countered.

"It's yours too. How do you think you got here?" She winked at me. "Now, what's the other thing?"

"It concerns Jaime. Cora's little brother—"

She cut me off. "Cora's the girl with the makeup?"

"Yeah."

Grandma sat up straighter, and her tone became cautious. "What about her brother?"

"I was thinking of writing him a story. Or writing it *with* him." The idea had come to me after Cora had left. I wondered if I would've come up with it had she not disapprovingly called me a superhero.

"That's very sweet of you, but why?"

"He loves adventures. If he's sick, he probably can't go on any."

She exhaled a sharp breath. "Are you sure about this? It's a huge commitment."

"What do you mean? It's just a story."

"What I mean is, you can't quit on him if something comes up in your life."

I thought about the Alphas and the upcoming championship, and then I wondered if I could swing it all.

"And what happens when the story's done?" Grams continued.

"I haven't thought that far ahead."

"You have to consider these things."

I pushed away from the kitchen island, upset that my grandmother wasn't being more supportive. "His dad probably won't okay the project anyway," I mumbled.

"His dad will approve."

"How do you figure?"

"He's a father. He's facing the most difficult thing a parent can go through. If there's a way to allow his baby to dream, he'll do it. He'll do just about anything."

A long moment of silence ensued, interrupted by my mother calling a quick goodbye to us before slamming the front door. The walls vibrated.

"What if Jaime doesn't like the idea?" I asked.

"There's only one way to find out."

"What if I fail at writing it?"

"Failing is not an option, but it's also not a possibility. Just by being there, by spending time with this boy, you'll make his life better."

I snorted. Of course my grandmother would say such a thing.

"I'm not just saying that because you're my favorite grandson."

I gave her a half smile. "I'm your only grandson."

"I know that," she said softly. "Ask his father tomorrow."

"You think he'll say yes?"

My grandmother's face was crowded with so many emotions that her wrinkles seemed more pronounced and more numerous. "Yes. But, Duke…If this boy doesn't make it—" She set her glass down. "Are you ready for that?"

A chill ran through me. Grandma rose and walked toward me. A lock of hair fell across my forehead, and she combed it back. And then she hugged me.

"I'm proud of you," she said.

I felt like an impostor, accepting her praise. A horrible thought hit me while I was still in her arms. What if I was helping Jaime to make up for the future havoc I was about to unleash on my school's pool? What if it was my subconscious's attempt at redemption?

Chapter Twenty-Six

Grandma agreed to keep our talk private as long as I swore to empty my heart and mind to her. Apparently, it was something I'd need to do often—my grandmother had been a psychiatrist back in the day, so she knew what she was talking about.

"Duke?"

Soft hands rested on my cheeks and drew my face down.

"Du-uke?" Amanda chanted. "Did you hear anything I just said?"

"Umm…no. What did you ask me, babe?"

"I asked if you, like, wanted to go to that bonfire concert with me."

"When?"

"On Saturday night. We're going with Liane and Joss. I was thinking that maybe, if you're not busy, you'd want to join us. The band is good and there'll be free s'mores and beer. Ask Gabe to come."

"What about Owen?" I asked.

"Sure. It's just—" She shrugged. "It might be weird."

"I can't go without at least asking him. Not if Gabe's coming."

She sighed. "Fine."

The second bell rang. Amanda pushed herself up, kissed me, and then left while I opened the door of my English classroom and went to sit next to the guys. As we took out our copies of *Othello*, I asked them about the bonfire concert.

"I'm down," Gabe said.

"Liane'll be there," I told Owen.

Gabe flinched next to me. It was too subtle for Owen to notice.

"Whatever. Me and Liane are chill as ice. I'll ask Melissa to go," he said.

Melissa was the junior on the swim team he was after.

"Okay, great," I said, and flipped to the page number Miss Brown had scribbled on the blackboard.

She picked me to recite Iago's lines. I read them without hearing them, as though a fan were spinning full speed inside my head, blurring sounds. I was thinking about Jaime and I'd decided to ask Miss Brown what she thought before even approaching Principal Matthews. When the bell rang, I stayed in my seat and took my time putting my stuff away.

"Are you coming?" Gabe asked me.

"I'll catch up."

His eyes narrowed, but he left.

Once everyone else was gone—aside from my teacher—I rose and toddled over to her.

"Miss Brown, can I ask your opinion about something?"

She stopped packing her satchel and gaped up at me, pushing thick locks of hair back to clear her eyes.

"It concerns the principal's son," I added.

Her usual placid gaze turned sharp. "What about the principal's son?" she asked carefully.

"You keep saying I write well, and Jaime loves stories, and I was thinking of writing him one." She didn't say anything for so long that I added, totally plagiarizing my grandmother, "To allow him to dream."

"Oh," she said.

Slowly, she flipped the flap of her satchel over and hauled it off the table. It looked like it weighed more than her.

"Is it crazy?" I asked.

"No."

"Then why did you say *oh*?"

"Because I've never even thought about doing something like this. I was just surprised."

I stared down at the speckled linoleum, feeling a *but* coming.

"I think it's wonderful."

"Really?" I asked, raising my gaze back to her face.

"Yes. Really. Jaime likes you. He'll be—"

She stopped talking and her expression changed. I tried to read what was going on inside her head, but her mind seemed as jumbled as her haystack of curls.

"This isn't to enrich your college application?" she asked.

"Enrich my college application? No!" A large ball of indignation lodged inside my throat, soon replaced by my harrowing guilt. "You know what? Maybe I shouldn't do this. Maybe it's a stupid idea."

I was about to spin around and leave, when Miss Brown touched my arm.

"It's not a stupid idea. It's the nicest thing I've ever heard. Please forget what I said."

The hallways were so quiet that I knew I was late for my next class.

"You'd have to get Colin's—I mean, Jaime's father's—permission. Do you mind if I talk to him before you ask?"

I shrugged.

"I'll do it today. Come and find me after school. I'll wait for you in the teachers' lounge."

"Okay," I said.

"Now go before Mr. Renfrew tells me I coddle my students too much."

Heart pounding, I cruised down to the chemistry lab. I

nearly rammed into Cora in the basement stairs. She flattened her back against the wall, and I sailed right past her but stopped three steps below and turned around. Her black eyes resembled holes, as though they'd sunk into her face and bruised her skin. I noticed she had a new piercing—a small silver hoop hooked into her lower lip.

"You mutilate your face because of your brother, don't you?" I asked.

She started climbing the stairs again. "Mind your own business, Meyer."

And I did. Before I could say anything else to piss off the girl I'd finally solved.

Chapter Twenty-Seven

On Wednesday, Miss Brown had told me that Jaime's father wanted some time to think about everything before making up his mind. He hadn't jumped on the occasion like my grandmother had told me he would, and that made me uneasy. I evaluated and reevaluated my idea. Maybe it was insane. Maybe it was mean.

Make a kid dream about stuff he can never have…Who thinks up crap like that?

I played basketball during lunchtime and sweated out my restlessness. The shower helped too. Even my hour with Shagdar was a welcome distraction. Especially, since my assignment was mopping the huge glass pool house connected to our school by a pathway. I took my time checking each and every corner for cameras—there were none—while Shagdar worked on the water filter.

"Mr. Darcy, how much chlorine does this pool need?"

His narrow gaze tapered. "Why do you ask?"

"Because my parents put in a system that's all natural, and now we don't use chlorine anymore," I rambled. I'd done way too much research.

He returned his attention to the filter. "They installed an

ozone generator last year, so we only put thirty percent of what you find in normal pools."

"Does it work?"

"Seems to. Had no complaints about the water." He put the filter back. "Do you have an ozone generator at home?"

"No. We have some sort of titanium pump." We didn't. I just remembered reading about something like it.

"Those are expensive."

"I guess." I concentrated on swishing the mop. "Do you ever have to change the water?"

He frowned. "Do you realize what a pain it would be to switch out 600,000 gallons of water?"

"That's a lot of water."

We didn't talk the rest of the hour, which gave me plenty of time to compute the numbers he'd just fed me. I'd read about tablets that dechlorinated water. It was mostly for home use, but they could probably work in the Olympic-sized pool.

The following day, April faded into May. The air was the same warmth, and the birds perched in the bright pink trees next to our house were chirping the same melody, but something felt different. My mother had once complained how fast time flew by. I'd never believed her. But at that moment, at 7:45 a.m. on May 1, while I reversed onto North Street, bumping into my neighbor's large plastic bins, I believed her. Soon, I would have to play the best game of basketball of my life and fill a pool with three hundred goldfish. But before that, I needed to toss ten thousand Campden tablets into the water. How would I ever score that many?

I anxiously roamed around school all morning. When lunchtime arrived, I sought out the guys to discuss my pool problem, but both were out. Gabe was on a campaign family photo shoot, and Owen was checking his mother into a rehab clinic for her alcohol problem. To top off my sucky luck, Amanda had to catch up on some science project.

"Yo, Dukey!" Dirk, our school's star football player, called from somewhere below me.

I rolled up from my reclined position on the bleacher.

"Heard you were going to the bonfire concert," he said.

"Yeah."

"I'm going with some of the guys. We were going to carpool, so only one of us needs to be responsible." I got that he meant stay sober. "Want a ride?"

"Let me check with Amanda," I said.

"Sure thing." He took off his silver football helmet. Sweat trickled down the blond sideburns he kept trimmed but long.

"Is the entire school going to this thing?" I asked.

"Probably."

"Have you ever heard Bare Bones play?"

"On YouTube. Their guitar player grew up here. Apparently he's dating Goth Girl."

"He is?"

"I know, right? Cora Matthews has a boyfriend. Who would've thunk it?"

The bell rang in the distance.

"Catch ya later," Dirk said, running toward the locker room with the rest of his team.

His statement hurled me back to that day I'd picked her up by the hospital bus stop, dripping with rainwater. She'd told me she was dating someone. I hadn't believed her, but I'd been wrong. Not only was she dating someone, but he was also in a band! I couldn't compete with that. Not that I wanted to compete with that. I had Amanda. She was great and normal and had lips that weren't black and punctured.

As I walked back toward school, I began imagining what the guitar player could look like, and by the end of the school day, I'd painted a clear picture of him in my mind: long hair, black liner around his eyes, and black polish on his nails. I researched him on my smartphone to see if I was close. The band was made up of three musicians. None of them had long hair. They were all very preppy looking, with neat hairdos, but the guy holding the guitar did sport eyeliner *and* nail polish. *Aha!*

"Checking out the band?" Amanda asked, peering down at my phone.

I jammed it inside my pocket.

"Did you listen to 'Bonnie Blue Eyes?'" she asked. "It's, like, one of my favorite songs."

"I didn't," I said abruptly.

The flecks of gold in Amanda's hazel eyes churned. "Is everything okay?"

"Yeah." I exhaled a short breath. "Sorry, babe."

"Can you wait with me at the bus stop, or do you have to start on your janitorial duties right away?"

I extended my hand. "Shagdar can wait."

She smiled as she closed her fingers around mine.

"Do you want me to pick you up on Saturday?" I asked.

"Liane was going to swing by. Unless you want to pick me up."

"Doesn't matter to me."

She pulled her hand away and placed it on the shoulder strap of her purple backpack. I tried to take it again, but she kept it out of my reach and stared beyond me at the bus pulling in.

I frowned. "What? Did I say something wrong?"

Her gaze flicked to mine, and then away again.

"Amanda?" I asked. "What just happened?"

A breath quivered out of her. "I want you to pick me up."

"Then why didn't you say that?"

"Because I wanted *you* to want that," she said, which didn't make much sense.

How was I supposed to guess that Amanda wanted me to swing by if she said that Liane was coming? She stepped inside the bus. Before the doors shut, I asked her, "What time?"

"You don't need to do it," she said.

"I want to. What time?"

She blushed. "Six."

"I'll be there at six," I said.

After she left, I texted Dirk that I would meet him at the concert. With all of my friends there—and my girlfriend—how bad could it be?

Chapter Twenty-Eight

It rained on Friday, which was refreshing considering it had been in the high eighties all week. When I walked into school, I found Amanda removing her yellow raincoat. Her hair was dripping with water, while Liane, who was standing next to her, was totally dry.

"The weather's such crap," Liane said.

"I hope they don't cancel the concert," Amanda said, as I circled my arms around her waist.

"We'll just do something else," I suggested. *Like spend some time in your house. Alone.*

"I know. I just really wanted to hear them play," she said.

"Babe, I'm sure it's not their last concert."

Liane closed her locker. "Did you know that Cora's dating the guitarist?"

I nodded.

"He's so hot. I wonder what he sees in her," she added, pulling her shiny blond hair up into a ponytail.

There was a long moment of silence.

"You're a guy. What does he see in that girl?" Liane asked.

Amanda stepped out of my reach. I could feel both their gazes on me, hot like branding irons. I shrugged. "I don't know what he sees in her." Which was true. I didn't know what *he* saw in her. The only thing I knew was what *I'd* seen in her. Past tense. "I'm late for English. I'll catch you at lunch."

I bent down and kissed Amanda, but her mouth stayed hard. Hadn't I answered appropriately? I decided not to dwell on something that was obviously out of my control and trotted to class.

As I moved through the whirring room toward my usual spot, Miss Brown called out to me. "Duke, Principal Matthews wants to see you."

"Someone's in trouble," Gabe snickered softly.

Owen grinned. "Maybe his office needs sweeping."

"Shut it," I muttered. "I'm not in the mood."

"I was just raggin' on you," he mumbled.

"Right now?" I asked Miss Brown.

"Yes. In his office," she said.

I marched out of the classroom and up to the third floor. His secretary gestured me in. Principal Matthews looked up from his computer when I entered.

"Take a seat."

I sat while he rose and came around to lean against his table, arms crossed.

"I had a talk with Maria on Tuesday."

I cocked an eyebrow. "Maria?"

"Miss Brown. She told me about your idea. For my son," he said. "As much as I appreciate your enthusiasm, I'm worried about—"

"I would never use Jaime." I was sick and tired they were all jumping to that conclusion.

He gave me a heavy nod. "I know."

"You do?" I frowned. "Then what are you worried about?"

Exhaustion and grief battled on his face. "I'm worried about him. About how he's going to take this. I understand you want to give him the gift of going on an adventure, but I'm afraid—" His voice caught. He coughed to clear it. "I'm afraid that if we offer this to him, he'll know his days are numbered."

"Doesn't he already?"

"I think he feels it." His lids drooped and lifted over his eyes, which appeared gray, like the piece of sky framed by the window behind him. "I haven't mustered up the courage to talk to him. He's eight, Duke. He still has some of his baby teeth."

He inhaled a thick breath, and then fell silent for a long minute.

"I'm going to talk to him over the weekend, about everything," he finally said. "I'll ask him if he wants to do it. But, Duke, do you understand what you're getting into?"

"Yes."

"Okay," he breathed. He pressed himself away from his desk. "Okay," he repeated, touching my shoulder and giving it a squeeze. "Come see me Monday." He returned his hand to his side and let it hang there, limply.

I stood up and, heart blasting against my ribcage, left his office. *Cora will declare war on me if Jaime accepts.*

I cracked my neck.

I could take her.

Chapter Twenty-Nine

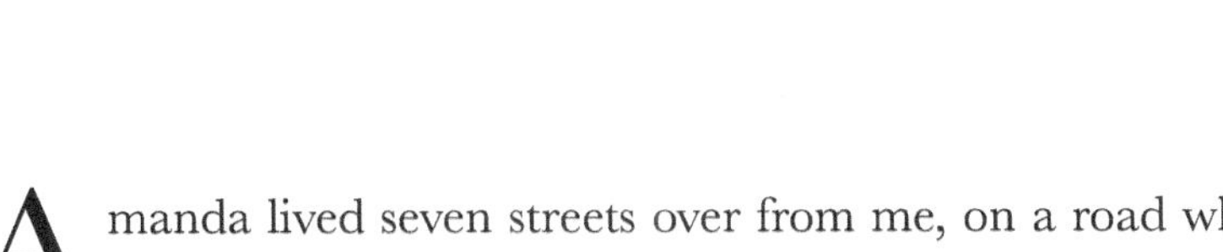

Amanda lived seven streets over from me, on a road where all the houses were built exactly the same. They were all two-story, painted an eggy yellow, with white shutters and a white picket fence.

I honked twice to let her know I was in front. In under a minute, she swung out of her house in a red dress with a hemline that hit midthigh, and lipstick to match. The color made her eyes pop. The effect it had on me—not so much her eyes, but the hemline—was instantaneous. I shifted in my seat, aware of the soft crackling sound in my jean pocket.

"Remind me why we have to leave your house?" I asked her as she settled next to me and strapped herself in.

She was flushed with excitement. "Because, it's going to be, like, supercool and everyone in school's going."

I leaned over to give her a light kiss, careful not to smudge her red lipstick. "Is your mom home?"

"She has a date with one of her coworkers. She usually sleeps over at his place afterward." Amanda turned to look at me. "Come to think of it, how about we throw an after-party at my house?"

"That would be cool," I said, trying not to sound overly excited.

I pulled away from the curb and drove toward the pier and down the sandy road that led to the beach. Dozens of cars were already parked, most of them on the grassy shoulder of the road. I slid into an illegal spot, switched off the engine, and hopped out to reach Amanda's side.

"Thanks," she said, wrapping her fingers around my outstretched hand.

They felt small and soft. I couldn't help thinking how they would feel on the rest of my body. The wrapper in my pocket crinkled as I walked. I thought about moving it to my wallet, but I didn't want her to catch me red-handed. Amanda quickened her steps at the sight of our friends. We moved toward them and split—she went to join Liane and Joss while I went to find Gabe, who was fidgety as hell.

"What's up?" I asked.

Before he could answer, Owen came up from behind and pounded my back. He'd already had a few beers. His breath stank. "Dukey!" he exclaimed. "Shoes off. Beers on."

He dragged me toward a large wicker basket heaped high with an assortment of shoes. I toed off my loafers and dropped them in the pile, and then grabbed the red goblet he half-tossed my way. Some of the contents sloshed onto my gray polo shirt. I tried not to mind, and reminded myself I'd probably reek of alcohol by the time the night was over. I scanned the beach, still lit by the sun. Amanda was whispering in Liane's ear. The second our eyes met, she grinned.

"There's a swim meet on Memorial Day weekend," Owen said, throbbing with excitement. How could he be excited? His membership was in jeopardy.

"Good to know," I said, as apprehension spiked through me. I had to get my hazing over with, if only for my sanity. I wanted to focus on other things than goldfish and chlorine.

Groups of girls girdled the white stage. I looked for the

guitarist. He was tuning the strings on his electric guitar, eyes closed. When his eyes opened, he smiled and shot his fans a large wink. The girls went crazy, yelling his name, reaching out for him.

Beer slipped down my fingers to my wrist from squeezing my plastic cup too hard. I released the pressure and the cup regained its original shape. Owen was saying something, but I couldn't concentrate on his voice; I was trying to locate Cora. Maybe the rumors were false. Maybe she wasn't dating the sleazy guitarist. Tendrils of acoustic music drifted in the air, quieting the concertgoers. It was nearly as though everyone had stopped breathing. *Seriously…*

"Goodnight, Greenwich!" the singer announced. He had a British accent that sounded fake, and his eyes were smeared with black liner like his two band mates. "What an honor to be playing for you tonight!" he yelled.

Everyone—except for me—clapped and cheered.

"Are you ready, Greenwich?" he yelled into the mic.

Yes! was hollered back.

"Because we are going to rock you!" he bellowed.

And with that, the drummer started battering the drum set, while the guitarist fondled his guitar, and the singer gave his microphone mouth-to-mouth. People swayed. Amanda was up front while I'd stayed back next to the wicker basket filled with shoes. I drained my glass and walked to the keg for a refill.

When I returned, Gabe said, "They don't suck."

I hated to admit he was right. They weren't as terrible as I'd hoped. "Amanda mentioned an after-party at hers after. You guys in?"

"Hell, yeah," Owen said. Something behind me caught his eye. "Melissa's here." He chugged his beer, squashed his red Solo cup, tossed it, and pushed his way toward his new prospect.

"Twenty bucks he plants one on her right now," Gabe said.

"I say he waits another song."

"You're on."

We watched Owen lean over and say something to Melissa. Soon, they were moving toward the darkening sea where they talked, heads close. And they swayed. The song finished and a new one started, and then it happened.

"Pay up," I said, holding out my hand. He slapped a twenty in my palm just as Liane and Amanda danced their way toward us.

Amanda wrapped her arms around my neck and pulled me down for a kiss. Her bare skin was balmy and smelled sweet, like warm honey.

When Gabe and Liane began dancing, I pulled away from Amanda. I didn't want to be a cock-blocker, but just because Owen was making out with Melissa didn't mean it was okay for Gabe to act on his feelings. I latched on to his upper arm and gestured toward the keg.

"Let's get the girls some drinks," I said, attempting to be subtle.

He scowled, but I hauled him away.

"Owen's going to rearrange your features," I said.

"Oh, come on. He's over Liane."

"*She* dumped *him*. He'll never be over her."

He pried my fingers off his arm. "Thanks for your concern, but I'm a big boy, and Liane's a big girl."

"Gabe—!" I called out, but he'd already stalked away.

Seconds later, his entire body was pressed against hers. Amanda shot me a smile as I walked back to her.

"Owen's going to truss him up," I said.

"I doubt it. He's doing that slut Melissa," she said.

"Slut?" I asked, one eyebrow pulled up.

"Melissa slept with half the football team, so yeah, major slut."

I turned my whole body toward her, forgetting all about Owen and Gabe and the shit that would hit the beach in a few moments. "Have you ever…?"

"Slept with the whole football team?" she asked.

Her eyes sparkled with mischief while my heart thumped, low and hard.

"Nah. Just one guy," she said. "But that was last year."

The music felt like it had stopped. "Really?" I'd thought we were on equal footing, but apparently Amanda stood a few bases ahead of me.

"Haven't you?" she asked.

I didn't hesitate. "Two chicks this winter."

She frowned. "Really?"

"Yeah," I lied.

Her brows evened out and she pressed herself on tiptoes. "Good," she whispered. "I'm not a fan of virgins."

I grappled with the collar of my shirt that suddenly seemed too tight. I undid a button. Still, I had trouble breathing. "I have to go to the bathroom. I'll be right back."

As I jogged toward the porta-potties, the scent of roses hit me full on. I stopped in my tracks and skimmed the swaying crowd. Being a head taller had its advantages. I spotted her right away. Cora's long black hair spilled over her shoulders and down her back like swirls of ink. As though she felt me watching, she turned around and held my gaze. Neither of us moved. We just scrutinized each other like prey surveys the hunter.

A shrill yelp made me spin back. Owen was charging Gabe like a bull. From Gabe's bleeding lip, I realized he'd already landed a few punches. I raced back to my friends and grabbed Owen's arm in midair. I had to struggle to keep it away from Gabe.

"You asshole! I trusted you. What the fuck?" Owen hollered.

The sun was setting and someone had lit the bonfire. The flames crackled in Owen's bulging eyes.

"You fuckin' asshole!" he repeated, trying to shrug me off. "How long have you been gettin' dick butterflies for my girl?"

"She's *not* your girl," Gabe said coolly.

Liane stood huddled behind Amanda, whose amusement had waned behind a look of stupor.

"Let's go," I told Owen.

"Two-timing nigger," he muttered.

I blinked.

"What did you just call me?" Gabe asked, his voice no longer calm.

The band had stopped playing. They were watching, along with everyone else on the beach.

"He's drunk, Gabe," I said.

"What the hell did you just call me?" Gabe roared, his face inches away from Owen's.

"Enjoy my seconds," he said.

Gabe punched him and Owen's head bounced back. Blood trickled from his nose across his pale skin. Owen threw me off and grabbed Gabe by the shoulders. They wrestled.

I scanned the horde of rubberneckers. "Dirk! A little help," I shouted as soon as I spotted him.

He seized Gabe around the waist while I trapped Owen. Together, we pried them apart.

I pushed my friend toward the wicker basket. "Grab your shoes. We're going." I held my arms out to corral him.

"I'm not done," Owen growled.

"You are for tonight. Come on. I'll drive you home."

One of his eyes had already puffed up. "Did you know?"

"Let's just go. Put your shoes on."

He bent over, grabbed his red loafers, and followed me off the beach.

Amanda caught up to me. "I'm taking Liane home."

"Okay. I'll throw this one in bed and meet you at your place," I said.

"Better you don't. Liane needs me. She's shaken," she added.

There went my plan.

From afar, I saw Gabe wrap an arm around Liane, who was trembling. He glared at Owen, who glowered right back. As we walked to my car, all I could think of was that I would remain a virgin for yet another excruciating day—perhaps longer. The condom wrapper crinkled in my pocket, a bitter reminder of my cosmic bad luck. I pushed my friend into the Jeep, pissed at him, at Gabe, at Liane, at Cora…If I hadn't gaped at her like a freaking idiot for way too long, I would've spotted Owen barreling through the crowd and prevented the fallout.

<h1 style="text-align:center">Chapter Thirty</h1>

The fallout was epic.

When I walked through Francis Academy's hallways with Owen on Monday morning, having spent all of Sunday trying to make him cool down, the entire school watched us with bated breath. I nodded to Gabe as we passed him by his locker. He avoided Owen. Liane was fortunately not by his side. They'd spent the better half of Sunday in each other's company, so I knew it was just a matter of hours before they would be seen together, but at least it wasn't the first thing Owen had to take in.

I shoved him into our art class just as Mr. Walker distributed handouts about our newest project: pottery. Mom would be happy, I thought, as I dropped into the chair next to Owen's. I spied Gabe approaching. He went to sit as far away from us as possible, next to Annabelle with the pink hair and the cross lodged between her big breasts.

Owen's vase resembled an ashtray. He grabbed it at some point, squished the still soft clay, and then he got up and walked out of class. Mr. Walker stared at him, along with the rest of us. Toward the end of the period, someone poked my shoulder. I jolted and my elongated piece of clay was thrown off-kilter. I stopped pressing on the pedal.

"Christ," I mumbled. I tried to correct the crooked chunk before me, but it kept drooping to one side.

Gabe slumped into Owen's seat.

I sighed and wiped my hands on the towel on my lap. "Owen's seriously pissed."

"I'm mad too," he said, voice low.

"I know. You guys need to talk it out."

He shot me a dumbfounded look. "Like hell. He called me the n-word."

"He didn't mean it."

Gabe snorted. "How would you have reacted if he'd called you a *kike*? He's a fucking racist. I always knew it."

"He's not."

"His whole family's racist. They don't vote for my dad."

"That's not true," I said.

"Ask him. They don't."

"Okay. But that's not because your dad's black."

"Believe what you want," he said.

Annoyed, I fixed my warped vase. "You guys have been friends forever. Owen didn't turn racist overnight," I whispered. "This is about Liane."

"Whatever."

"No. Not whatever. Don't blow this out of proportion."

"Me?" he shrilled.

People turned to stare.

"You're taking his side, aren't you?" he asked.

"I'm not taking sides, but I'm not letting you throw away five years of friendship over some girl."

The room grew silent as everyone tried to listen in. Even Mr. Walker.

"Lunch. Bleachers," I said in a low voice. "The three of us."

"No way in hell am I talking to Owen. Not today, Duke." He rose and walked back to his seat just as the bell rang.

Before I'd even returned from depositing my sorry-excuse-for-a-vase on the drying rack, Gabe had bolted out of the classroom. In an attempt to catch up with him, I ran out the door and nearly rammed into Principal Matthews.

"Duke. Just the person I was looking for," he said. "Do you have a minute?"

His worried expression instantly dispelled my irritation.

"Yeah," I said.

I followed him on autopilot up to his office, took a seat, and waited for him to speak. He rounded his desk, gaze flickering over everything but my face, and then he lowered himself into his seat before finally lifting his head and staring at me.

"Jaime—" he started.

The bell sounded through the school.

When the ringing petered out, he continued, "Jaime wants to see you this afternoon." He was wringing his hands, but stopped abruptly. "You *are* free this afternoon, right?"

"Yes," I said.

He rifled through the lopsided pile of paper on his desk until he came up with a pad of sticky notes. He pulled one off, scribbled something down, and gave it to me. "My address," he said.

I already knew where he lived, but didn't tell him. "Is Cora aware of…this?"

"No."

"Are you going to tell her?"

"Eventually. But I want you to know that what she thinks won't impact my decision."

"She's going to hate it. I mean not the story part, the me-hanging-out-with-her-brother part," I said.

"Possibly, but her boyfriend's in town for another week, so she'll be out of the house."

I was shocked that he knew she was dating that slimy guitarist and seemed fine with it.

"So, I'll see you this afternoon?" he asked.

I nodded and rose.

"My secretary will give you a tardy slip," he added.

I nodded again and walked out of the office, blood gushing inside my ears, inside my body, inside my head. Why was I nervous about facing an eight-year-old boy?

Chapter Thirty-One

All the trees in Greenwich were in full bloom, including the stocky magnolias that lined the Matthewses' street. The only reason I recognized them was because they were my mother's favorite.

One spring day, twelve trees had been delivered to our doorstep. Although Mom insisted she bought six, the delivery guy refused to take the others back to the store. At first she'd been furious and had planted only six, keeping the others in their pots. After a week, when the store still refused to reimburse her, she'd huffed and taken out her shovel and found spots for the rest of them.

I parked behind the Volvo woodie, but kept the motor running. I became hesitant, second-guessing myself. How would we go about this? I hadn't pondered the technicalities of the project. *Screw it…*It was too late to chicken out. I was going in there, and that was that. I scraped in a massive breath and cut the engine. Laptop wedged underneath my arm, I hopped out of the car.

A twinge of guilt flickered through me as I walked past the principal's ride. There were no traces of white paint, yet my drawing still glowed inside my mind. I chewed on the inside of my cheek, skipped up the front steps, and pressed the doorbell. A shrill ring resounded throughout the house. Footsteps came next. When the door swung open, I clamped my fingers into fists and rolled my shoulders back.

You can do this, Duke.

Principal Matthews stood in his open doorway. He drew the door wider. "Come in."

"Thank you." I spotted a bunch of shoes lined up against the wall underneath a wooden console, so I took mine off and added them to the lineup.

"I was just making some cookies," he said. "Do you like chocolate chip?"

"Yes." One of my eyes twitched. I blinked but it didn't go away.

"Jaime's in—"

"Yo," came a springy voice.

"Hi, Jaime," I said.

His black hair was all mussed up, as if he'd woken from a nap.

"I set up in here." He pointed to the room on his right.

It was a living room with a white L-shaped couch that took up most of the space and a square glass dining table covered in bowls.

"Lead the way," I said.

I trailed him inside the living room. The ceiling was low so I hunched over, which was probably overkill.

"Dad insisted on baking cookies, but I thought you might like pretzels and chips better."

"I eat everything."

"But what's your favorite?" he asked, sitting on one of the chairs.

"Chips." The twitching stopped.

"Me too."

I set my computer down on the table and took a seat.

"Do you cook?" he asked.

I shook my head. "You?"

"Sometimes. But Dad doesn't let me touch anything, and Cora is *super*bossy."

I snorted. I could totally picture his sister being overbearing. "Is she here?" I asked, straining to hear all the sounds around me. Metal clattered in the kitchen.

His nose wrinkled. "Nope. She's off with her boyfriend."

"You don't like him?"

"I don't know him. Cora doesn't bring people around here. I don't like him because when he's in town, I don't see much of my sister."

"I heard him sing two nights ago," I said.

"You went to his concert with Cora?"

"Not *with* her, but yeah, I went to his concert."

"Was he good?" Jaime asked, placing his elbows on the table and tucking his chin against one of his open hands.

"Not bad. I didn't stay very long, though."

"Why not?"

"I had to take one of my friends home early." I lifted the screen and powered on my laptop.

"Why?"

"He got into a fight over some girl."

"Like a fistfight?"

"Yup."

"Was there blood?"

I shifted in my seat. "Some. I pulled them apart before they could really do damage."

"I've never gotten into a fistfight," he said, somewhat dreamily.

"They're not that great."

"Some days, I feel like punching things. It's probably my Colombian genes. Warm blooded and all."

His dad arrived with a gigantic plate of golden cookies. The smell of chocolate filled the air. It was intoxicating.

"Don't mind me," he said, placing the dish on the table.

"Duke, do you want something besides water? I think I might have some juice."

"Water's perfect, Mr. Matthews." I grabbed the Brita pitcher that stood next to the bowl of tortilla chips and poured myself a glass.

"I'll be in my room. If you need anything, just come find me," he said.

"*O-kay*, Dad," Jaime said, clearly trying to get rid of his father.

Mr. Matthews didn't move.

"Dad?" Jaime said. "You can go."

"Yes. Of course." And he finally left.

When his bedroom door closed, I said, "I've never done this before. I mean I've written stuff, but never *with* someone else."

"I read your rock star story."

"You did?"

"Yeah. Maria gave it to me. It was really cool."

"Thanks," I said, surprised. I picked up a cookie and stuffed half of it inside my mouth.

"I wanted to be a rock star when I was small."

Small? I wanted to say, *you're eight, Jaime*, but I chewed on my cookie instead. His years could not be counted the same. "Not anymore?"

"Nah. I grew out of it."

I smiled. And then it occurred to me that he wouldn't grow out of many things, and my amusement dissipated. "And today? What would you want to be?" I asked, reaching for another cookie.

"A supe."

My fingers froze in midair. "Soup?"

He giggled. "Not soup! A superhero."

"Oh. *Oh*! What kind of superhero?"

"The powerful type."

I snorted. "Why did I even ask?"

"Being a powerless superhero would be stupid." Jaime smirked.

"Obviously. So, what sort of power are we talking about?"

"Invisibility."

"How do you become invisible?" I asked him.

"You're the writer."

"But you're the superhero."

He scrunched his brow and lowered his hand to the chip bowl. "I click my fingers."

"That's too easy," I said.

"I spin around five times," he said, chomping on a chip.

"You'll get dizzy."

"Okay, fine. *How* do I become invisible?"

I leaned back in the chair and folded my arms and thought. And then I thought some more. My gaze coasted over the room, finally settling on my glass of water. I jerked up in my seat. "I got it! Water."

"Huh?"

"You become invisible when you're wet," I said.

"But then I'll be cold all the time."

"Superheroes are not superheroes all the time."

"Okay, but still, I'll be cold when I'm powerful. That's stupid."

We both resumed thinking. I cracked my knuckles. I didn't like the sound of bones cracking, but I was hoping it might inspire me.

"How about I become invisible when I *drink* water?" Jaime suggested.

"Yes! That's perfect. *And* when you get wet, like in the rain."

He bounced his feet excitedly against the rung of the chair. "But that would mean that every time I wash my hands, they'll become invisible."

"You're very thorough, aren't you?"

"Yep."

I typed everything down. "And what would your superhero name be?"

"Ghostboy," he said, without hesitation.

I gaped up. I supposed ghosts were invisible, but ghosts were also dead. I wondered if he'd thought of that.

"What?" he asked.

I blinked my reasoning away. "Nothing. Ghostboy it is." I typed it out.

"What?" he asked again.

I kept my gaze averted.

"Tell me," he said.

"It's just…it's a bit depressing, no?"

"I don't think so. I like to think ghosts exist. That my mother's still around, watching."

A shiver ran through me.

"Is it the name you don't like?" Jaime asked.

"No. I like the name."

The tension in his shoulders released. "Good, because you're writing a whole book about him." He began bobbing his feet again. "I mean, you don't have to write an entire book, just a few stories—You don't even need to write anything about him at all if you don't want t—"

"Jaime," I cut him off. "*I* suggested this. I *want* to write Ghostboy's story."

"Okay." He stilled. "So I was thinking…I do that a lot."

I chuckled.

"Ghostboy needs a sidekick, and I thought of who it should be."

"Your sister?"

"No." He stared straight at me, eyes a blazing blue. "You."

"Oh." This story was for and about Jaime. Not about me. Him including me meant something; something that worried me.

"If you want to be my sidekick," he added shyly.

I shoved my worries aside. "I'll make a stellar sidekick, but for that, I need a kick-ass power."

He cracked a gap-toothed grin.

"So what can the Duke of Graffiti do?" I asked, typing out the nickname he'd bestowed upon me back at the hospital.

"I have an idea."

"Why am I not surprised?"

Chapter Thirty-Two

"He's not coming, Duke." Owen cracked his knuckles as though getting ready for a fight.

"He said he'd be here."

"Well, it wouldn't be the first time he lied about something." Most of his body was steeped in the shadow of the bleacher; only his face was visible, slashed by a sliver of sun. It made his eyes glow like a cat's.

"He'll be there," I said, mostly to convince myself.

A twig snapped, and then Gabe and Dirk appeared. I didn't dwell on the fact that he'd brought Dirk along. He'd come—I'd been right—and having Dirk there was probably a good thing.

Owen and Gabe stared at each other, stone faced and more rigid than the metal structure over our heads. Both folded their arms at the very same time.

Owen spoke up, "You brought a bodyguard."

"You never know what a dumb inbred will do to you," Gabe said.

"You guys gotta stop. You're brothers," Dirk said.

"No, we're not," Owen said.

"He's right," Gabe agreed. "We're not. God forbid he would have a black brother."

Owen's pale skin flushed, but then he shook his head and snickered. "Good one!"

It was quiet for an awful minute.

"I spoke to the Wolf, by the way. I want you out, and they'll take a vote on Saturday. The first rule is respect and you fucking disrespected me," he said.

Stunned, I gawked, but then I jerked my gaze to Dirk. If Owen was speaking about the Wolf in front of him, it had to mean he was an Alpha. Dirk nodded as though reading my thoughts.

"*Me?* Disrespect *you?*" Gabe hissed. "You called me a nigg—"

"That's what you are, aren't you?"

Gabe bolted forward but Dirk restrained him. I jumped between my friends.

"Whatever. At least I don't have a pencil-sized penis," Gabe said.

Owen's eyes bulged, and he rammed into me to get to Gabe. I wobbled, but stood my ground.

"You fucking bastard!" he growled at Gabe.

Owen gripped my shirt and attempted to push me aside, but the only thing he managed was to rip the fabric. I stared down at the gaping material and wondered how I would get through the afternoon. *I could staple it closed or*—Owen took advantage of my lapse of attention. He shoved past me and banged his fist into Gabe's cheek. Dirk pushed him back.

"Quit it!" I yelled.

"You're being a couple of assholes!" Dirk shouted.

"And all this because of a girl," I added.

"This has nothing to do with Liane." Gabe's voice was unnaturally calm. "This has to do with him not getting everything he wants."

"This has to do with you fucking going behind my back! You should've manned up and told me about it," Owen said.

"I didn't go behind your back. Plus you were hooking up with Melissa."

"The second before you jumped on Liane. A whole whooping second, Gabe!" he snapped.

"The way you spoke about her last week—I thought you were over her." When Owen didn't respond, Gabe sighed. "Look, I'm sorry." He said it so softly and so quickly that I thought he'd just sucked in a breath.

"You should be," Owen spit out.

No one spoke for a long time.

Finally, Owen sighed too. "My dick is not pencil-sized."

I would've laughed had I not been worried about the way it would register in his head.

Gabe smirked. "I know."

"We *all* know." Dirk rolled his eyes. "I don't think I've ever met anyone who whips it out as often as you do."

A gust of hot wind hit my bare skin and made my shirt flap like a white flag. *How appropriate.*

Gabe chewed on his bottom lip. "Did you really talk to the Wolf?"

Owen eyed the dark earth underneath his feet where no grass ever grew. Seconds ago, I'd been certain he was bluffing, but now I didn't know what to think. He tucked his shirt in, hands shaking. Then he pulled at his collar.

"Owen?" Dirk asked. "Did you?"

When he finally answered, his words were like bullets exploding out of a gun barrel, blasting the brittle truce into chunks. "I'll fix it."

"Shit," Dirk whispered.

Owen scratched the back of his neck. "I'll talk to the Wolf on Saturday at the meeting and tell him it was a misunderstanding."

"You shouldn't have involved him in the first place," I said.

"I know," Owen said.

"Not cool, dude," Dirk said.

"I know," he repeated.

Gabe's features were pulled tight, and he didn't speak.

"You blew this out of proportion," I said.

"I know! And I feel like shit about it." Owen's voice was so loud that I was certain anyone sitting above could hear him. "Look, if they do kick you out, I'm kicking myself out too."

"You don't have to," Gabe said.

"Oh, shut it," Owen said. "That's the least I can do. Anyway, we might both get dropped if this one doesn't perform."

Dirk approached me. "I meant to tell you. My uncle owns a company that breeds freshwater fish down in Florida. He offered to ship us the goldfish, free of charge."

"Three hundred of them?" I asked. "Won't he ask questions?"

"Nah. My uncle's cool."

"That would be amazing," I said.

"When do you need them?" Dirk asked.

"Memorial day weekend apparently."

"Okay." He looked around. "So, are we all good?"

Gabe gave him a curt nod, Owen slugged Gabe's shoulder, and we all walked back to school.

Everyone noticed the truce, including Liane who marched through the front quad at the end of the school day straight for me.

"They're *fine* about it?" she asked. Her voice was so shrill it had lost its airiness.

I was standing with Amanda in the shade of the big elm tree, planning a minigolf date. "Yeah. It's all good," I said.

"But it shouldn't be all good. What Owen called him is inexcusable!" Liane continued.

"And yet, Gabe excused it. What are you so worked up about? Now you can date him."

She huffed and shook her head like I had no idea what I was

talking about, and her flaxen ponytail swished around. "What happens when he goes crazy on him again?"

"He won't," I said.

She stuck her hands on her hips. "I have a tough time believing that."

"Liane." I sighed. "Stop overthinking this and revel in the peace."

"Who uses *revel* anymore?" she asked.

"No one since Shakespeare," Amanda said.

I winked. "Well, I'm bringing it back."

Chapter Thirty-Three

After giving the principal the first chapter of *Ghostboy*, I felt excited. I didn't know if it was the story or the upcoming game or my friends' truce, but my pulse thrummed as though a swarm of bees were pollenating my ribcage.

When I spotted Amanda standing by the entrance of her classroom, I grabbed her by the waist, lifted her, and gave her a kiss worthy of a kick-ass rom-com. I set her down without a single word and strolled down the hallway to my first class, and then to my second and third.

During lunch, I went to find her. She was with the cheerleaders on the bleachers. I straddled the bench she was sitting on and kissed her. She kept laughing and asking what had gotten into me. I was about to tell her—minus Jaime's story—when I decided I should play it to my advantage.

"I'm just really…*really* glad to see you," I said.

Her friends cooed and snickered, which made Amanda blush.

I pressed my mouth to her ear and added, "Will your mom be home after our date?"

"I don't know. I'll check." She angled my head so that her lips were pressed up against *my* ear this time. "Come prepared."

My earlobe tingled and so did the rest of my body.

"What are you two whispering about?" Joss asked.

"I'm warning Duke how, like, badly he's going to lose at minigolf."

I pushed myself up. "Yeah. In your dreams," I said with a wink. I desperately needed to walk around campus to divest myself of the tingling. "I have to check on a homework assignment. I'll pick you up at seven?"

"I'll be ready. Will *you*?"

For minigolf, yes, but I doubted she was talking about minigolf.

The second I got home that afternoon, I barricaded myself inside my room and closed my blinds. I grabbed the box from underneath my bed and went through it item by item, spreading everything out on my American flag comforter. I flipped through the magazines, read the warnings inside the condom box, and popped two different types out. Then I started getting dressed and gelled my bangs out of my eyes. My scar was just a thin white line now, still visible but subtle.

I thought about ninja blades, which made me think of Jaime. I wondered if he was reading the pages. I wondered what he thought of them. Would he find the hallway full of lollipops over the top? Granted, he'd come up with the Duke's power. Anything my alter ego drew or wrote in paint materialized. The Duke had spray-painted the word *suckers* on a bunch of lockers and *poof*...a hundred green lollipops had rained down on him.

I looked over at my desk, and located the pop. It battled for space in my pencil holder.

"Honey, are you out for dinner?" my mother asked from the hallway.

When I saw the doorknob move—even though I'd locked my door—I swept my arm across my comforter, funneling the magazines and ripped containers back into the shoe box. I shoved it underneath the bed and sprang to the door. I counted to three and unlocked it.

"Hey, Mom." I was breathing harder than during a basket-ball game.

My mother's fist was poised in midair, ready to knock.

"I'm out for dinner. I have a date. We're going to play minigolf," I said in one breath.

"Really?"

I nodded.

"Do we get to meet her?"

I rubbed the back of my neck. "Yeah. Maybe. Sometime." I wanted to push the door closed, but Mom held it open.

"What time will you be home?"

"Umm…around eleven."

"Eleven? Doesn't the minigolf close at nine?" She peered past me, straight at my nightstand. "Oh."

When I spotted the condom wrapper, I slammed my lids shut, wishing I could spray-paint a pink elephant and have him materialize on my bed to hide the little foil packet.

She patted my forearm. "Have fun."

"Thanks," I said, daring to look at her again.

Suddenly, she launched herself inside my arms. "My baby's all grown up. You'll be leaving the house soon," she cried.

"Estee?" came Grandma's voice from down the hallway. "What happened?" She bounded out of her bedroom.

"Nothing," I said, patting my mother's back. I was praying Grams's eyesight wasn't as sharp as Mom's.

"Duke's growing up," Mom wailed, soaking my black T-shirt with tears.

"Right now?" Grandma asked, gaze darting between the ceiling and my head. "He seems about the same size he was this morning." She winked at me.

Mom made a sound that was a cross between a wheeze and a giggle. "He has a girlfriend."

I patted my mother's back some more.

"That was bound to happen," Grams said, touching my mother's heaving shoulders. "I know he said he would marry you someday, but you knew he was just saying it to wrap you around his pinkie."

Mom let out a yelp of laughter.

"Hand her over," Grams said, extending her arms to take her daughter. "Now go! I'll hold her back."

I gave my grandmother a grateful grin, grabbed my wallet, car keys, the condom on the nightstand, and raced out of the house, feeling pumped for the night ahead and weird about my mother's outburst.

I drove over to Amanda's and held my breath for what felt like the entire night.

Chapter Thirty-Four

I was still holding my breath the following morning. The evening had sucked so bad that I didn't want to think about it. I tried to keep all of my miserable thoughts in check during practice, but they kept popping up, each one squashing my ego a little harder.

I missed so many shots that the coach threatened to have me benched. I convinced him it was a fluke and swore to be on my A-game the next day. I would not let the whole team down, nor miss a chance to land a scholarship. *Yes*, my parents could afford to send me to college, but how proud would they be if I could manage on my own?

When I arrived at the Matthewses' house at a quarter past twelve, I was still reeling. I didn't think I could write anything. I whacked on his front door and waited, kicking a small pebble off their doorstep. It landed noiselessly in the flowerbed below. It had seen better days.

The door flew open. Jaime stood in his Batman pajamas.

"Did I wake you?" I asked, shifting the weight of my laptop to my other hand.

"Nope. I put these on to channel Ghostboy."

I smiled and the breath that had clogged my lungs all night

finally snaked out. Why did I even care that I was still a virgin? It didn't matter. Cancer mattered. Jaime mattered. "Good thinking."

"Do you have any costumes?" he asked.

"I might have something leftover from Halloween."

"Any superhero ones?"

"Maybe, but I doubt they'd fit anymore."

"Even the one from last October?" Jaime asked.

"I was Drampton. You know, from *Pursuit of Kings*."

"Don't leave Duke outside," Mr. Matthews said, drying his hands on a kitchen towel. "Come in, come in."

I did. A rush of aromas hit me—menthol, barbecue sauce, and roses. "Is Cora home?" I peered into the narrow, darkened hallway but didn't spot any movement.

"No. She didn't come home last night," Jaime said.

"Jaime!" his father interjected.

His comment shoved my botched date right back into my face. It also thrust a very unwanted image inside my brain: Cora sleeping next to the guitarist, her tanned leg draped over his. *Ugh!*

"Your sister values her privacy."

Jaime just shrugged. "Did you eat lunch yet? Dad made ribs."

"I can smell that." I filled my lungs with barbecue sauce instead of roses. My stomach grumbled. "Are you sure there's enough?"

Principal Matthews nodded. "I have trouble with quantities. I used to cook for the squad back in my army days."

"You were in the military?"

"Stationed in Colombia. That's where I met my wife." The little lines around his eyes softened. "Enough about me though. You boys get on with your story while I prepare lunch."

Jaime led the way into the living room. I still experienced the need to hunch over.

"Mom was a beauty queen when she was young. You want to see a picture?"

Before I could answer, he moved toward the media unit in front of the white couch and grabbed a frame decorated with seashells.

"That's her," he said proudly.

I stared at the image and blinked. It was Cora underneath her layer of goth makeup. I tried to memorize the bronzed-skin and black-eyed woman so that the next time I saw Cora, I could imagine what lay beneath the mask.

"She looks a lot like my sister, doesn't she?" he asked.

I nodded.

He put the frame down with a reverence I'd never known boys his age to possess, nor boys my age, for that matter. "I read the pages." His expression didn't give anything away. "And…"

My mouth went dry. "And?"

"Aaannd…I loved them!"

"You did? I mean, you did."

"The suckers turning into lollipops were so cool! I could totally picture them!"

His enthusiasm made me grin. "You didn't think it was over the top?" I asked.

"Nuh-huh. It was awesome." He made his way to a chair and sat. "What are we writing about today?"

As I took the seat next to his, I said, "We need to send Ghostboy on a mission."

"Ghostboy and the Duke," he corrected.

"Yes." I powered on my laptop and brought up the file. "What have you always dreamed of that's impossible in real life?"

"Besides winning against my brain?"

"Huh?"

"I have brain cancer. Grade four glioblastoma." He spoke this with so little emotion that it made my skin clammy.

"I don't know what to say," I whispered.

"You don't need to say anything. I was just telling you…so you knew."

I gaped at my keyboard. A thick silence developed between us.

"I'd like to fly," he said. I must've appeared dazed, because he added, "My dream. It's flying."

Fingers trembling, I typed it out on the keyboard. A long moment of silence ensued where I desperately tried to unravel the knot in my stomach, but it was more twisted than the chains my mother tossed my way when she couldn't disentangle them.

"I know!" he exclaimed suddenly.

"You know what?" My voice cracked. *Stupid voice.*

"The Duke can paint them wings, and they could jump off a cliff."

Whoa! That got my mind off cancer. "I'm afraid of heights."

"Yeah, but the Duke of Graffiti isn't. He's not afraid of anything."

"You're right. He's not." I wished I were more like my doppelganger. "Are we talking feathery wings or a glider?"

"Definitely wings. Black wings. Maybe bluish-black, like ravens."

Ravens made me think of ghosts that made me think of—I swallowed the hard ball that was lodged inside my throat. Thankfully, Mr. Matthews came in carrying a platter stacked high with ribs.

He took in his son's perkiness. "Why do I feel I won't approve of what Ghostboy's about to do?"

Jaime grinned. "You're not in my story, Dad."

"Is that right?" he asked, taking a seat at the table and distributing the pile of plates and the cutlery. "Is your sister in it?"

Jaime scrunched up his nose. "She would totally tell me what to do."

Mr. Matthews smiled and it blunted some of his worry lines. "That she would."

"What would I tell you to—?" Cora froze in the doorway. "What's *he* doing here?"

Her face was white but splotched with gray smears, and her eyes were bloodshot, as though she'd cried or hadn't slept. It was probably the latter.

Their father stood up so fast his chair tipped back, falling over with a loud thump. "Where were you?"

"What's he doing here?" she repeated.

"Duke is—" her father began. "He's uh—"

I so wished he would keep grilling her on where she'd been.

"He's writing me a story," Jaime filled in.

"He's what?" she exclaimed. Her gaze was so sharp it seemed like knives were sticking out.

"Writing me a story," Jaime said again.

"Since when?" she asked, her tone lilting.

"Since last week. You want some ribs?" Jaime asked, stacking some on his plate. "They're my favorite."

"Get out, Meyer," she hissed.

I rolled my shoulders back and hiked my chin high. "Jaime, you want me to leave?"

"No."

"Then I'll stay."

"It's either me or him," Cora said.

No one spoke.

"Dad?" Her deep voice sounded like an earthquake.

"It's what Jaime wants, honey," he said.

She stepped further and further back until the shadowy hallway swallowed her whole. I was certain she hated me now, probably more than she hated me before—if that were even possible. When the door slammed shut, it dawned on me that I'd won, but it didn't feel like a victory.

It felt like the beginning of a war.

Chapter Thirty-Five

When I got home, I tried to work on *Ghostboy*, but it made me think of Cora's murderous gaze, and I didn't want to keep picturing it, so I played *Lands of the Fae* instead. I settled my character in a new encampment by the river with Gabe's fae, a flat-faced, bare-chested demon-warrior. We were waiting for Owen's avatar to join us. My character was pale like the moon, tall and clothed with a suede poncho-like garb he'd sewn from the hide of a beast he'd slaughtered. He was a skilled swordsman now and was learning how to engrave magical incantations onto the blades he made.

A knock on my door made me jump. "Dinnertime," my mother called out.

I tore my attention away from my laptop and, rubbing my stinging eyes, went downstairs to take my seat around the table. A cork landed in my salad. I thought it was some furry brown spider at first, but then I spotted the bottle of champagne in my father's hands and the geyser of foam spilling down his wrist. Mom raced to the kitchen to grab some paper towels while Grandma arrived holding four glasses.

"What are we celebrating?" I asked, lifting the cork out of my salad and spinning it between my fingers.

"You know that situation with the medication and the boy?" Dad asked, giving my mother and grandma two filled glasses of bubbly, and me, a half-full one.

"Yeah," I said.

"The complaint was thrown out." His face was so bright that his undereye circles didn't seem as purple.

"Really? How?" I asked.

"Well, the medication came with an appropriate warning."

"That's great news, Dad," I said. But then a thought made my skin crawl. "Is the kid from this town?"

Dad frowned. "Why do you want to know?"

"Curiosity."

Dad fixed me. "He is."

"How old is he?"

"Duke, I don't see why—"

"How old, Dad?"

He shrugged. "Five, six maybe."

I let out a deep breath.

"Why? Do you know someone with cancer?" Dad asked.

I set the cork down. "No."

When Dad looked at Mom, I peeked at Grandma. She gave a subtle head shake. At least my secret was safe. I debated telling my parents about Jaime and what I was doing, but I didn't know how they would react. Maybe they'd tell me I needed to focus on school…that I didn't have time to go around writing stories for sick kids. Or worse. Maybe they'd call my idea cruel, like Cora had. I couldn't risk it.

"What's the second thing we're celebrating?" I asked.

Dad, Mom, Grandma…they all looked at me, and they all smiled. Actually, Dad's mouth twitched more than curved. *Oh, crap! No, no, no*…I grabbed the glass of champagne and guzzled half of it, and then ogled the small bubbles popping on the surface.

"I told you we shouldn't have put him on the spot," Dad whispered to Mom.

"I was just trying to be supportive," she answered.

Grams leaned over and patted my arm while my parents argued. "Don't worry, honey. First times are always bad. My first time with your—"

Yuck, no. I had to cut her off so I mumbled, "Nothing happened."

She lowered her voice. "You mean, down there?"

"No," I said.

My parents were thankfully still at it.

"Was it the girl? Was she not ready?" Grams asked.

"I don't want to talk about it."

To my great surprise, she dropped the subject. She even changed topics. "Do you know what I heard at the beauty parlor this morning?"

That put an end to my parents' quarreling.

"No. What?" Mom asked, sitting up straighter. She loved gossip.

Dad kept observing me, but he didn't ask any questions. Finally, he sighed and stopped trying to excavate my brain. I didn't talk for the rest of the meal. I just ate my two heaping servings of spaghetti and went straight up to my bedroom. After stripping down to my boxers and turning off the light for an early night, my phone lit up with a call. When I saw Amanda's name, I groaned, still too embarrassed to discuss last night. I willed sleep to overpower me. It didn't, so I grabbed my phone and dialed her back.

"Hey!" she said. "I tried to, like, call you all day."

"I was busy."

"I'm sorry about last night."

"Whatever."

"No. Not whatever." Silence. "Mom swears she didn't see anything."

"You said she'd be out," I muttered.

"That's what I thought," she said softly. "Can we try this again?"

I sighed-groaned. Of course I wanted to try it again, but I could never go back to her house. Not after her mother had caught me with my pants down in the bathroom, rubbing one out. "I'll call you after the game tomorrow."

"You promise?"

"Yeah."

"I got a whole lecture on safe sex, by the way," Amanda said before I could hang up.

I cringed.

"Mom wanted me to make an appointment with my gynecologist for the pill and everything."

"Why? I have condoms." *Boxes and boxes.*

"Says it's safer, you know, if we're in a relationship."

The word startled me.

"We are in a relationship, aren't we?" she asked.

We'd dated two weeks. I had no clue what we were in. Out of nowhere, Cora's face popped into my mind, but it wasn't her usual pale one. It was Cora with golden skin like her mother's. I tried to erase her image, but it was seared in my retinas.

"Duke? Are we—Is this going somewhere?" Amanda asked.

"Yeah," I breathed.

Cora and I were going nowhere. At least nowhere good. She had a boyfriend, so I should have a girlfriend. That way, she wouldn't think I was obsessed with her.

Which I wasn't.

Chapter Thirty-Six

We won the championship. Gabe scored the winning shot. The excitement was explosive in the stadium, in the locker rooms, on the plane ride back to Greenwich. When I stepped inside my house at six thirty that evening, I was a changed man, brimming with self-assurance and serenity. Within the week, we would hear from college scouts. We were only sophomores but if we caught someone's eye, that person would follow us during the next two years, until we were ripe for college.

"Mom! Dad!" I exclaimed as I kicked off my sneakers and chucked my gym bag on the floor.

"We're in here," my mother called out from the living room.

I trod excitedly toward the entrance to tell them about the game when I spotted Amanda sitting next to my grandmother. She was propped up against a navy throw pillow, sipping a cup of tea, legs folded neatly.

"I got a tweet that you guys won." Amanda was grinning so widely it made her square jaw look as quadrangular as SpongeBob's.

"Honey, you okay? You're very pale," Mom said, patting the cushion next to her on the couch.

"Yeah, yeah." I moved toward her without stopping by Amanda.

Amanda's grin vanished. What exactly had she been expecting? That I make out with her in front of my family?

"I'm just tired," I said. "Long day."

Mom suddenly shot off the couch. "I forgot about the shepherd's pie."

"What shepherd's pie?" I asked.

"The one for dinner," she said. "Mom, I need your help."

Grams lifted an eyebrow. "To take it out of the oven?"

"I can help, Mrs. Meyer," Amanda suggested.

"No, no. You stay here with Duke. Mom!" She tipped her head toward the kitchen.

Grandma groaned, but she got up and followed her. They glided the double doors shut.

"I shouldn't have come over," Amanda mumbled. She uncrossed her legs and placed her cup on the coffee table.

"No. It's okay. I just—You caught me by surprise. My parents never met any of my girlfriends," I said. I didn't add that it was because I never had any.

"Your mom mentioned that." She studied the geometric pattern of the cream rug. "Still. I should go," she said, but it nearly sounded like there was a question mark at the end of her sentence.

Did she want me to tell her to stay? Would she stay through dinner? Did I want her to stay for dinner?

"Do you want to stay for dinner?" I blurted out.

"Do you want me to?"

Hadn't I just asked her that exact question? Instead of pointing it out—I was beginning to understand that girls, or at least Amanda, needed double confirmation—I nodded.

Amanda's smile was back. She rose and skipped toward me. My heart pounded, but not with excitement. I eyed the sliding doors with dread. They were still shut, but for how long?

Knowing my grandmother, she probably had her ear pressed to them.

"So? Did you meet Michael Jordan in Chicago?" Amanda asked.

"Nah. He never showed, but some of the current Bulls were there. That was pretty sweet."

"I heard Owen's throwing a huge party next weekend to celebrate your win."

"Yeah."

"Can I take you out to dinner before the party?"

"Take me out?" I didn't like the sound of being taken out.

"Yes."

"I'd rather take *you* out," I said.

Amanda laughed. "Afraid of being emasculated, Duke?"

"No. How about you choose the place, and I cover the tab?"

"Defeats the purpose of taking you out," she said, pouting.

"I'll feel more comfortable picking up the check. I'm old-fashioned."

She sighed. "Fine. Tony's?"

"Sure."

She started leaning in for what I imagined was a kiss when the front door banged shut. I bounded off the couch, straight onto my feet.

"I'm home!" Dad called out.

My pulse pitched as his heavy footsteps approached.

"Oh. Duke. You're…entertaining," Dad said, looking from me to Amanda.

"You must be Duke's father." She stood up and made her way around the coffee table to shake his hand.

"And you must be—his girlfriend?"

She nodded. "Amanda," she said.

Eyes and cheeks glowing, my mother popped back out of the kitchen. I would never have guessed that meeting a girlfriend would make her this ecstatic.

"Amanda's staying for dinner," I said.

"If that's okay?" she added.

"Of course," Mom said. "We have lots of food. And everything's ready."

"Good. I'm starved." Dad pressed a kiss to my mother's bright cheek before marching past her through the other set of double doors that led to the dining room.

"Give me five minutes. I need a shower," I said.

"Okay. Hurry," Mom said. "Amanda, what can I get you to drink?"

I raced out of the living room and up the steps, locked myself in the bathroom, threw off my clothes, and jumped underneath the warm spray. I lathered up quickly and roughly, grating off a whole layer of skin, toweled myself dry, finger-combed my hair, and then rushed back to my bedroom to yank on a pair of jeans and my Beatles T-shirt. Barefooted, I plodded down to the dining room where everyone seemed to be getting along. I took my place between Grandma and Amanda.

As Mom served the mashed potato and minced meat dish, Grams asked, "Are you friends with Cora?"

"Cora?" Amanda squeaked.

I was so surprised, I jabbed my knee into the table.

"No." Amanda was staring at me. "Did Duke tell you I was?"

"No. Duke doesn't talk much about school."

"But he told you about Cora?" Her tone was flat. Her mouth too.

"Who's Cora?" Mom asked.

"No one," I grumbled.

Mom's gaze shot over to Grandma as Amanda sat up straighter, clearly seething. She didn't look at me during the rest of dinner even though she chatted pleasantly with my parents. As soon as we'd eaten dessert, she thanked them for their hospitality.

I walked her out, or rather, tailed her out. "Do you need a ride? It's late."

"I'll walk," she said.

We stood there for a second, both watching a kid bike down my street. The air was seething between us.

"What's the deal with Cora, Duke?"

"There's no deal."

"You spoke about her to your grandma!"

"I speak about a lot of people to my grandma."

"You didn't speak to her about me. She didn't even know my name, let alone that we were dating."

"I don't like talking about my private life."

"But you don't mind talking about Cora?"

I bit my lip. Perhaps I should've pinned Amanda down with a kiss, but I didn't want to kiss her. "Just let it go, Amanda. Nothing's going on with Cora. She's dating someone, in case you forgot."

"What if she wasn't?" Amanda asked, her voice cracking.

"Don't do this," I said. "Don't be the jealous girlfriend."

Amanda blinked and her eyes got all watery. She took off running down my street. For a second, I debated whether to run after her, but I was barefoot, and by the time I put on shoes, she'd be halfway home. So I watched her fade off my street, wondering if we were over.

Somehow, I hoped we were.

Chapter Thirty-Seven

Amanda and I were definitely over.

We didn't have the breakup talk, but she acted as though we'd had. I didn't mind…one less conversation to suffer through. I tried to act civil, letting out a *hi* when I saw her that morning. Her response was a glare. I avoided her the rest of the day. As soon as the last bell rang, I hopped into my Jeep and drove over to Maplewood Drive. I wasn't supposed to meet with Jaime before Tuesday but decided to stop by his house to tell him about the basketball game. Holding my laptop, I rang the doorbell, only then noticing that the principal's woodie wasn't in the driveway, which probably meant no one was home. I started to turn away when the door swung open.

"Hey," I said.

"I didn't know you were coming over," Jaime said excitedly. "I have to change into my *outfit*." He winked, pulled me in, and then shot down the short corridor to what I imagined was his bedroom.

I entered the little house and slipped my shoes off in the entrance. It was hot and it smelled hot. It also smelled minty, like that ointment for sore muscles. I wanted to crack open one of the windows in the living room, but didn't know if I should. Maybe air packed with pollen wasn't good for Jaime.

"Ready!" he said, bursting into the room, dressed in his Batman pajamas.

I took a seat at the glass table and set down my laptop. "I have to admit I didn't have time to work on the story."

His smile slackened. "Oh."

"I'm going to write it this afternoon."

"Why did you come then?"

"Because—" *I wanted to escape everyone.* "Because I wanted to tell you that we won the championship," I said. Jaime wasn't a diversion; he was a friend.

"Really?" he exclaimed. "Did you score a lot of points?"

"I did."

I spent the next ten minutes giving him a play-by-play of the entire game. He didn't blink once during my storytelling.

"I wish I could've been there," he said. "I've never been to a basketball game."

"Ever?" I asked, reclining in my chair. The wooden frame creaked.

"Nope. Cora hates sports and Dad doesn't let me out of the house often."

"So you stay here all day by yourself?"

"Not by myself. Our old neighbor comes over as soon as Dad and Cora leave and stays until they get back."

"But they're not back," I said. I peered around the darkened foyer. "Are they?"

He shook his head. "Not yet, but she had an emergency…a water leak or something."

"And she just left? Just like that?"

Jaime shrugged.

"That's not very…responsible of her," I said.

He bobbed his head and swung his legs, his bare feet grazing the carpet.

"So what do you do with her all day?" I asked.

"I draw. Read comic books. Play video games."

"She plays video games with you?"

"Nah…she sits on the couch, watches talk shows, and rubs this cream on her wrists." He wrinkled his nose. "It's stinky. And she farts a lot."

I chuckled. "She sounds awesome."

"She's a retired nurse, so she knows what to do if I have a seizure."

The laughter froze in my throat. I hadn't even thought of Jaime having seizures. "Do you have them often?"

He shrugged. "I did for a while, but then they stopped. I've only had one in the past month. That's why I was in the hospital." His gaze drifted toward the window. "That's how they knew my tumor was back."

"I'm sorry, Jaime." I didn't know what else to say.

"About what?"

"That you have to go through this."

"You mean spend my days on the couch with smelly Bengay lady watching people yell at each other on TV? You're not sorry. You're superduper jealous."

I hoisted up a smile.

"So I was thinking…Ghostboy's mission," he said.

Ghostboy, right. I powered on my laptop. "Yeah?"

"We fly to reach a dragon's nest," he said.

I drummed my fingers. "Dragons are overdone. How about, we fly to locate the river of immortality?"

He smirked. "Overdone. How about…we fly because it's the only way to find the girl who doesn't exist?"

"How can we find her if she doesn't exist?"

"She's just hidden. Like a chameleon."

"How would flying help us find her?" I asked.

"Because flying is way cooler than walking." His eyes looked bluer, brighter, like fragments of sky. "That's all I have."

"Maybe from above, she shines or something," I suggested.

He pushed his thick black bangs off his forehead. "Yes!"

I typed everything before asking, "So who's Chameleon?"

"Cora. *Duh!*"

"Cora?" I trilled. "She won't want to be in our story."

"She doesn't have a choice. It's *my* story."

I gulped. Cora the chameleon, besides being an alliteration, sounded like a risky idea. "She'll hate being the damsel in distress."

"Too bad. I choose her. She's Chameleon from now on."

I was about to protest, but Jaime seemed dead set that his sister needed saving. I was fairly certain she would think it absurd. But then, I reminded myself we were talking about Chameleon, a fictional character, not Cora.

"Chameleon's power is that she can blend into the landscape," he said.

"So she's kind of invisible like you?"

"Yep. She *is* my sister after all."

"In the story too?"

He nodded without hesitation.

"Does she control it, or does it just happen to her?" I asked.

"It's Cora. She controls *everything*."

I chuckled. "Why does she want to disappear?"

"Because she's scared." He was twirling something between his fingers—a small, silver hoop. Probably one of Cora's.

"Scared of what?" I asked, keeping my attention on the hoop. He buried it in his palm.

"Scared of being found."

I could feel my brow lift. "By whom?"

"By the bad guy. *Duh.*"

"Oh. So now we have a bad guy?" I asked, smiling.

"Every story has to have a bad guy."

I positioned my fingers over the keyboard. "Does our bad guy happen to play the guitar?"

"Nah. He's not important enough to her."

I sat up straighter. "He's not?"

Jaime shook his head even though he seemed lost in thought.

He crumpled his small brow and spread his fingers wide, contemplating the silver hoop with such intensity that I wondered if he was communicating with it. Suddenly, he snapped his hand shut. "This person took our mother because she had powers, and now he's after us because we inherited her powers."

Goosebumps crawled over my skin, because the line between fiction and reality was blurring.

"Chameleon was protecting Ghostboy, but then they lost each other, and now she thinks the bad guy has Ghostboy and is coming after her. She doesn't know that her brother got away thanks to the Duke and the lollipops and—" A tiny crease appeared between his eyebrows. Just as quickly, it vanished. "And smoke! When Ghostboy saw the lollipops, he asked the Duke to spray-paint smoke, and it materialized, and the sprinklers came on, and Ghostboy became invisible!" Out of breath, Jaime leaned over to peer at the computer screen. "Why aren't you typing? Is it silly?"

"Silly?" I asked, jolting out of my enthrallment. "No. It's great. I was visualizing the whole thing."

He flashed me his gap-toothed grin.

"Sometimes I forget you're eight," I said. "You're a million times more mature than my friends."

"Really?" he squeaked. "I mean, *duhhh*. I'm the superhero who's going to save the world after all—Well, not the world— Just my sister."

"Save me from what?" Cora asked, leaning against the door frame.

Both Jaime and I jumped.

"The boredom of Greenwich or the stupidity of the people in school?"

Chapter Thirty-Eight

Cora was staring at me with her debilitating black gaze. "Meyer, a word."

I swallowed.

She pressed away from the door frame. "Outside. Now."

"Cora, please don't be mean to him," Jaime said.

Her squared shoulders rounded. "I'm not. This is about school."

I lifted an eyebrow. She wanted to discuss school? Had some great crisis happened I wasn't aware of? "I'll give your dad the pages on Wednesday," I told Jaime, rising from the chair and collecting my laptop, phone, and car keys.

"Drop them off here if you want…I mean, if you have time," he added. He was toying with the little silver hoop again.

"Yeah. I can do that. See you on Wednesday then."

"Bye, Duke," he said.

I stepped past Cora, put on my loafers without bending over, and exited the house. Seconds later, she came out and shut the door. We stood on the porch facing each other. Well…not facing; I was an entire head taller.

"This isn't about school, is it?" I asked.

"No." Her raspy voice was barely above a whisper. "Jaime

likes you, but I know he's just a project to you. I don't want you to lead him on and promise him that you'll come over all the time. I don't want him to think you're friends. You could never be friends. You don't have time to build a friendship."

"It sounds to me like you don't want me to be his friend," I said, my tone crisp.

"I didn't say that."

"I'll make time for him."

"It's not about *your* time." Her eyes held this sheen that made them look lacquered. "The doctors—" Her voice faltered. She took a deep breath that rattled her triple-chain necklace. "They gave him three months." She stared down at her combat boots. "Last month, they gave him three months," she repeated, her voice barely above a whisper now. She wiped her downcast eyes, leaving a black smear over her golden knuckles. "They say it's moving fast because he's so young."

"And there's really no cure?"

She shook her head. After a few very quiet minutes, she looked up, eyes narrowed and dry. "They made us believe there was one the first time around. They don't know shit about the brain. The tumor's pressing against his left frontal lobe. But he's still able to speak. They can't explain that," she hissed.

"Have you gotten second opinions?"

"We got second and third and fourth opinions! They're all the same."

After a beat, I waded into unknown territory. "Did your mother die of the same thing?"

"She died giving birth to Jaime. From complications. He got cancer because of a treatment they gave him as a newborn. To help his lungs develop."

*So the bad guy's death…*The idea made me queasy. If Jaime said the bad guy was after him, it meant he knew it was the end. But then he'd mentioned the bad guy was after Chameleon…I shook my head. I had to stop taking things so literally. There was nothing fatally wrong with Cora…At least I didn't think so.

"Are *you* okay?" I piped up.

She frowned.

"Your health. You're not sick or anything?"

"We've already had this conversation, Meyer. No. I'm not sick. Do I look it?" she asked. She'd placed her hands on her waist, which looked funny on her. Cora wasn't a hand-on-hip sort of girl. She was the type of girl who gave you the finger.

"Don't freak out. It was just a question."

The blistering sun was making my shirt stick to my back. I untucked it and pried the damp cotton off my skin, trying to make some air circulate. A dog barked somewhere. Cora's gaze wandered in the direction of the bark just as a motorcycle appeared, barreling down the street. It was black, and so was the rider's shiny helmet and leather jacket. When I spotted a guitar strap, I knew exactly who was coming.

"What time will your dad be home?" I asked, still staring at the douche bag.

"In another hour. He had a meeting with the board of trustees."

I felt unbearably warm. Each lungful of air was searing my lungs, especially now that it was mixed with motorcycle fumes. "I can stay with Jaime."

"Why? I'm here." She swerved her attention back to me.

"Yeah, but so is your date," I said flatly.

"I noticed," she said. "He's not going to eat my brother."

"Maybe Jaime doesn't want to hang out with him."

"He offered to play him some songs. Maybe even teach him a melody."

"Jaime wants to fly, not learn to play a freaking instrument."

"Because you know him so damn well, don't you?" She jabbed her finger into my chest.

My heart vaulted along with my temper, as though she'd pressed some hidden switch embedded in my skin. "Jaime worships the ground you walk on. Did you know that? Do you know what he wants to save you from? From trying to make yourself disappear!" I snapped. "He's sick and yet the only person he gives a fuck about is you. Not himself." I gripped my computer so tightly the edge bit into my flesh. "I know you keep saying I don't know him—and maybe I don't—but you don't know him either if you think he wants to learn to play the freaking guitar with this wannabe."

Cora gasped just as the motorcycle veered to a stop next to my car. It was so close that I would probably need to kick it over to open my door.

"Have fun," I said, and flattened the pebbles in the driveway under my rapid footsteps.

"Hey. This guy bothering you?" the guitarist asked.

I pushed past him and shoved my door open. It nipped his ride.

"Watch it! That's a forty grand Ducati," he yelled.

I glowered at Cora. I didn't bother looking at eyeliner-dude.

"Who the fuck are you?" the guitarist asked.

I closed my door without answering, flung my laptop on the passenger seat, and started the motor. I didn't stick around to watch him slide his slimy tongue down Cora's throat. There was only so much I could take.

Poor Jaime, I thought as I gunned the car through his neighborhood much too fast. But suddenly, uncertainty superseded sympathy. What if I'd been wrong? What if he wanted to learn the guitar? What if he asked me to write that in our book the next time we met? I slapped my steering wheel and muttered curse words before pumping up the volume of the radio so that it would submerge my mind and every clinging, stupid thought inside.

Chapter Thirty-Nine

I was about to stick some books inside my locker when it slammed shut. I just managed to pull my head out of the way. I spotted thin fingers topped with bruise-colored polish.

"Good morning to you too," I said.

"What is wrong with you?" Cora's eyes were so wide that she looked like the charcoal drawing I'd done of her a month back.

"With me, nothing. With you, though—"

Even through the thick layer of white makeup, her cheeks appeared pink. "Were you trying to get back at me?"

"Okay. Rewind. I have no clue what you're talking about."

"Don't lie to me."

"Lie to you?" I asked, trying to control my tone. "Lie to you about what, Cora? Enlighten me. Please."

The pink lingered on her cheeks, but her voice dropped a few octaves and became raspier, almost a growl. "When your buddies asked what you were doing at my place, you told them we were hooking up. I know I asked you to keep quiet about Jaime, but telling people we're sleeping together…that's just disgusting."

I wasn't certain what part offended me most, her belief that

I would think up such a rumor or the fact that she actually felt disgusted by me. "Good to know."

The silver hoops gleamed as her eyebrows converged. "What do you mean *good to know*?" she asked, her tone devoid of the earlier venom.

"Do you seriously think I would say something like that? Hooking up with you is social suicide."

The flare in her eyes blunted and her hand skated off my locker.

Keeping my voice low, I said, "My *buddies* have no idea I was at your house. No one knows. And yeah, I wouldn't discuss Jaime, but I also wouldn't make up some lame excuse about you and me."

Many people were watching. I rolled my shoulders back and glowered at everyone. They turned away.

"Better not spend too much time standing next to me or new rumors will start," I added.

Cora blinked.

I was about to tell her I would uncover the culprit when a better idea popped into my head. "Hey, everyone!"

The people who'd turned away spun back like boomerangs.

"You've all heard the rumor by now. As much as Cora and I appreciate your enthusiasm about our alleged relationship, we are *not* hooking up, and we have no future plans to do so either. Please spread the word. Thank you for your time."

I tipped my head toward Cora who hadn't moved an inch— even her breathing seemed to have halted—and proceeded to my classroom, realizing I didn't even have the right book. *Oh, well.* I couldn't return to my locker now. I readjusted the strap of my heavy bag, distributing the weight across my shoulders.

Someone slugged my shoulder. "Duuudde…" Owen said, drawing out the word. "Stellar speech."

"Thanks."

"Just wanted to tell you I didn't believe the rumor. I mean, Cora? You'd have to be desperate to tap that."

I nearly, just nearly, shoved Owen against the lockers. Common sense stopped me. I couldn't fight for a girl I didn't like. "Who started the rumor?" I asked.

He gave me a crooked grin. "Take a wild guess."

"Amanda…"

"Bingo! What did you do to her? She's totally pissed at you."

My gaze fired across the hallway. When I spotted my ex, I stalked over to her. She went quiet, and so did Liane and Joss. All three scowled at me.

"What the hell, Amanda?" I said. "I didn't think you were the kind of girl to fabricate rumors."

"Rumors?" she yelped. "You went to her house! I, like, saw you—"

"You followed me?"

She flushed. "I…I," she stammered. But then she folded her arms tightly. "You're not denying it."

"No. I'm not. I did go to her house, which is also our principal's, by the way. It was about my community service."

Her jaw wobbled.

"Sadly, this is making me happy we broke up," I said.

"Go to hell, Duke."

The hurt that flooded her killed my anger. I even felt bad as I watched her dash away with Joss.

Liane stayed back. Once they'd disappeared in the girls' bathroom, she said, "It's not too late. You can still fix things."

"*You're* giving *me* relationship advice," I teased.

Liane punched my upper arm. She was struggling to keep a serious face.

"I don't want to fix things. Maybe that makes me a jerk, but I don't like Amanda enough to fight for her."

"Because you like someone else?" she asked.

Her gaze wandered to someone behind me. I turned, expecting to find Cora, but I found Gabe instead. He was sauntering over to us.

When he reached us, he grabbed Liane by the waist and pulled her against him. "Dukey, I just heard the whole drama."

"Just now?" Liane asked.

"Give me some cred, woman. At least I heard it *before* I spoke to the two of you." Gabe was grinning his too-many-teeth grin.

"Where were you?" she asked, laughing.

"My alarm failed me. Just got here."

When he kissed her, I looked away. I found myself staring at Cora. Then I found myself walking toward her. I realized I didn't give a crap if people assumed anything about us.

"How did it go yesterday? Did Jaime play the guitar?" I asked.

"I thought befriending me was social suicide," she said, gazing out at a fat elm tree whose branches seemed to extend all the way to the window.

"Doing you is social suicide." I gave her a crooked grin. "Talking with you is less lethal. So, did he play?"

Even though her thick black hair was fanned out around her cheeks, I could detect a smile. "He listened," she said.

I chuckled. "I'm guessing he's not gonna pick up guitar playing anytime soon."

She shook her head. "No. It wasn't for him. He's more of a nerd, like you."

"*Shh*…I don't want anyone to uncover my secret," I said, smiling widely. "How did you meet him by the way?"

She twirled her head toward mine, her hair pitching the sultry scent of petals right into my nose. "Ricky? You want to know how I met him?"

"That's what I just asked."

Her—not forked—tongue darted out and toyed with the small hoop hooked into her blackened lower lip. My mind went blank as heat engulfed my entire body. *Wow.* Something was seriously wrong with me.

"At one of his concerts. A friend of mine was producing his show and took me backstage."

"That's cool," I said, adding, "He's good."

She snorted. "Yeah, right. You hate his music. I saw you at his concert. You had this perma-frown."

"How long were you watching me?"

She cast her attention on the elm again. "There were fifty people. And you're a whole head taller than everyone else. You're hard to miss."

I shifted my heavy bag to my other shoulder. I really had to drop some books off in my locker. "And I thought you were going to mention my pretty face again."

She rolled her eyes and smiled, and with that smile, I knew that Cora Matthews wasn't totally immune to me.

Chapter Forty

Between writing twenty pages for *Ghostboy*, playing more basketball than I had in the past month, and getting Jaime to one of our afternoon games—Miss Brown took him—the week faded into Friday before I'd even stopped dribbling. In my haste, I'd nearly forgotten about the art exhibit and cocktail organized for our parents in the school gymnasium that night. Gabe begged me to go. Even though I didn't want to schmooze with forty-year-olds, I donned the new suit Mom had gotten me —the one I'd worn at New Year was already an inch too short in both the legs and sleeves—and followed my parents in my own car.

The second I stepped into the gym, Gabe ambled over.

"Are we the only kids who came to this thing?" I asked.

"No. Liane's here. Joss, Dirk, and a couple other people too. Oh. And Cora's hanging around the back with Miss Brown and Shagdar and some kid. She probably had to make an appearance, being the principal's daughter and all." When he noticed my parents talking to his, he added, "Gonna go say hi to Estee and Michael. Be right back."

Some kid? I looked around and caught sight of Jaime standing next to her. I waved and he waved back excitedly. I was about to walk over when an arm snaked around my waist. From the light pressure and papery skin, I knew it was Grandma.

"Hey, Grandma P.," Gabe said, already back. He leaned over and planted a big wet one on my grandmother's cheek.

"Hi, honey. You don't come around anymore."

"Dad's campaign is taking up most of my free time."

I snorted. "Your dad's campaign, or Liane?"

"You're dating the pretty blond? I thought she was going steady with Owen," Grams said.

Gabe shifted on his shiny dress shoes. "Duke's not dating Amanda anymore," he blurted out.

I shot him an icy stare.

"You're not?" she asked.

I shook my head, still scowling. He shrugged apologetically.

"Your mom will be disappointed," she said.

A waiter came by with a platter of drinks. Grandma grabbed some wine.

"So show me which piece is yours, honey."

"I don't think there's anything of mine up."

I scanned the row of drawings I could see. They were hanging from ropes that had been strung across the gym and wrapped with string lights. The effect was rather neat.

"Walk with me anyway?" Grams asked.

"Of course," I said.

"I'm going to go see Dirk. He looks more bored than you do during home ec. Catch you later, man."

I watched him leave, sort of wishing I could go with him.

"I can ask your mother to walk me through," she said.

I patted her hand. "Night's young, Grams."

We strolled through the aisles of paintings and drawings, stopping a few times to take a closer look. One piece was particularly good. Unsurprisingly, it was Annabelle's. She'd dipped the bottom half of her canvas in bright pink paint—maybe that's where the idea for her hair had come from.

"And you said none of your pieces were up." Grandma pointed to the one across from Annabelle's.

I turned to see what Mr. Walker decided to exhibit and froze. My first instinct was to tear it off the rope before anyone else could see it, but it was too late. Three people were huddled around it, commenting on the depth of the brushstrokes that contrasted harmoniously with the powdery finish of the charcoal. Their words; not mine.

"Is that—?" my grandmother started.

"Don't say it."

"I was going to say a face." Grams studied me before asking, "Is she here?"

Had Cora seen it? Had she recognized herself? It wasn't *that* obvious. My own grandmother hadn't grasped what I'd drawn. Most people would just think it was a black-and-white picture of holes. They wouldn't know that Cora's face contained no color.

"Well, is she?" Grandma repeated.

"Maybe."

"Point her out."

"No way," I mumbled.

"Okay, then. Tip me off as to where she's standing."

"In the back. Near the fire exit," I mumbled.

Grandma peered through the rows of canvases. "I don't see her."

"She's pretty hard to miss."

I followed her gaze, but Cora was no longer there and neither was Jaime. Maybe she'd left…but then I caught sight of her in my aisle, Jaime in tow. Dragging Grandma along, I dashed over to them.

"Hi," I said, slightly out of breath. "This is my grandmother."

Panting, Grams looked from me to them, stunned about the impromptu introduction. But quickly, her surprise dissipated and was replaced by a smile. "Thrilled to meet the two of you." She bent over and lowered her voice to a whisper. "I hear I'm in the presence of a superhero," she said. "Do superheroes shake hands?"

Jaime grinned sheepishly. "I'm not a real one."

"That's what Clark Kent used to tell me." She winked. "Your secret's safe with me."

He giggled. Even Cora smiled.

"And you must be Cora." Grams extended her hand.

After a brief hesitation, Cora shook it.

"The girl with the penchant for makeup and facial jewelry," Grams added.

Jaime snort-chuckled while I started perspiring. It got worse when Cora scowled.

"I had my nose pierced back in the day," Grandma said.

"You did?" I squawked. I desperately wanted to take off my jacket, but I was afraid of sweat stains.

"Uh-huh. When I lived in Kerala. I was a yogi, and in India, piercing your nose was said to relieve a woman of the pain of childbirth."

"I didn't know that," Cora said.

Jaime groaned loudly. "Ah, crap. Now she's going to pierce her nose."

"Language, Jaime," she said.

He rolled his eyes, which made me chuckle.

"Shall we continue touring the aisles?" Grams asked.

Both Cora and I nodded at the same time. When she started walking in the direction of my drawing, I blurted out, "Nothing to see down here."

Grams searched my face. "Duke's right. Let's go to the next aisle."

She dropped my arm and latched on to Cora's. I was expecting her body to go stiff, but she seemed relaxed next to Grandma.

"So tell me about your piercings. Which came first?" Grams asked, starting back down the aisle.

I followed close behind with Jaime.

He craned his neck to look at me. "Thanks for talking Maria into taking me to the game the other day. It was *so* cool!"

"Glad you liked it. I didn't play too well though."

"You made that shot from the middle of the court!"

"Yeah, but I kind of sucked the rest of the time. Anyway," I said, "what did you think of the new chapter I wrote?"

"I felt like I was flying. How cool would it be to float in the air?"

"It's called hang gliding."

His face fell. "You have to be eighteen, so I took it off my bucket list."

His comment made my chest ache. "You have a bucket list?"

He swiped his dark bangs out of his eyes. "Yeah."

"What's on it?"

"Driving a car," he whispered. "Doing something illegal."

"At eight, driving a car *is* illegal," I said.

"I know. I just sort of want to do something *really* illegal. Like spray-painting a wall."

"I'm a terrible role model."

"No, you're not."

"How about you let Ghostboy get in trouble? I can have him rob a bank and do jail time."

"Fine." Jaime sighed. "But not a bank. How about he hacks into some government database to find Chameleon?"

"Sounds good." I was already running the scene in my mind.

"What time are you coming tomorrow?" he asked.

"Two thirty okay?"

He nodded.

"So what else is on your bucket list?" I asked as we meandered down the last row.

I spotted his father speaking to mine. Hopefully, they were discussing what a remarkable student I was.

Jaime tugged on my arm. "Going to a fair."

"Huh?"

"What's on my bucket list."

I stopped worrying about what my father and principal could be discussing. "You've never been to a fair?"

He shook his head. "I also want to try beer."

"You never tasted beer?"

"I'm eight," he said.

"I keep forgetting."

"Getting a dog. A big one."

"Anything else?"

"I want my sister to stop wearing her makeup. I'm okay with the piercings, but she's not pretty with all that gooey crap. You should see her without it. She's *sooo* beautiful."

"Have you asked her?"

"I'm scared to bring it up."

"Are you two paying any attention to the art?" Grandma asked, appearing next to me.

"Yeah," I said, while Jaime said, "No," at the very same time.

"Which is it?" she asked.

This time, I said, "No," while Jaime said, "Yes."

Grandma laughed. "Need a minute to straighten out your stories?"

Both Jaime and I grinned.

"Where's Cora?" I asked, realizing she was gone.

"She needed to see her dad about something."

I nearly unhinged my neck from the swiftness with which I scanned the room. "*Ah, crap,*" I muttered, breaking into a slow jog. I pushed past a waiter, spilling some of his drinks, and dashed down the aisle toward her. But then I stopped in my tracks and studied her profile as she contemplated her charcoal reflection. She was going to take out a restraining order on me. Instead of confronting her and making up some excuse that it wasn't her, I backed away and left the gymnasium.

Chapter Forty-One

After massive hesitation, I drove over to the Matthewses' house the following day, starting and stopping my car engine three times before finally pulling out of my driveway. I couldn't stand Jaime up because I was a coward.

I sucked in a lungful of humid May air and rang the doorbell. I was greeted by a Batman-pajama clad little boy.

"You left without saying goodbye," he said.

"I had a thing," I said vaguely. "Is Cora here?"

"No. She's out. She went running."

I slipped off my Converses. "She runs?"

"Only when something's bothering her." He led the way into the living room.

My left eye began twitching. "What's bothering her?"

"Don't know, but she's been acting weird since last night. Pretty much after you left."

He'd set up two big bowls of candy, all green. I guessed sour apple.

"Maybe you leaving without saying goodbye made her mad."

I dropped into a chair. The legs creaked underneath my weight. "On a scale of one to ten, how mad was she?"

"Seven…and a half. Did you guys fight again?"

"Again?" I asked.

"The other day, outside the house. Before Ricky arrived. I heard you arguing."

I gulped. "You heard us?"

Jaime's cheeks turned crimson. "I shouldn't have listened; it's just—you were talking really loudly."

I touched his shoulder. The small, sharp bone protruded into my palm. "You don't have to apologize, Jaime. If anyone should apologize, it should be your sister and me. We shouldn't talk about you behind your back."

He skewed up his lips. "I feel so good right now—" His voice broke and his shoulders quivered. "Life's so unfair."

When he started crying, I made a decision that was crazy. I shoved my computer under one arm and told him to follow me out of the living room.

"Where are we going?" He sniffled.

"On a little ride."

The red tinge in his eyes made them look radioactive. "I should tell Dad."

"I'll do it. Where is he?"

"In his room, doing some paperwork."

Jaime pointed to his father's bedroom while donning his neon sneakers. I knocked. The door swept open.

"What is it? Is Jaime all right?" Principal Matthews soared out of his room, rushing past me. "What happened? Is it—? Did you—"

"I'm fine," Jaime mumbled.

"I wanted to take Jaime for a ride," I said, breaching the thick tension.

"A ride? In your car? You're only sixteen."

"Just down to the park," I said.

"Please, Dad? Pretty please?"

"Why don't I give you boys a lift?"

Him driving would completely foil my plan. "I'll be very careful, I promise."

"Please, Daddy."

The *Daddy* broke him. "Fifteen minutes. After that, I call the cops."

Jaime swung his arms around his father's waist and hugged him.

"Duke, Jaime rides in the back with his seat belt on."

"Absolutely."

"Come on." Jaime's gaze was bright but no longer watery. He'd already opened the door. I put on my shoes and trailed him to my car.

"Keep your phone on," the principal said. He was about to close the door when he forced it back open. "What's your number?"

I gave it to him, and he placed a missed call so that I could record his digits. After Jaime clicked himself in, I backed out of my spot. I drove up Maplewood and turned on an adjacent street, and then turned again.

"That's not the way to the park," he said.

"I know." I pulled to a stop. "Seat belt off. Climb in front. Behind the wheel."

Trembling—I hoped with excitement and not fear—Jaime popped off the strap while I jogged over to the passenger side.

"No way," he whispered, as he settled in the driver's seat.

"We're doing your bucket list. All of it."

"All of it? But—"

"But nothing. Today, I'm teaching you to drive."

He giggled nervously, covering his mouth with his palm. "Dad would flip. And Cora—"

"Let's not think about her right now." I should've said *them*, not singled out Cora, but Jaime was too agitated to notice.

"First things first. Adjust the seat so that your feet touch the pedals. The levers are on the left side."

As he moved the seat forward and down, I lowered the steering wheel as far as it could go.

"Can you reach the pedals?"

He scooted to the edge of the seat. "Yeah."

"The right pedal is the accelerator. The left is the brake. You use your right foot for both. Your turn signals are here." I flipped the lever up then down to show him. "Once I put the car in drive, it will start moving. You have to press on the brake to make it stop. Got it?"

"Got it."

"Ready?"

"Yes!"

I put the car in drive. "Go, Ghostboy."

He shot me a humongous grin. The car lurched forward.

"Eyes on the road," I said.

The Jeep screeched to a stop. Forward, stop. I cracked my window open to avoid throwing up. It took him six attempts to manage something akin to cruising. He took his first turn a little widely but used his blinker. He stopped in front of the stop signal. And on and on we went, until I read the clock on the dashboard. We'd been gone twenty-five minutes.

"Crap. We have to go back." I slid my finger across my phone's screen to send his dad a text before he called the police.

The car tires squealed as Jaime hit the brakes. Queasy, I looked up. I thought that one of his old crotchety neighbors had caught us. Instead, it was some girl with a long ponytail.

"*Ah, man,* Cora's going to tell Dad for sure," Jaime said.

Cora? I gawked. *No way…*

I stuck the car in park and jumped out.

"Jaime Matthews, what the hell do you think you're doing?" she yelled.

I still couldn't believe it was her. Without makeup, she was so different. So…normal. A car honked somewhere, snapping me out of my daze.

I broke into a slow run to round the Jeep. "It was my idea."

"I bet it was," she hissed. "Jaime, out of the car. Now."

Panicky, he unhooked his seat belt and scrambled out. "Please don't tell on me," he mumbled.

A vein in Cora's temple throbbed. From exertion or from rage, I didn't know. I was hoping for the first, that she'd run hard. Her sports top was drenched; a dark V marked the space between her breasts.

"Meyer!"

"Huh?" I jerked my face up so quickly that my neck cracked.

"Are you insane?"

I momentarily forgot what we were talking about.

"It was my idea, Cora," Jaime said.

My eyebrows pulled together. *Oh, right. Jaime driving.* "Don't listen to him. It was my idea, and I take full responsibility for it. Please don't tell your father though. He might handcuff me to Shagdar again."

"Shagdar?" Jaime piped up.

"Mr. Darcy," I said.

"How did you come up with Shagdar?" he asked.

"Shaggy from Scooby Doo and—"

"So not the point!" His sister was shaking her head, her black ponytail swishing around her shoulders.

I inhaled a breath of rose-heavy air. "No one got hurt."

"Thank God! He's eight, Meyer. Eight!"

"And I'm never gonna be nine, Cora!" His voice took on an intensity that rivaled hers. "Never. Never ten. Never sixteen. This is it for me. And I don't want you to be mad at Duke. It was one of the best, coolest things I've ever done!"

She gasped.

"I don't know why you've been pissy all day, but don't take it out on me or on Duke. We didn't do anything to you."

Her gaze drifted to me, and then away again. Her lashes were so thick and long, something I'd never noticed when she wore black eye powder. And her lips were red. Not pinkish red, but crimson. I'd detected the potential for Cora to be nice-looking; I hadn't detected the potential for her to be drop-dead gorgeous. Yet that's what she was. *Gorgeous*. A work of art I hadn't done justice to with my limited painting skills.

"Give me a lift? My legs are killing me," she said.

"Sure," I said.

"I wasn't asking you."

My brow furrowed.

"Jaime, will you drive me home?" she asked.

"Really?" he squeaked, rocking on the balls of his feet. "Hell, yeah."

"Language."

He rolled his eyes at me before clambering into the driver's side.

"I call shotgun," she said. "Coming, Meyer?"

Pulse hammering, I darted into the backseat and leaned over the armrest to spin the volume dial up. It was an Eagle Eye Cherry song about saving tonight. I didn't know about saving tonight. What I did know was that I was going to save today. I was going to record Jaime's smile and commit Cora's face to memory before she hid it again behind her impenetrable, mono-chromatic mask.

"Hey, guys?" I said before Jaime took off.

They both turned around.

"Say cheese." I snapped a picture of brother and sister.

At Owen's party that night—the one to celebrate the basketball championship—I studied the picture of Cora and Jaime, zooming in on her face, examining her features carefully, memorizing the color of her skin, the redness of her mouth, and the length of her eyelashes.

"Who's *that?*" Owen asked, startling the hell out of me.

"A friend," I lied, shutting off my phone and stuffing it in the back pocket of my jeans.

He hooked his arm around my shoulder. "That's one fine-looking friend."

"Yeah," I said, pushing his arm off.

Part of me couldn't believe he hadn't recognized her; another part reminded me that I hadn't either.

Chapter Forty-Two

I saw Cora twice that week, but we didn't speak. Mostly because she wasn't the type of girl you made small talk with. If I approached her, I needed a solid subject of conversation and I didn't want to use her brother as a topic.

On Wednesday afternoon, I went over to Jaime's and discussed the pages I'd written. Cora wasn't there. Apparently, she was studying for her finals in the school library. The following day, I headed there at lunchtime and, sure enough, found her sitting at a table, sandwiched between two piles of thick manuscripts.

"You know, you can use the Internet for nearly everything nowadays," I said.

She glanced up at me, surprise registering on her white and black face. I missed the girl I'd seen on Saturday, yet part of me was relieved she was wearing her ornamental mask. The real *her* would remain my secret for some time longer. I wondered if Ricky had seen her without makeup. I hated the thought that he might have.

"I need to study, Meyer."

"I do too," I lied, lobbing my bag into the chair across from hers.

She gestured to the free tables around us. "Library's empty."

"You're right." I tried to wipe my expression clean of emotion as I heaved my bag up and started toward another desk.

She sighed. "But you can stay if you promise to be quiet."

Like I would ever stay after she'd pulverized my ego. I shot her a sour smile. "You take up too much space."

And she did. Cora was everywhere. Her scent was everywhere. I considered leaving. Instead, I went bookcase by bookcase and read the leather and paper spines, scanning the collection that extended up two floors. Glossy wooden ladders were hooked into the railing so you could access even the highest shelf. A stained-glass window stretched to the ceiling and filled the cavernous space with speckled light. The room had been the last owner's private church. There was even a confessional behind the rows of bookcases, which had, ironically, become a place of sinful behavior.

The thought of sex reminded me of Amanda and of my botched attempt. It made my foul mood flair, and I punched a shelf. All it achieved was smarting knuckles and toppled books. As I set them straight, I felt a presence beside me.

"I need a book and I can't reach it," she said.

"Use a ladder," I said flatly.

"It's right above you."

I sighed. "Which one?"

Her gaze flew up to the shelf. "*Umm…*"

That second of hesitation made me question if there truly was a book.

"*The Anthology of Mayan Constellations*," she said.

I grabbed the encyclopedic publication and passed it to her. "What class do you need that for?"

She kept her face in the shadow. "It's for Jaime."

My ego took another hit. And there I'd thought she'd come to talk to me.

"What book are *you* looking for?" she asked.

I was about to make up a title but didn't want to lie. And not because I felt bad about it, but because it would bring me nothing. "I actually came here to talk to you."

"Please, don't—"

"It's about Jaime, not about my screwed-up feelings."

She flinched and her gaze swung away from mine. "Don't have feelings for me."

I snorted. "Like I can control that. Anyway, you're dating someone and I'm not…pathetic." I totally was.

For a second, she was silent. But only for a second. Then her gaze climbed back up, and she met my eyes. "What was it you wanted to tell me?"

"Did you know he has a bucket list?"

"No."

"Well, he told me about it on Friday. That's why I took him driving. That was on the list."

"What else was on there?"

"He wants a dog. A big one. That's what I came to talk to you about. Could he get one?"

"A dog?" she mused. "He hasn't talked about a dog in years."

"Do you think your dad would flip?"

"Are you free after school today?" she asked.

"I have basketball, but after that, yeah. Why?"

"To get him a dog."

"Shouldn't you run it past your father first?"

"Meyer, Jaime looked happier yesterday than he's been in months. If there's any way to keep him that way, I'm game."

"What time does the pound close?" I asked.

She lobbed the book at me, which I just managed to catch, snapped out her phone, and typed on it. After a minute or so, she grimaced. "Five thirty."

"Could we go tomorrow?"

"I guess so."

"Meet me by my car at three thirty?"

Her cheek dimpled. She was biting the inside of it. "It will start more rumors."

"I don't think you've understood this about me, but I don't care about rumors. Especially in this school. Now if you're worried it'll reach your boyfriend and screw up your relationship, I'll pick Jaime up, and we can just meet at the pound."

She bobbed her head up and down a few times. "Yeah. Let's do that. It's the one in Westport."

"Okay."

She retreated the way she'd come. In the stained-glass light, her black hair was dotted green and blue and copper like the wings of a butterfly. As I watched her leave, I realized I was still holding the book. I marched over to her desk and plopped it on top of the lopsided pile.

"You forgot Jaime's book," I said.

She glanced up at me, confused, but as soon as she saw the anthology, she pushed a lock of hair behind her glowing red ear. I snorted. Cold-hearted Cora had had no intention of bringing the book home. At least my intuition wasn't completely screwy.

"See you tomorrow," I said.

"Yeah. Tomorrow."

I grabbed my stuff and left, humming to myself, because I no longer felt pathetic.

Chapter Forty-Three

"Are we there yet?" Jaime asked. "Really?" I caught a sideways glimpse of him smiling. His nose was pressed against the car window. "Can you give me one tiny clue?"

"Nope. So, did you read the pages I dropped off?"

"Maybe," he said. "But I'll only tell you what I think of them if you give me a hint."

"You're impossible," I fake-grumbled. "Think receptacles." I was hinting at dog bowls.

"A container store?" He sounded so disappointed that I couldn't help but chuckle.

"I upheld my side," I said. "Now spill. What did you think of them breaking into the hospital's database to locate Chameleon's health record?"

"I was scared they were going to get caught by Dr. Goor. You made him sound so creepy."

"He did study Chameleon and Ghostboy's mother."

Jaime nodded. *He'd* suggested the villain being an evil doctor/scientist after our driving stunt. "I don't want Chameleon to live on the street though."

"Where do you want her to live?"

"How about in the forest?" he asked. "She can hunt fish and rabbits to feed herself."

I raised an eyebrow. Cora with a weapon was a frightening thought.

"The Catskills. She can live there," Jaime continued excitedly. "In a hunting cabin where she has to make her own fire. We went two years ago. It was *sooo* cool. And Cora loved it."

"Your sister's a nature girl?"

"Yup. She would take me swimming in lakes, and we'd roast marshmallows at night. It was the best trip ever."

"Okay. I'll move her to the woods. And when we look at the doctor through the peephole I draw on the wall of his office, we catch him studying a map and making an X on the Catskills."

"And when he spots us, you should paint some banana peels on the hospital floor so he trips."

"That would definitely slow him down. Or..." I spun into the parking lot of the animal shelter. "I can draw a lock on the hospital doors so he can't get out."

"Get out!" he shouted.

"That's what I just sai—" I stopped talking when I realized Jaime wasn't listening to me. He was gaping at the shelter awning, his eyes sparkling like firecrackers.

"Dad said yes?"

"Cora said yes," I told him. "I don't know if she ran it past your dad though."

"No way!" He tore the seat belt off his chest but didn't pounce out of the car. Instead, he rested his head back and took measured breaths.

"Are you okay?"

"Yeah. Just give me a sec."

I got out, went over to his side, and opened the door. Slowly, he lowered himself from the backseat.

"Jaime? Are you—?"

"I'm okay. I'm okay." He added a small grin to convince me, but it didn't. "Ricky's here," he said.

He pointed to the black motorcycle parked against the curb. I couldn't believe Cora had brought along her douche bag guitarist. Reeling, I slowed, trailing Jaime through the front door.

"Yo, little man." Ricky knocked fists with Jaime. When he spotted me, he added a curt, "Hi."

"Hey." I kept my tone civil even though I wasn't feeling very civil. I shot Cora a disgruntled look.

A man in a sweat-stained, short-sleeved shirt arrived with a clipboard. "I'll be with you in a second, sir," he told me.

"I'm actually with them," I said.

The man gawped at the four us.

"He's my other brother," Cora said quickly.

I cocked an eyebrow.

"You brought the whole family, huh?" The guy handed the clipboard to Ricky.

"Well, we're all going to be living with the dog, so we thought we'd choose him together," she continued.

"Good thinking. It's important that your companion feels comfortable with all of you," the man said. "After you sign these papers, I'll introduce you to our three bigger dogs, Mr. Davos."

My temper flared, until I noticed the age restriction written in bold on the form—you had to be eighteen or older to adopt a pet. Then I understood why the guitarist was there and my frustration lessened. After he signed, Sweat-stain took us to the backroom toward three large cages.

"This here is Android. He's a spaniel mix."

He pointed to a dog lying down, muzzle resting on his paws. When the canine saw us, he twisted away.

"This is Mitzy," the man continued.

A chocolate lab peered at us through large coffee-colored eyes. When Jaime placed his palm against the cage, she shied away from him, cowering to the back of the cage.

"We found marks that she was beaten. I won't hide that earning her trust will be tricky."

A dog with a missing leg whimpered and pushed against the metal screen in the third cage. When Jaime pressed his hand against the grate, the dog licked it.

"This is Rita. She's an eight-year old collie. Had an infected paw when we found her. Coyotes. We had to amputate it, but she healed and adapted quickly."

"Hey, Rita," Jaime said. "Hey, girl."

The man stared at Jaime, and then at Ricky who was running his fingers over his short hair. He didn't sport eyeliner today, but he did wear a leather and grommet jacket that screamed wannabe.

"You are aware you can't give the dog as a present, right?" Sweat-stain said.

Ricky nodded.

"Why do you look familiar?" The guy tilted his head to examine Ricky.

"I'm in a band. Bare Bones. Maybe you heard us play?"

"That's it! I love you guys," he said.

I rolled my head around my neck and it cracked. I tried to focus on Jaime scratching Rita's ears, but Ricky was hogging all the attention. I couldn't take it anymore.

"I need to call Owen," I said. "I'll wait for you by the car."

"No, wait, Duke. What do you think of her?" Jaime asked, jumping out of his crouch.

"I think she'll be great."

His gaze bounced back to the collie. "She's awfully sweet."

"I'll let her out so you can get to know each other," Sweat-stain said.

The second he opened the gate, she walked up to Jaime and sniffed his arms.

"That tickles," he said, laughing.

"Mr. Davos, what do *you* think of her?" Sweat-stain asked.

"She seems nice," he said.

Cora's head snapped up and her piercings gleamed in the bright light. "Why don't you pet her?"

He narrowed his eyes, kneeled, and clucked his tongue. Rita trotted toward him and sniffed him. She gave a small snort and returned to Jaime.

"She likes the boy a lot," Sweat-stain said.

"Good thing, considering she'll be spending a good deal of her time with my fiancée's family," Ricky said.

"Fiancée?" I exclaimed.

The man frowned until Cora explained I considered her too young to get hitched. To prove her point, she slung her arm around Ricky's waist. I'd reached my breaking point and retreated to the lot. Jaime was oblivious to my escape, much too absorbed by Rita.

A minute later, Cora shot out of the pound. "Meyer, what the hell?" She marched right up to me, angry, furious even.

"You're engaged? You're seventeen! He's in a band. What happens when he leaves to go perform all over the country?"

She folded her arms. "Will you stop it?"

"Yeah. I'll stop it, but he's not gonna make you happy, Cora."

She closed her eyes and drank in the hot air. When she raised her lids, there was a stone-like sheen to her black gaze. "We're not engaged. He owed me a favor. I'm not eighteen and neither are you. Ricky and I aren't even together anymore."

"You're not?"

She shook her head.

"Why?" I asked.

A soft breeze blew through her hair. She tried to catch the flyaway strands, but more wind wafted around us as the sky turned grayer. Cora shivered and lifted her face. "It's going to rain any second," she said, hugging her arms to her torso.

The clouds moved quickly, revealing a sliver of sun. "It's not."

"It is. I'll bet you anything."

"It's not. And anything?"

"Yes. Anything," she said.

"Dinner tomorrow night?"

She gave a small nod. "But if I win—"

"You're not going to win."

"But if I do. I want you to take Amanda to dinner."

"Absolutely not!" I said. "Why would you ask me to do that?"

"Because I think you didn't give her a fair chance."

"I don't want to give her a fair chance."

"That's my deal," she said. "Take it or leave it."

I checked the sky. The air crackled with heat, but it was dry, as dry as my throat. "Fine. You're on."

Not a drop of rain fell that evening, but at half past midnight, it stormed.

One of Jaime's dreams had come true today…as had one of mine.

Chapter Forty-Four

I spent Saturday morning rewriting Ghostboy and the Duke's close escape from the hospital. Then I started on a new chapter where Duke spray-paints a truck on the grimy brick wall of an alleyway and the thing materializes. I hesitated to change the pickup truck for a motorcycle, but that made me think of Ricky. So I kept the pickup and added tons of features to it, like a sick sound system and a motorized camping tent.

Which gave me a brilliant idea for my date tonight…

"Did you lose your phone?"

I snapped the lid on my laptop closed.

Gabe was leaning against my door frame, smirking. "Were you watching porn again?"

I lurched off my bed and carved my shaky fingers through my hair. "Yeah. You know me." Watching porn was sadly easier to explain than the book. I still hadn't told anyone about it, besides my grandmother.

"Come on. We have a recon meeting over at the Modley's."

"About what?" I asked.

His eyes widened. I still didn't catch on.

He checked the hallway before whispering, "About next weekend."

The blood drained out of me. I hadn't thought about the Alphas and their goldfish in over a week. The second I did, the thrill of writing the story and planning my date with Cora drained out of me. "Right. I *should* go over my plan."

"Damn right. Now put on your sneaks and let's go."

When we were outside, he gestured toward his Prius.

"We can take my car," he suggested. "I'll drop you off on my way home."

"Nah. I'll take my own. I need to go to the supermarket and grab some stuff for my mom," I said.

"I need to grab some stuff too," he said. "Party supplies for next weekend, if you catch my drift."

"Maybe we won't be celebrating."

"Oh, we will. Just wait and see the turnout of aiders and abettors waiting for you."

"Seriously?" I asked, folding myself into the Prius's passenger seat.

He turned on the ignition and pumped up the radio. "It's going to be epic."

Or an epic fail, I thought, but kept my negativity bottled up. Gabe was in too good a mood to drag down. I watched my neighborhood slide out of view. Soon we were driving parallel to Long Island Sound, where properties were so large they required mechanical gates and caretaker houses. Gabe punched in the code that activated Owen's wrought-iron gate and angled the car down the long, winding driveway.

He wasn't kidding when he told me I would have a support system. Six cars were parked in front of the Modley's mansion. We got out of the Prius and followed the sound of rap music all the way down to the lake, where everyone was playing ultimate Frisbee.

"The man of the hour!" Owen yelled, jogging toward me. He draped his sweaty arm around my shoulders.

I recognized Dirk and another junior from the football team.

Pablo was there too, as well as Owen's older brother Eddy, who'd driven over from Yale. The other two were seniors whom I knew only by name. There was Max, leader of the Glee Club, and Remo, the brawny German senior whom all the girls were nuts about.

Owen led the way to a sculpted picnic table, which was more of a statue than a table. He flipped open the cooler beside the table, grabbed a bunch of soda cans, and passed them around.

As we popped the lids open and took seats, three house-keepers brought out lunch: burgers on brioche buns, hand-cut fries, and homemade ketchup. They placed pitchers of ice water on either side of the table before scurrying back up the slope toward the massive house.

"How's Yale?" I asked Eddy.

"Full of hotness. Especially at this time of year. Microshorts and tank tops, Dukey. If I fail my finals, I'm blaming it on the indecent amount of skin I'm subjected to everyday." He winked at me.

I'd forgotten how identical he looked to Owen, in spite of their three-year age gap. And how identically they thought. Both had been obsessed with girls long before any of us even noticed they existed.

"How's Francis Academy? Heard you were dating Amanda," he continued.

"You know Amanda?" I asked.

He leaned in and winked. "I taught her a thing or two about the male anatomy. I hope it paid off."

"You slept with her?" I asked.

"Yeah. Last summer. Took her virginity."

The fry dangling between my fingers plummeted to my plate. I couldn't believe Amanda had lost it to Eddy.

"I should ask for payment for all the deflowering I did around the academy," Eddy said.

"Man whore," Owen coughed.

"You should pay them for doing *you*," Remo added with a grin.

Eddy chuckled. "You say things like that, and I'll make you my bitch in the fall." He caught Remo in a chokehold and rubbed his hair with his fist. "My first little Yale minion."

Laughing, Remo pressed him off.

"The plan! The plan! The plan!" Owen banged his palms against the table each time he shouted the word.

Everyone turned to stare at me. I took a swig of soda and laid out my strategy, from dechlorinating the pool on Friday night and cranking up the water temperature to help with the process, to turning it back down a good hour before throwing the fish in. The swim meet was at ten thirty, which meant the swimmers would start warm-ups around ten. I needed the fish in the water by nine.

"I'm receiving the goldfish on Friday," Dirk said. "My uncle told me they can stay in the travel tank overnight, so I'll drive them over in the morning."

I nodded my thanks.

"I brought you a little present from New Haven," Eddy said.

I frowned.

"The tablets. Why do you think I'm here?"

"My guess was to collect more hymens," Max said.

"Any virgins in the Glee Club?" Eddy asked, taking a huge chunk out of his burger.

"Not anymore," Max said with a sly smile.

Was I the last virgin in Francis Academy? "Thanks for the tablets, Eddy," I mumbled.

"No prob, Dukey. But I do want something in return."

"What?"

"Video footage of Shagdar when he discovers the fish."

Laughter rippled through the small assembly. I gulped. Video footage would require me to stick around. After I dumped the fish, I wanted to hit the ground running.

"Hell, yeah. We're getting front row seats. Mel's gonna flip," Owen said.

I was surprised he hadn't told his newest girlfriend about it. He wasn't known for his discretion. I gobbled down my burger to soak up the acid swishing around my stomach. As I chewed, a thought grew and solidified inside my mind, a thought that involved Jaime and his bucket list. What I was about to do to our school wasn't noble, but it would thrill Jaime.

The goldfish could be his "something illegal."

Chapter Forty-Five

That evening, jittery as hell, I rang the Matthewses' doorbell. I was surprised when Miss Brown opened the door, and even more so when she told me that Cora was out.

"But Jaime's in the living room, trying to train Rita to sit. He's been at it since this morning."

She gestured me inside, so I came in, took off my shoes, and went to find Jaime. Rita leaped toward me, tail wagging.

"Hey, girl," I said.

Jaime's cheeks were flushed with delight. "I thought you were coming tomorrow."

"I had to see your sister about something. Do you know when she'll be home?"

"Don't know. She left about thirty minutes ago."

"Do you know where she went?"

"Didn't say. Wait. You gotta see this." He whistled. "Rita, sit."

The collie stopped licking me to glance at Jaime. I patted her head and she went back to licking my hand.

"She really did it. A few times even," he said.

"I believe you."

He whistled, and this time, Rita returned to him. When he told her to sit, she sat.

"You see!" he said excitedly.

I nodded. "Well done, Jaime."

"Apparently, we have you to thank for our newest family member," Principal Matthews said, balancing a big lasagna dish on his oven mitt.

I bit my lip. "Yeah. Sorry."

"I said thank, not chide. She's precious." He placed the dish on the table and crouched to the dog's height. Rita bounded toward him. "Do you want to stay for dinner?"

Cora had probably stood me up. It was in part my fault, though. I hadn't thought of asking for her number, and we weren't Facebook friends. I'd had no way of contacting her besides calling her father, which would've been weird. Too bummed to eat, I made up some excuse about checking on Rita, and then left, promising to be back in the morning.

I kicked my tire before getting in the Jeep and backing it out of the short driveway. At the stop sign down the street, I decided to head over to Owen's house. Considering Eddy was home, there would definitely be something going on at his place.

As I was about to turn left, the passenger door flew open. I pressed down on my brakes, and Cora launched herself inside my vehicle.

"Jesus! Are you crazy?" I yelled.

"Certifiably, according to you."

"What is that supposed to mean?"

"You asked Mr. Darcy if Dad was abusing me," she said.

"He told you?"

"Yeah. He told Dad too."

"Crap," I muttered.

She snorted. "Dad thought it was sweet you were worried about me."

"So he doesn't hate me?"

"What can I say? The men in my family have a special place

in their hearts for you, Meyer." She shot me her taunting, squinty-eyed look.

"What about the girl in the family?"

She turned her head. "Don't."

"You've accepted to come on a date with me."

"It's dinner, not a date. And it was a bet." Cora pulled her seat belt across her chest. She was wearing a low-cut navy dress that clung to her like Saran Wrap.

"You wear short dresses to all your nondates?"

"It was the only clean thing left in my closet."

Yeah…right.

"Where are we going?" she asked.

"You'll see," I said, taking the route I knew by heart.

"I don't like to see. I like to know."

"Well, you'll *know* soon enough."

"I don't like crowds," she said.

"It'll be crowd-free. Just relax. It's a thirty-minute ride."

"Thirty minutes! Geez, Meyer, could you have chosen a further location?" she grumbled.

"I could've," I replied calmly.

I wouldn't let her fluctuating temper bother me. I had a plan, and it was as airtight as my goldfish-dump. We drove in silence. Cora toyed with the radio dial incessantly. She was nervous. Ironically, I wasn't anymore. I turned sideways a few times to glance at her. The waning sun softened the sharp line of her nose and made the silver hoops in her brow glisten. She'd chosen a deep crimson lipstick, almost brown, instead of her usual black one, but the rest of her makeup was unchanged.

When we turned onto a dirt road, she broke the silence. "Where the hell are we?"

"You don't recognize this place?"

When she shook her head, the tip of her ponytail brushed against her breasts.

"You've never been to the bluffs?"

"No."

"Really?"

"Yes, really," she said. "I don't drive, remember?"

"Ricky never took you?"

"Do you seriously want to talk about Ricky?"

"No. I don't." My knuckles whitened around the steering wheel. "It's the nicest place to watch the sunset from," I added after a bout of silence.

She kept her attention on the foaming sea that glittered gold underneath the setting sun. I parked where the road ended and jumped to get Cora's door. She'd already pushed it open, but I held it out anyway. As I spread out my American-flag comforter and unpacked the basket of food, she walked around, her gaze locked on the horizon. It reminded me of when she'd stared at my drawing of her. She seemed lost in some other dimension.

"I haven't had a picnic since the summer we spent in the Catskills," she said, returning toward me.

"I heard you loved it up there."

"How…? *Oh.* Of course. Jaime." She sank down noiselessly onto the blanket and crossed her legs. "I did love it…until—"

"Until what?"

I passed her a plate and a glass. When she took them from me, our fingers collided. She dropped the glass, and it landed softly onto the blanket.

"Until his first seizure," she said, staring down at it. "We thought it was heatstroke. It was a really hot day."

We were both quiet for a moment. The only noise came from the warm wind brushing through the grass.

"Sometimes, I forget he's sick," I said, righting her glass.

"I do too. Ever since we stopped the treatments and he started spending time with you, he's been better. I don't want to ruin that."

"How would you ruin that?"

"Do I seriously have to spell it out?"

"You mean if we got together, and then had a nasty breakup?"

"You catch on quick," she said.

Her sarcasm didn't irk me. She considered me boyfriend material. "Why would we break up?"

"I don't know…Why did you break up with Amanda?"

"She was jealous. Why did you break up with Ricky?"

"He was dating me to upset his mom."

"Really?"

She pointed to her face, before grabbing a bagel from the bread basket. "His mom is this very waspy socialite. She thought I was the devil incarnate."

"Is that why he owed you one?"

"Sort of. After admitting to using me, he asked me to sit through one last dinner with his mom."

"Don't tell me you accepted?"

She bit her lip ruefully.

"Why would you put yourself through that?"

"To annoy her. She's awful to Ricky."

"And apparently he's paying it forward…You shouldn't have stayed with a guy like him."

She tore a piece off her poppy seed bagel and nibbled on it. "I'm not pretty like you, Meyer. I don't have people falling at my feet."

"Are you kidding? You're beautiful. You just don't want people to see it." When she stayed silent for too long, I added, "Can I ask why you put on so much makeup? Is it a religious thing?"

She gave her head a small shake. That was all I thought I would get, but I was wrong.

"When Mom died," she began, "Dad spent all his time with Jaime. He forgot I was only nine…he forgot to take care of me. But I don't hold it against him. Jaime needed him more than I did. Anyway, one day, the school bus drivers were on strike, so I had to walk home. Dad was with Jaime, and I didn't have a phone to call him. I got lost, but some woman found me." She flicked a piece of bread into the grass. "I remember being scared of her because she had all this makeup and piercings and weird hair, but she helped me find my way home. The next day, the strike was still going on. I don't know if I did it on purpose, or if I was just directionally challenged, but I went the wrong way—again—and she was there—again." Cora took a breath of night air. "She made me feel safe, which I hadn't felt since my mother died."

It took me a second to absorb her revelation, because I hadn't been expecting it. "Do you still see her?"

"No. She disappeared one day."

"What happened?"

"Don't know. She just wasn't there anymore. I think she was hiding from someone and that someone found her. At least that's my theory."

"Who are *you* hiding from?" I asked.

"I'm not. I'm honoring her."

My speculations crumpled like a long line of cascading dominoes. "Jaime doesn't know that, does he?"

"Only Dad knows."

"And me now," I said. "I'm honored."

"Oh, please." She rolled her eyes. "You never would've let it go."

"Are you saying I'm nagging?"

She smiled. "Impossibly."

"Thank God I'm pretty then."

She laughed. It was the first time I'd heard her laugh. It sounded like the rustle of silk, heavy and soft. It faded much too quickly.

"What else was on my brother's bucket list?" she asked.

"Actually…your makeup."

"He wants my makeup?"

I chuckled. "No. He wants you to take it off." When she didn't respond, I added, "Is it something you can do?"

"I can do anything I want." The thick armor was back.

"Let me rephrase my question…*Will* you do it?"

The tip of her tongue darted out and toyed with the hoop. "I'll do anything for my brother."

My heart bounced in my chest at the idea of the entire school discovering Cora's real face. They'd already discovered her knockout body the day she'd been subjected to the leather getup. If they saw her without makeup, I would no longer stand a chance with her. Some heartthrob like Remo would swoop her off her feet.

"What else was on there?" she asked.

"He wants to go to a fair," I said, trying to curb my distress. "I checked the dates and the next one's on August fifteenth—"

A noise escaped her throat, and her body started trembling.

"What?" I asked.

She raised her face toward mine, eyes glistening as wildly as the sea below, and I remembered the doctor's prognosis. I moved to her side, slung my arm around her shoulder, and tucked the top of her head under my chin. A second ago, I'd heard her laugh for the first time, and now I was hearing her cry for the first time. I stroked her hair, trying to pitch away her pain.

"I can't imagine the world without him," I said softly.

Her sobs swelled and her body softened into mine. I inhaled her. Cora was like a drug, and I craved her like an addict. I ran my fingertips up and down her spine, keeping my touch light. She snapped straight and pressed away from me.

"Don't," she croaked. After a long stretch of silence, she added, "You probably would've had more fun with Amanda."

"Probably. You have some serious baggage."

She laughed and swiped my arm. I caught her hand and spread her fingers with mine before she could pull them away. Slowly, I tugged her close and she yielded. Our foreheads touched, then our noses, then our lips. The earth moved and the ocean swelled as Cora's thorny roses twined around my heart like barbed wire.

<h1 style="text-align:center">Chapter Forty-Six</h1>

"A sonar system?" Jaime said, glancing at my computer screen.

"So that Ghostboy can locate Chameleon," I explained. "He can send out a mental signal that hits the girl's body and echoes back to him, giving him a physical grasp of where she is."

"Cool!" Jaime said. "Way cool."

Rita, who was nestled on the couch, laid her head on Cora's thigh. Jaime's sister petted the canine and then turned a page of her newest read, *Catch-22*. I let my gaze drift over her bare, glowing face.

"Duke?" Jaime said.

"Uh-huh."

"What if she's really far? Can it still work?"

"Uh-huh," I said, distractedly.

"What does Ghostboy see when the signal comes back to him? A flashing map or Chameleon's actual surroundings?" Jaime asked.

"Uh-huh."

"And then the Duke paints a purple rabbit that poops gold coins," Jaime said.

"Uh-huh."

"Cora, you need to leave," Jaime said.

I swiveled my attention back to him.

"Why?" she asked.

"Because you're distracting *us*." He gave me a meaningful look.

She petted Rita's head. "I'm not even talking."

"Pretty please," he said.

"Fine." She tried scowling but her attempt was dire. "I'll take Rita out for a run."

"Thanks, sis. And by the way, you look beautiful today." Jaime tilted his head to study his sister. "You look like Mom."

Cora's eyes misted over. "You think so?"

He nodded. "Yup. Duke can't even concentrate."

Her cheeks flooded with heat. It was a weird sight to see so much color on her face. "He's a guy, Jaime. He checks out anything with a pulse."

"Not anything." I chuckled. "I have standards."

"Yeah, right," she said as she left, shooting me a crooked smile.

When she came home later, flushed and glistening from her run, I became so unfocused that I told Jaime I had enough material to write two solid chapters. Thankfully, I did—on my computer. My brain hadn't processed any information, too filled was it with the white noise of my hectic pulse.

"So, you like Ghostboy and Chameleon's mental sonar?" I asked.

"Yeah. It's supercool." He hopped down from his chair, and kneeled next to Rita. Panting, she licked his cheek, which made him giggle. He ran his hand through her white-and-brown coat. "Do you think Cora knows she's Chameleon?"

"I can ask. I have to drop by her room before I go."

"Nah. Don't. I'd rather she doesn't know. I don't want her to tell me it's silly," he said. As I left the living room, he added, "Why do you have to stop by her room? Are you two friends?"

"It's about a homework assignment."

"She's a junior."

Jaime was too smart for me.

"She had Mr. Walker for art last year," I said. "I wanted to ask her about a project he gave us."

He blew his bangs out of his eyes. "The Duke of Graffiti needs help with an art project? From my sister? She's sucky in art."

"Okay. Fine. You got me. I need to discuss something I have planned for you."

His eyes widened, becoming big pools of blue. "Really?"

"Don't get too excited. I need her approval."

"Go!"

"I'll tell you what she says."

"Okay. Go," he repeated eagerly.

I started toward the small hallway that led to the bedrooms, before doubling back. "Which one is her room?"

"The one at the end."

Maybe visiting her bedroom was totally inappropriate—especially considering she didn't know I was coming. My fist hovered in midair. What if she was in the shower, or half-naked, or fully naked? My heart thumped against my ribcage so loudly that it sounded like my fist pounding the door, which flew open. Had I knocked?

"Yes?" she asked. She was towel drying her long hair, which was bleeding water on her tight tank top and on the waistband of her low-slung sweatpants.

"Did I knock?" I asked, trying to keep my gaze leveled on hers even though it felt weighted down.

"You breathed."

She'd taken out her piercings. I wondered if she had to take them out before each shower. That was a lot of metal to remove and put back.

"What?" she asked, lowering the towel.

I snapped out of my daze and rubbed my palm against the back of my neck. "Can I come in?"

She nodded slowly. "You're having second thoughts aren't you? I was too."

I froze. "Second thoughts? About what?"

"Last night."

"No. Absolutely not." I shook my head for emphasis. "But you are?"

She grabbed my arm and dragged me into her room. Then she shut the door. "Jaime. He doesn't want to share you, and I understand. The two of you probably bond more when I'm not around."

"He doesn't want to share our *story*. He's excited you and I are talking. Okay. Maybe not excited. But definitely not angry." My fingers were still clenched. "Is it really about Jaime, or is it about me? I know I'm a sophomore, but I'm turning seventeen in July."

She sighed, folding her towel over the back of her desk chair. It was turquoise, as was the rest of her room, or at least what was visible of it. She'd painted quotations over nearly every inch of wall. All were black, but varied in size and style.

We age not by years, but by stories, was in italics.

A wise man once said nothing, was in block letters.

"Meyer?"

"Wait. I'm getting to know you." I approached the piece of wall with the smallest-written quote. I nearly had to squint to read it.

Fear does not stop death, it stops life.

I traced the last letters with my fingers before turning around. She'd squared her shoulders defensively, trying to appear tough; it was cute.

"What?" she shot out. "I like quotes."

I smirked. "This is not liking. This is a true passion." I read more. There were two common themes, unsurprisingly time and death. "It's really neat."

She was watching me watch her walls. Fueled by a streak of boldness, I swooped down and kissed her. It was as brief as an eyelash flutter. It took her a few seconds to react, but when she did, she forced me back.

"What are you doing?" she whispered.

"Most people call it kissing." When she didn't say anything for too long, I sighed. "It was our last, wasn't it?"

She bit down on her lower lip.

"Can I get a do-over? It was a pathetic last kiss," I said.

She released her lip. "Just one more."

I weaved my right hand through her hair, gently lifted her face, and moved my mouth toward hers slowly, trying to make the moment last forever. I pressed my nose against hers, brushed my lips against hers, but then instead of kissing her, I drew my lips along her jaw, all the way up to her ear.

"If I only get one more, I'm saving it," I murmured, before straightening. I winked at her and continued observing the quotations.

Cora didn't say anything. She didn't move. I wanted to believe it was a side effect of my smoothness. In reality, I had no idea. I snuck a glance at her—her eyes were crowded with that sad, faraway gleam.

"I actually came in here to ask for your permission again," I said. "Can I take your brother to the school swim meet on Saturday?"

She finally came back to life. "He wants to go to a swim meet?"

"Can I take him?"

"I guess," she said.

I turned to go, relieved that she'd said yes, even though she had no idea what she'd agreed to.

"I can come too," she said.

I stiffened, closed my eyes, and swept my mind for a solution. The one I came up with made my heart twist in my chest. "I'd rather not. As you said, we bond more when you're not around."

She gasped. It was quiet and deep, like the bang of a

cannon in the night. For a second, I wanted to tell her the truth, but what if she told her father? Then I would definitely spend my last month of sophomore year attached to Shagdar's garbage pick. Worse though, I would never become part of the exclusive brotherhood and I would let down Gabe and Owen.

If I couldn't have Cora, then I wanted the Alphas.

Chapter Forty-Seven

I t was late and quiet. Armed with confidence and cartons full of Camden tablets, I parked next to Francis Academy's glass-domed pool house.

That afternoon, I'd gone for a furtive stroll through the swimmers' changing rooms and left a window open in the boys' locker room, right above the last shower stall. That was my entry point.

Checking my surroundings, I ambled up to the window and pressed my fingertips into it. It gave way. Beads of sweat were collecting on my brow. I wiped them off and pushed the first box in. It fell to the floor with a satisfying thump. I shoved the next box through, and then returned to the car and grabbed the four others, balancing them in my arms. After thrusting them all in, I hoisted myself up and landed in a crouch with the stealth of Spiderman—Jaime would be proud.

I stood and stacked the cardboard boxes in the shower, and then jogged over to the control closet—the one I'd seen Shagdar visit the day I'd helped him mop up the pool house. My sneakers squeaked on the cement floor. I still didn't know how I was going to get away with dumping the goldfish without conse-quence. Just as I had that thought, there was a pounding noise.

Heart in my throat, I stood flush against a wall, hoping to become one with the shadows. The knocking resumed. Maybe it was in my head…or in my chest.

Silence.

Then suddenly, a hissed, "Duke, open up. It's me," jolted me out of hiding.

Gabe had mentioned he'd come but hadn't answered his phone all evening. I raced to the entrance and flipped the lock open. My friend came in, smiling like the cat who'd gulped down the goldfish—pun intended.

"You scared the shit out of me," I hissed.

He winked. "Said I'd help. I'm here. What can I do?"

"Grab the boxes. They're in the last shower stall," I whispered.

"On it." He sprinted to the locker room.

During the time it took me to turn up the temperature, Gabe had fetched all the boxes. We tore them open and dumped the contents into different segments of the pool. The tablets fizzed down to the bottom.

"And now, we pray this works," I said, watching the tiny bubbles snake up to the surface.

"It'll work."

"I need to come back at six to turn down the temperature."

"You're on your own for that. Six is way too early, man. I'll hitch a ride with Dirk around eight. Is that good?"

"Yeah. But don't be late."

"This is going to be an epic blast."

"You keep saying that," I grumbled.

"Because it will be! You gotta chill out, Dukey," Gabe said. "Tell you what. Come over to my place. We can watch the play-offs. That should help you relax."

I sighed. It wasn't as though I would sleep tonight anyway.

"You can do this," I told myself.

At four 4:48 a.m.—an hour ahead of schedule—strung up on tepid milky coffee, I walked into the foggy, glass pool house. I trotted over to the control closet and brought the temperature dial back down to seventy-seven degrees, before retracing my steps out to my car, which I'd forgotten to turn off. My hands trembled and so did my right eyelid. I shivered from the cold anxiety gnawing at my bones. With an hour and a half to kill before collecting Jaime from his house, I decided to go home and shower.

I tiptoed into my dark house and tried to climb the stairs without being caught, but of course, Grandma P. trapped me. She tipped her head toward the kitchen.

"I was worried about you. Is Jaime all right?" she asked, when I walked over.

"Jaime?"

"You told me you were going over to his place for dinner. When you didn't come home, I thought the worst. I left you a message." She was nursing a cup of coffee.

"He's fine," I said.

She exhaled a soft breath. "Thank God." When I didn't say anything for a long time—mostly because my weary brain couldn't construct sentences for the life of me—she asked, "How's the story coming along?"

"Good." I drummed my fingers against the marble.

"Are you done with it?"

"Nearly."

She looked at my hands. I stopped fidgeting.

"You look nervous, honey," she said. "Is everything—?"

"I-I'm fine."

"Where were you?"

"At Gabe's."

She cocked her head to the side, trying to find an angle to see into my head. Since I wasn't lying, I kept my gaze locked on hers. After a few minutes, she asked, "Did you sleep?"

"No. Couldn't. Really need a shower. Bye." I turned to leave.

"Why the rush?"

"Taking Jaime to a swim meet," I said.

"Oh, that's sweet of you."

It wasn't sweet of me. It was downright bad of me. I was dragging an innocent eight-year-old into the murky waters of criminality. I gave a sharp nod and headed back to the stairs.

"By the way. Your dad—" Grandma started.

I whirled around. "Yeah?"

Although the kitchen glowed warmly, Grandma's skin was pale. "Never mind."

My pulse throbbed inside my throat. "No. Tell me."

"He just wants to talk to you."

"About what?" I asked.

When her brow puckered, my shoulders wound up as tight as the string of a bow.

"You told him?" There was reproach in my tone.

"He found out."

"How?"

"At your art exhibit. He saw you with him," she said.

"Oh." I bit my lip and calmed down. "I'm not going to stop seeing Jaime."

"That's not his intention."

"Then what is? Why do I need to talk to him?" I asked.

"You just do. That's all I know. Now go to bed. You look like you're about to keel over."

Like I could ever relax now! Grams had just smeared a new layer of anxiety over my already thick one. What could my father possibly want to discuss?

Chapter Forty-Eight

____

True to her word, Cora brought Jaime out to my car at seven forty-five sharp.

"Be careful with him," she said, after shutting the back door.

She tightened the black cardigan around herself even though it was far from cold. She wasn't wearing makeup this morning, and her skin glowed, but so did her undereye circles. They rivaled mine.

"I'll drop him off after the meet," I told her, absorbing every inch of her bare skin. She'd kept it covered all week in school.

"I'm ready!" Jaime bounced in his seat, seat belt digging into his abdomen. He looked like he'd gained a little weight. Even his cheeks seemed fuller.

I nodded goodbye to Cora and pulled away from the curb.

"We're going on a mission," I announced.

His mouth gaped open. "A real one?"

"Yes. And it's very illegal."

"Get out!"

"Remember when I painted your father's car?"

"Yeah."

"Well, it was a dare. To get into this club called the Alphas. It's ultrasecret. You can't tell anyone about it."

He bobbed his head up and down.

"This is my second chance," I continued, and told him about the goldfish and the footage I needed of Mr. Darcy.

In my rearview mirror, I could see his eyes sparkle like streamers. Which reminded me of the school dance coming up in two weeks, the one for which I was dateless. For the briefest of seconds, I thought about asking Cora, but I stomped out that crazy plan.

Soon, we were pulling up in front of the pool house. I spotted Dirk's car and parked next to it. Before leaping out, I turned toward Jaime. "You sure you want to be involved? You don't—"

He'd already unstrapped himself. "I'm sure." He gave me a thumb's up before jumping onto the pavement. His enthusiasm exacerbated the nervous excitement that had been building up inside of me all month.

I switched off the engine and came around to join him at the back of Dirk's truck. He was gaping at the four corrugated cardboard boxes.

Dirk tipped his head toward Jaime. "Who's the little guy?"

I touched Jaime's bony shoulder. "Jaime. This is Dirk and Gabe."

"Hey," he said.

"Aren't you Cora's brother?" Gabe asked, his eyebrow hitching up. I wondered how he knew. Probably the art show…

"Yeah. But she doesn't know anything," he said.

Gabe smiled. "And your dad?"

Jaime stepped out of my reach. "I'm not a tattletale."

Dirk chuckled. "Good. If you are, I'm taking my fish and hitting the road."

I tucked my fingers under one of the crates. "How much do these things weigh?"

"Don't know. Delivery guys put them in my trunk. Nothing I can't handle, though." Dirk flexed his biceps. "Out of my way, weakling."

"You're never lifting that on your own," I said, stepping back.

He heaved. The box lifted an inch, and then came down hard. A swishing noise filled his trunk. "Gabe? A little help."

Gabe snickered. Together, they lifted the first crate.

"Jaime, can you get the door?" I asked.

As he ran to pull it open, I placed my palms underneath the package. We walked quickly, carefully, depositing the package at the edge of the pool. Before going back for the three others, I stuck my hand in the water. It wasn't cool yet, but I doubted it would simmer the goldfish. At least I hoped it wouldn't. A bunch of floating, dead fish would not earn me a spot in the Alphas.

"Duke," Jaime said. "Come on! They got the second box." His cheeks were splotchy red.

I jogged back out. Ten minutes later each one of us stood behind a box. I started tugging on the heavy-duty packing tape but couldn't rip it open.

"Anybody brought scissors?" I asked.

"Nope," Dirk said.

"Shit," I muttered.

"Why don't you use your car keys? I see Dad do that all the time," Jaime said.

"The little dude has some serious brains," Dirk said.

"I'm not little. I'm eight."

I chuckled as I crouched and tore through the tape with my keys while Dirk and Gabe did the same. Then I attacked the package at Jaime's feet. Inside the crenellated crates were Styrofoam boxes, and inside those were plastic sacks filled with water and frolicking fish.

"Will it kill them?" Jaime's voice echoed in the cavernous glass house.

"I took most of the chlorine out of the pool, so hopefully not," I said.

Jaime observed the fish with a somber expression.

"Are you okay?" I asked him.

He raised his eyes to mine; they were all shiny.

Gabe sighed. "Not to interrupt, but we gotta hurry."

I wanted to tell Jaime I didn't have to go through with this. But I did have to go through with it. For Gabe and for Owen. If it had been just for me, I would've walked out with the boxes and set the fish free in Bruce Park Pond.

"You want to wait for me by the car, Jaime?"

He shook his head, and his bangs fell in his eyes. He pushed the dark locks away. "I'm your sidekick, remember?"

I felt Gabe's quizzical gaze on me as I slashed open the sturdy plastic bags with my keys and tipped the crate—an orange and gold waterfall spilled out. For a second, the fish seemed stunned, but then they flicked their tails and swam away as quick as thieves.

"Are you just going to stand there, or are you going to make yourselves useful?" I asked.

"On it." Dirk bent at the waist, hacked through the packaging, and tilted his box.

As I hewed through the one at Jaime's feet, Gabe unloaded his fish. When the last bunch went in, I monitored my handiwork.

"They look happy," Jaime said.

I had no clue if fish could sense happiness or grief, but they lived—perhaps that was what Jaime meant.

I bent down and released a few whispered words in his ear, "And Ghostboy does it again."

A beaming Jaime held up his hand for a high five, and I delivered.

"I'll lock up after you guys. Meet me by the car," I said.

"Can I stay with you?" Jaime asked.

"I don't know if that's a good idea. I have to climb through a window."

"*I* want to climb through a window," he said eagerly.

"Okay. Gabe, can you go around the back to catch him?"

For a second, Gabe didn't move. He just stared between Jaime and me, trying to understand our connection. He probably thought it was Cora. Dirk seemed equally puzzled.

"Guys?" I gestured toward the door.

After they filed out, I locked up and told Jaime to follow me. We sped toward the locker rooms. We'd covered a very short distance, yet he was panting.

"You okay?" I asked.

Though he dug his hands into his waist, he nodded.

My pulse felt like it was about to burst my aorta. "Are you sure?"

He was breathing so hard he couldn't get any words out, but he did give me a thumbs-up. Cora's advice ricocheted through my mind. I was acting recklessly with her brother. We had all the time in the world. We should have walked, not sprinted.

"Ready for the pass." Gabe's pleasant tone cut through my gloomy thoughts.

I twined my fingers together, creating a stirrup, and coaxed Jaime to step up. I lifted him as cautiously as Mom carried her vases, and then held on to his legs until Gabe took delivery of him. I heaved myself up and over the ledge, fire racing through my veins and perspiration soaking my T-shirt.

Jaime's chest rose and fell more steadily now, but what duress had I put his body under? How much more could he endure? Enough to finish his bucket list, or would Ghostboy be the only one who got the adventures?

Chapter Forty-Nine

"So? Are you in?" Jaime asked the second he answered the door.

Rita circled me excitedly, giving me a few licks to attract my attention. As I petted her, I let out an overly dramatic sigh, at which Jaime's face fell. But then I grinned and said, "You're looking at member number sixty three."

"Yay!" He clapped and performed a little victory dance, twirling on himself. He seemed more excited than I was.

"Is your dad here?" I asked.

"No. He's dealing with some very angry parents," Jaime said.

"Yikes."

"Had anything to do with it, Meyer?" came a familiar, deep voice from inside.

Jaime blanched as his sister tugged the door wider.

"Of course not," I said, my tone flat. "But it was something, wasn't it, Jaime?"

He nodded with great enthusiasm, hair flopping around his face. "I wouldn't have minded jumping in. It was *super*cool, sis."

Cora snorted. "I bet. But it was also *super*stupid."

"She's so annoying," he told me. "So…ssso…annoy…ying."

"We get it," she said, smiling. "I'll just grab my stuff and get out of your way." Cora retreated toward her room.

"Are you ready to write? Because I have lots and lots of ideas," I said.

Jaime blinked. He was staring past me.

I twisted around, but no one was there. I wiggled my fingers in front of him. "Yoo-hoo. Jaime?"

He kept staring beyond me.

"Are you okay, buddy?" I asked, inspecting his face. "Jaime?" My voice sounded nearly like a shout now.

He started raising his hand, but it dangled in midair before slumping down against his side.

My pulse jackhammered inside my throat. "Cora!"

In a second, she was out of the house and at her brother's side. She crouched down next to him. His eyelids twitched and his fingers trembled and his knees jerked. Rita nuzzled his side and started whimpering.

"Call nine-one-one! He's having a seizure," she yelled. It sounded like she was standing at the bottom of a well. "Meyer! Nine-one-one! Now!"

I jumped, dropped my computer and keys on the ground, and yanked my cell phone out of my jeans. My fingers shook so much that it took me several attempts to dial the number. When someone answered, my mind went blank. Thankfully, Cora snatched the phone from me. In a surprisingly calm voice, she explained the situation, all the while keeping one hand around Jaime's arm. Her fingers were pale as snow, and her face, although not made-up, seemed dusted with white powder.

Jaime was staring up at me, his eyes empty. I dove down to my knees. "It's going to be okay," I rattled, hoping I wasn't lying.

Rita whined.

A single tear snaked down his face; it plopped on the doormat underneath his feet. I bent my finger and brushed away the wet trail from his cheek. Suddenly his head lolled back and his lids shut and his little body crumpled. I shot my hands out and caught his fall. Slowly, I lowered him to the floor.

"Lay him on his side," Cora said.

Carefully, I rolled Jaime onto his side. She ran into the house and returned with a cushion. She placed it underneath his head. She was still on the phone. Fleetingly, her gaze touched mine. Afraid she would spot the terror raging inside of me, I looked over at her brother, whose chest now rose and fell evenly.

A siren filled the air. It was so soft at first that I thought I was imagining it, but then it grew louder, strident. It was everywhere, in the magnolia trees, in the mowed grass, in the grubby flowerbed, in Jaime, in Rita, in me. Everything vibrated. And then nothing vibrated. The shrill sound stopped. Doors slammed, metal clanked, footsteps pounded, wheels spun. Two people sprinted toward us. A bodiless voice asked me to move. Jaime shook his head. I saw his fingers twitch out to me. I fought to stay next to him but someone pulled me back.

"Please, sir. We need room," the voice said.

"I'll stay right here," I told him, my voice surprisingly steady.

After a quick examination, they lifted Jaime and laid him out on the stretcher. I followed them back to the EMT van. The paramedic jumped into the back and strapped an oxygen mask to Jaime's face. It seemed to cover every inch of it. Cora scrambled up and sat next to her brother, her hands clasped around his. My fear hardened into a jagged ball that clogged my throat. I tried to swallow, but it wouldn't go away. The ball grew larger when her eyes locked on mine. They looked like black vortexes that had sopped up all the misery and horror of the world. They pulled me forward.

I was about to climb in when the second responder told me to step back. "Family only," he barked, shutting the doors.

"Where—Where are you taking him?" I sputtered.

"Greenwich Memorial," he said as he hopped into the driver's seat. He turned on the siren again, and it screeched inside my ears. Seconds later, the van was just a blip on the horizon.

I swallowed. My palate felt parched, and my tongue as arid as a dried-up cornhusk. For several seconds, I couldn't move. Slowly, I started twitching, unclenching my fingers, bending my arms, breathing. Each breath burned the hell out of my throat.

Rita was sitting at my feet, gaping at the horizon.

"What happened?" someone said.

It was an old woman who smelled so strongly of peppermint it made my eyes water. I rubbed them.

She tightened the belt around her royal blue bathrobe. It was the exact shade of Jaime's eyes. "It's the boy, isn't it?"

I nodded. "I have t-to…go." I wanted to call Jaime's dad when I realized Cora had left with my phone. "Do you have… Mr. Matthews's…phone number?" I struggled to get the words out. The ball was expanding, plugging my entire throat.

"Yes," she said.

"Call him. Tell him…Jaime's with Cora…at Greenwich Memorial."

Rita in tow, I jogged to my car while patting my pockets for my keys. They weren't there…I remembered dropping them. I jumped up the porch stairs, swooped down, seized my laptop and fallen keys, shut the house's front door, dashed back to the Jeep, bounced inside, and shut the door. Swerving out of the driveway, I barreled down Maplewood and just missed the old woman who smelled like menthol and the collie that now sat beside her, as helpless as I'd been a few seconds ago. I didn't slow down, burning through stop signs and red lights. I threw the car into a parking spot and ran into the hospital, my keys jingling in my pocket like tolling church bells.

Chapter Fifty

I couldn't feel my feet or my legs by the time I located Cora in the waiting room. My mouth was filled with the taste of metal and my heart had slammed against my ribcage so many times that it had definitely bruised it. I ached for Jaime, for Cora, and for Mr. Matthews who arrived seconds after me. He looked like he was wearing his daughter's makeup.

As he vanished down the hallway to gather information on his son, I slumped in the seat next to Cora's. She was spinning her thumbs in her lap. Her silver rings flashed like the EMT van's revolving light.

"How is he?" I asked.

"They took him for a scan." She bit down on her lip and then released it. "They said he should be okay. For now. But I —" She swallowed. "I don't know."

My knee jiggled. I jammed my sole against the floor. "I'm sure he'll be fine."

"He told me he forgot my name. He remembered I was his sister but he couldn't remember my name."

I wrapped my hand around her restless one. For a second, she let me hold it. But then she pulled it away.

"You didn't have to come," she said.

"Are you kidding?" I was about to tell her how pissed I was that the paramedic hadn't let me ride with them, but decided to crack the stiff tension instead. "You ran off with my phone, and I'm expecting a booty call."

She snorted, but her lips twitched into a small smile.

When she didn't say anything, I added, "I'm kidding. But you did run off with my cell."

She stopped spinning her thumbs, shifted on her seat, and produced my phone from the back pocket of her black shorts. As I took it, our fingers brushed, which made her pallid cheeks flood with color. Her reaction pried some of the gloom off my soul. But then I remembered we were in the ER.

Cora suddenly leaped up.

Her dad was back, hunched over, but taking long strides. "He's okay. He's awake. His memory's fine."

She threw her arms around him and sobbed. Well, at first, I thought it was her, but then I realized it was him. I'd never heard a grown man cry before. It was almost more terrifying than Jaime's seizure.

He pulled away from Cora and blotted his eyes with his shirtsleeve. "Thank you for coming," he told me.

"Of course."

"Can I go see him?" she asked.

"Not yet, honey. The doctor wants him to rest. He promised to send someone out to get us." He took a seat across from me as Cora returned to her chair. Silence ensued, as thick as the humid heat outside the hospital walls.

"The tumor…it's everywhere," Mr. Matthews finally said. His voice was barely above a whisper. He planted his elbows on his thighs and leaned over, resting his forehead against his palms. His shoulders quivered, but no more tears escaped. Yet grief rocked his body. "What a day. What a day," he murmured, dropping his hands onto the armrests.

"How's the goldfish situation?" Cora asked, glancing at me.

I tried not to stiffen, but I did sit up straighter.

"Under control. Finally," he said. "Mr. Darcy even managed to save some."

"I thought chlorine suffocated fish," she said.

"The chlorine level was low." His eyes drifted over me.

I stuffed my mind with thoughts of ponies and spinach to barricade it from Mr. Matthews's scrutiny. When I spoke, I attempted to keep my voice even. "Jaime was stoked when he saw them."

His features softened. "I bet he was. He used to want an aquarium." He smiled. "Don't get him one. The dog's already a handful."

I laughed nervously while Cora gasped.

"Rita! I left her outside. And our door. It's wide open," she said.

"I closed the door," I reassured her. "And I left Rita with your neighbor. The one who takes care of Jaime."

"She can *barely* take care of him. She'll probably forget Rita outside or something."

"I'll go get her then. I can keep her at my place overnight, or for however long Jaime's here so you don't have to worry about her."

"That would be very nice of you, Duke," Mr. Matthews said, so I got up.

I started for the sliding glass doors, but stopped. "I'd like to see him. Whenever I can."

"Yes. Of course. We'll call you," he said.

For a second, I thought about staying and phoning my mother to pick up Rita, but I hadn't filled her in on anything. Not only would she be confused, but she would flip. "Give me news, okay?"

Cora was back to spinning her thumbs, each girdled with shimmering rings, but Mr. Matthews nodded. Reluctantly, I trod out of the hospital.

• • •

When I came home with a dog, it caused quite a stir.

My mother's gaze darted over Rita, from her shiny muzzle to her missing front leg. "You got a dog without asking us?"

"It's not what you think." I gestured to the living room.

Mom went in first, and then Grams, whose arms were folded tightly, and then me, and then Rita. I sat on one of the couches while the collie lay down at my feet.

"For the past month, I've been hanging out with this boy. His name's Jaime. You might have seen him at the art exhibit in school. He's the little brother of a friend of mine."

My mother furrowed her brow.

"Anyway, I've been seeing him because we've been working on a book together," I continued.

"A book?" she asked.

Grandma burrowed deeper in the couch, nearly disappearing.

Mom observed her. "Did you know about this, Mom?"

"I—umm." Grams glanced at me and I nodded. "Yes," she said.

"And you didn't tell me?"

"It wasn't my secret to tell. And it wasn't anything bad. It's pretty incredible if you ask me."

"Why are you writing this boy a story?" Mom asked.

"He has cancer. Terminal. I wanted to bring some fun into his life."

"You couldn't have *bought* him a book?"

I was taken aback by my mother's coldness. "I'm writing *his* adventures. Or at least the ones he wished he could have gone on. It's not some impersonal essay. It's his story."

"But why?" she asked.

"Because I have everything and he doesn't. And it's not fair." My voice broke. "It's not fair."

My mother smoothed down her long, flowy skirt. "What about the dog?"

"It's Jaime's."

"And why is it here?"

"*She*. Not *it*. Rita's here because he's back in the hospital. I offered to take care of her."

She stood up and began pacing the geometric-patterned rug. She didn't say anything for so long that I got up too.

"I'm going to take Rita for a walk around the block," I said. "Give you time to compute the news."

Mom halted her marching and stepped over Grandma's feet, nearly knocking over one of her glass vases. She grabbed my arm and held me back. "Don't go, honey. I'm not mad. I'm just surprised. I wish you'd told me."

Her eyes were shiny.

"And Rita can stay with us for as long as need be." She extended her hand toward the collie to let her sniff it. It took a few seconds for Rita to wag her tail, but when she did, my mother broke into a smile. "How about I take her out? Your grandmother needs a walk, and I wouldn't mind some fresh air."

"I need a walk?" Grams asked, unbinding herself from the couch.

Mom gestured toward the door, which she'd already pulled open.

"What's this?" My father stood on the threshold, arm hovering in midair, key jutting out.

"*She*—not *this*—is Rita," Mom said.

Dad lowered the racket bag slung across his shoulder and placed it by the door. "Is she ours?"

"No. I'll let your son fill you in. Mom?"

"I'm coming. I'm coming. Jeez." Grams squeezed my arm on her way out.

"That's it. I'm getting you a wheelchair," Mom told her.

"I'd rather rollerblades," Grams answered before my father closed the door behind them.

Staring at me, he asked, "Does she belong to the Matthews boy?"

"Maybe. How did you—"

"Let's sit," he said.

"I'd rather stand."

He sighed. "The Matthews boy. He's the one that I—" His voice broke. "That I told you about."

I frowned as I silently ran through our past discussions. When I got to the one he meant, I lost it. "Not Jaime! *No…* This isn't happening. This can't be—!"

"I'm sorry."

"*Sorry?*" I spat. "Sorry doesn't cut it. He had a seizure today! I was there!"

"What else do you want me to say, Duke?"

"I don't know, but not that you're sorry!" Anger replaced everything inside of me; it filled me like blood fills veins and air fills lungs. I was shaking. "Does Mr. Matthews know?"

"He does. We met in person after the case was dismissed. At your art show. I didn't want it to impact your school record, especially not after the spray paint incident."

"You did *not!*"

"Excuse me for caring about you, Duke," he said, raising his own voice. It vibrated through the foyer, against the stone, the mirror, and the wooden walls. "My actions shouldn't reflect upon my son. That was the only point I was making."

"What about *his* son, huh?"

My dad's jaw set. "I offered to pay for his son's treatment."

"There *is* no treatment."

"Oh, you know what I mean!" he barked.

"I can't believe this," I breathed. Children disappointed parents, not the other way around. I shook my head one last time before racing up the stairs to my room and slapping the door shut.

I hadn't thought this day could get any worse, but it just had. How could Jaime's father even stand to look at me? I represented the people who had robbed his son of a future. I punched my wall. The plaster chipped and my knuckles bled. As I watched the blood bead, I thought about Jaime.

Death wouldn't end our friendship; the truth would.

Chapter Fifty-One

All anyone could talk about on Monday were the stupid goldfish.

"Okay, what's going on with you?" Gabe asked as I slammed my locker shut for the tenth time that day. "And can you please explain to me how you happen to be best buddies with Cora's little bro?"

"I'm writing him a story," I said.

"Huh?"

I explained it to him.

"For real?" he asked.

"Yes, for real."

"Is this your way of getting into Goth Girl's leather pants?"

"Fuck you, Gabe," I said and started jogging away from him.

But he caught up. "I was joking, man."

"Well, it was a stupid joke."

He bit down on his lip. "I'm sorry. I was just surprised, that's all."

I sighed. "You and everyone else I tell."

"I feel like a huge douche now for my earlier comment."

"You *are* a huge douche," I told him.

He chuckled, which lightened my brooding mood.

When we entered math class, Liane sprang off the desk she was sitting on. "It was you, wasn't it?" she asked.

I pulled my brows in. "Don't know what you're talking about. I slept over at Gabe's house. Owen kicked us out of bed to see his girlfriend swim. Wasn't me."

Her certainty faltered. "But—"

Gabe tucked her hand in his. "I told you, babe. Duke had nothing to do with it."

"But—"

He shook his head emphatically.

I didn't think Liane would give up so easily, but she did, charging right into another topic. "So, who are you taking to the school dance, Duke?"

"I'm not going," I said, chucking my messenger bag on the table.

"Why not? I had a whole bunch of girls lined up for you."

"Well, get them out of line."

"Gabe? Drill some sense inside this party pooper. You already missed the Modley's big bash yesterday." She flipped her flaxen hair.

"I was busy," I muttered.

"Come. It'll be fun," he said. "Owen's spiking the punch."

I grunted. "I don't need to go to a dance for spiked punch. Grandma spikes all her drinks. I can just down one of hers."

"How about you ask—" Gabe started.

"Shut it," I said. "I'm not going and that's final."

Just then Miss Brown walked in, more frazzled and crazy haired than ever. The sadness in her eyes made my gut twist.

During class, my phone vibrated, lighting up with an unknown number. I never took phone calls in school, but raised my hand to be excused. Miss Brown nodded and I bounded out of my seat. Before I was out the door, I answered the call.

"I was going to leave you a message," Cora said.

"How is he?"

"Better. He wants to see you." I heard Jaime's voice in the background. "And he wants you to bring your computer."

"I'll be there with my laptop as soon as school lets out. Or I can come now," I said. "I just need to get a slip from your dad."

Another muffled voice came through the receiver. "Dad says stay in school. You have finals coming up."

"You do too," I said, pacing the hallway like a caged beast.

"No. I decided to drop out and redo the year in September."

I froze in my tracks.

"Meyer, you still there?"

"Uh-huh."

"Jaime wants to talk to you."

There was rustling. It sounded as though Cora was dragging the phone across the starched hospital bed sheet.

"Hey," I said when the noise stopped.

"Hey."

"I'm gonna need a heart replacement if you do that again," I said.

He tittered. "I'll give you mine."

My breath hitched in my throat. He must have heard it because he stopped laughing.

"How's Rita?" he asked, thankfully changing the topic.

"Keeping my mom and grandma busy. I think they gave her a fur mask and painted her nails."

"No they didn't," Jaime said, his tone light again.

"They didn't. But they did wash her with something. She smells like strawberry ice cream."

He giggled. "She won't want to come home with me."

"You've obviously never lived with the women in my family," I said. "I've been trying to crawl out of my house forever."

Mr. Matthews talked, but I couldn't make out his words. "Dad says, go back to class."

My jaw hurt from the grin that strained across it. "Okay, okay," I pretended to huff.

"Don't forget your computer. See ya," he said before disconnecting.

I stored Cora's number in my phone, running my thumb over the ten digits. When I stepped back into class, I must still have looked joyful, because everyone stared at me, including Miss Brown. I returned to my seat and tried to concentrate on her lecture, but all I could think about was seeing Jaime.

I was so full of adrenaline by the time school let out that I tore through the hallway like a bowling ball. In ten minutes, I was at the hospital. Another three and I was in Jaime's room. Mr. Matthews was there but Cora wasn't.

"She went home to rest," he said. "Do you mind if I do the same?"

"Of course not." I looked over at Jaime instead of at Principal Matthews, suddenly hobbled by the weight of my dad's confession. I wondered if he thought I'd known all along. Or worse, if he thought that was the reason I was helping his son.

"I'll be back before five," he said.

"Don't rush. I don't need to be home until seven."

"Finals start Wednesday, Duke."

"I can study here. Go home and rest. I promise I don't mind."

He sighed. "Call me…if there's anything." He crossed the room toward Jaime, pressed a kiss to his son's forehead, and then left.

I was assaulted by a déjà-vu. Two beds. It wasn't the same room I'd shared with Jaime when I had appendicitis, but it was a relatively accurate copy.

"So, how you feeling?" I asked, coming to sit on the chair pulled up to his bed.

"Been better," he said with a shrug.

His eyes glided over the small TV hanging off the wall. There was no sound, but there was an image: *Mike the Ranger*. Was that the only damn show the hospital antenna picked up?

"I was thinking…" he said. "When we find the log cabin

Chameleon's hiding out in, there should be broken glass on the floor."

I pulled out my computer.

"Because there was a fight. And there's blood. A lot of it," he continued. "Everywhere. Even on the walls. Ghostboy is scared it's Chameleon's."

My nostrils prickled at the idea of a room full of blood. "How about just broken glass. And dirty boot prints that lead us to suspect it's the evil scientist?"

"Blood adds more drama."

"Okay. But we don't need it on the walls."

"Why? Does the Duke faint at the sight of blood?" he teased.

"The Duke never faints. He drinks blood for breakfast."

Jaime smirked. "He's not a vampire."

"It was just a manner of speech."

"A little blood?" he begged.

"Fine."

"But don't worry, it's not Chameleon's." His reassuring tone made my heart squeeze. I was the older one; I was supposed to be comforting him.

"Okay. Do we find the weapon?" I asked.

"It's a broken vase."

"My mom would be inconsolable," I said, mostly to myself.

"Why?"

"Because she loves vases. Like obsessive love."

"My mother loved photo albums. We have so many, but most are empty." He pinched the sheet and then released it, absentmindedly running it between his thumb and forefinger. His nose suddenly wrinkled. "You want to see something?"

"From the look on your face...not really."

He turned his head. "Check out my new haircut."

His pudgy hand fingered the bald patch a few inches from the base of his hairline. It wasn't so much the bare area that caught my attention but the thickness of his fingers and wrist.

He'd gained more weight. Didn't an appetite mean good health?

"It's ugly, huh?" he asked. "They shaved it off for the scan."

"You can't really see it."

"Oh, *puh-lease*." He rolled his eyes. "You're such a bad liar."

"From the front, you can't see it."

He grinned. "I should get a hat. *That's it*! That's how they know it was Dr. Goor! They find his hat. He always wears a black felt hat."

"We never had him wearing a hat before," I said.

"Let's add it. Bad guys always have hats or ski masks."

"Fine." I made a note to add the hat. "Back to the story. How about the Duke draws a replica of Dr. Goor's office door on the cabin wall? You know, like a portal."

Jaime's enormous eyes brimmed with delight. "Yes!"

I willed my fingers to type fast. I needed to jot everything down before our time ran out. I refused for the pages of our book to resemble the Matthewses' blank family albums.

Chapter Fifty-Two

On Saturday, Jaime got out of the hospital. They'd kept him six days because they were running PET scans and CAT scans and all kinds of other tests to see how they could adjust his meds to slow down the tumor's growth.

Rita and I waited on the Matthewses' porch for the Volvo woodie to trundle down Maplewood. A huge platter of barbecued ribs covered in foil, a basin of mac 'n' cheese, and a tower of fudgy brownies sat next to me. Grandma and Mom had made them, thinking the Matthewses would be in need of a home-cooked meal. I'd remembered Jaime's favorite dish was ribs. I didn't know about the mac 'n' cheese, but according to Mom, everyone liked pasta with gooey cheese.

Rita was the first to spot the car. She barked and hopped on her three paws. Then she started doing figure eights, tail wagging so wildly that she nearly knocked over the brownies. After the car pulled in, I unhooked her leash and she bounded over to Jaime. Soon, he was covered in slobber and dog hair.

"She does smell like strawberries," he said.

Cora hitched an eyebrow while her father lugged up an overnight case.

"I brought sustenance," I said, pointing to the food.

"Thanks," she said, as she picked up the platter of ribs.

I carried in the other two dishes. We set the glass table for lunch. Miss Brown arrived so we added another placemat. Jaime was lying on the couch, Rita huddled up against him. When I was alone with Cora in the kitchen, I whispered, "Is he okay?"

"He's tired."

"What did the doctor say?"

She was gathering forks and knives. Her fingers wrapped more tightly around the cutlery. "It spread to his spinal cord."

I didn't ask if it was bad. I knew, without doubt, that it was.

"They wanted to keep him, but he insisted on being discharged." Her already low, raspy voice dropped more. "A few weeks, Meyer. Not months anymore. Weeks."

My first impulse was to hug her, but I was frozen in place, in space, in time. Even my heart felt like it had stopped beating. I thought about the night he'd listed all the things he wanted to do. "Okay," I said. "We have to hurry then."

Her grief was interrupted by a frown.

"To finish his list," I added.

When she caught on, she asked, "How? He's really weak."

"I'll carry him if I have to, but we're completing it."

"You're crazy," she said, but some melancholy lifted off her.

"And you're just realizing that?" I asked lightheartedly.

She smiled as we returned to the living room.

"Jaime, honey, you want me to make you a plate?" his dad asked him.

"I'm not hungry."

"Not even for ribs?" Cora asked.

He shook his head gently.

"You have to eat something," his dad continued.

He sighed. "Fine. But just one rib."

His father's face creased in pain as he placed a single rib on a plate. He put it next to Jaime, who didn't even touch it. He just kept patting Rita. At some point, he drifted off to sleep. We spoke quietly. Principal Matthews explained he hadn't eaten anything in weeks.

"But he doesn't look skeletal," I said.

"It's the cortisone. And painkillers," he explained.

And then we talked about the weather, and what I would be doing during summer break. I knew I needed to get a job somewhere—for the experience—but I hadn't applied anywhere yet. The summer seemed a long ways away.

Jaime stirred and rubbed his eyes.

"How's your head, honey?" his father asked.

"Okay."

"Does it hurt?"

"No." He gave his father a gossamer smile.

"Do you want me to reheat the rib?" Cora asked.

"Sure." Jaime lifted his hand and waved it around slowly, watching it. "Maybe we should change my superhero name to Balloonboy instead of Ghostboy."

"Not happening. We already added a hat to our villain. No more major changes."

Mr. Matthews's gaze ping-ponged between Jaime and me. "Do I get to read your book one day?"

"Yeah. When I'm gone," he said.

The bare bone his father was holding clattered onto the plate. "Excuse me."

He pushed himself away from the table and exited the room in rapid strides. Biting her lip, Miss Brown followed him.

"Shouldn't have said that," Jaime murmured.

"What happened?" Cora asked, returning with his plate, which she placed next to him.

"Nothing," he said. He reached for the rib and took a bite. It looked painful for him to chew and swallow, but he kept at it until it was picked clean of meat.

She eyed me but didn't push the subject. "I have some library books I need to return. Will you still be here in an hour?" she asked me.

"Not going anywhere before we finish our story."

"Today?" Jaime asked.

"Yup."

"Man that's a lot of thinking."

"Yup," I repeated, taking a seat on the couch next to him and turning my laptop on. "Go ahead."

"Where were we again?" he asked, puzzled.

For a second, I worried that the tumor or the seizure had tampered with his memory, but then he spoke about the spray-painted office door, and I relaxed. Cora, though, was stiff as a plank and as narrow as one. She'd lost weight. Even her black leggings sagged in places they weren't supposed to. Her arms were as thin as twigs, and her somewhat-round face appeared gaunter.

"Okay, then. See you later." She was about to leave when she doubled back and hugged her brother. "Glad to have you home, kiddo."

As she left, I had an idea. I shot up and placed the computer on the coffee table. "Give me a sec."

"Not going anywhere," he said as I went after Cora.

"Can I talk to you?" I asked her.

She hesitated—I could see it in her eyes—but in the end, she nodded. She led the way down to her room.

After she'd closed the door, I said, "Jaime mentioned your mom kept photo albums, but that they're all empty."

"Yeah."

When I told her my idea of filling one with pictures, a gust of emotion blew over her.

"Thank you," she whispered.

"For what?"

"For reminding me to do stuff like that." She shrugged. "You know…make him happy."

"You always knew how to make him happy," I said, gazing beyond her at a fresh quotation. It hadn't been there the last time I was in her room.

Maybe it's not about the happy ending; maybe it's about the story.

"It's always about the story," I said. "Jaime taught me that the first time we met. He told me that just because I knew the ending didn't mean I shouldn't read the book."

A strangled sob broke out of her. I closed the space between us with one giant step and crushed her against me. She was just bones and soft, cold skin. And roses. I held her as she cried, trying to be the mooring that would keep her from drifting away during this horrible storm.

Chapter Fifty-Three

On Wednesday, when I unbolted my locker, an envelope floated out. I knew it was from the Alphas before even breaking the red seal.

Gabe, who was standing next to me, leaned over. "It's probably for your induction. Open it," he whispered eagerly.

I broke the burgundy wax and took out the card. "It's the night of our promotion ceremony," I said. *June 19.*

"Where are we meeting?"

"At the pier."

He gasped. "They probably chartered some superyacht. Shit, that would be so cool. I need to go find Owen and Dirk to tell them."

Before he took off running, I said, "I need to postpone it."

"Postpone it? You can't postpone your induction. They choose, you don't."

"It's either that or I forfeit my place." I tucked the note back in the envelope. "I can't plan anything this month."

Gabe's excitement was replaced by a sulk. "Why not?"

"You know why not," I said quietly.

"They're going to be pissed, Duke."

"Just tell them. I don't need a confrontation right now."

"Thanks," he mumbled. "Can't wait. If they send my head back in a box, tell my mom I loved her."

I rolled my eyes. "Should I tell Liane too?"

He fiddled with the dial of my lock.

"Too soon?"

He nodded. "Yeah."

"Too soon for what?" Owen asked.

"Nothing," Gabe said.

Owen seemed confused.

I passed him the letter. "For this." I shot Gabe a look. "I'll let him explain. I need to revise some stuff for our history exam. I'll catch you guys later."

"Later, Dukey," Owen called out as I walked away.

When the week ended and exams were over, a weight lifted off me. No more school. No more tests. No more studying. I had no idea how, but I was nearly certain I'd passed…more than certain. The next time I would return to Francis Academy, I'd be a junior. With Cora, but without Jaime.

I pushed away my glumness, trying to focus on the fact that I was a free man. I wondered how to spend my first free evening. Since I wasn't attending the school dance, I decided to go home and work on the book. I was nearly done with it. It was a strange feeling, reaching the end. Part of me wanted to put the final dot, yet another part feared that if I finished the story, Jaime would let go.

A knock on my bedroom door made me jump.

"Honey?" It was Mom. "Can I come in?"

"Yeah," I said, saving my work.

"Why aren't you ready?"

"Ready for what?" I asked.

"The dance. It's tonight, isn't it?"

I nodded.

"Come on, sweetie. You have to go. It's your last day as a sophomore."

"I don't feel like it, Mom."

She puckered her lips. They were so shiny they reflected my desk light. "Everyone's going."

"Except me."

"You'll have so much fun."

"No, I won't," I said.

"That's it! I'm a patient person, but I can't take your moodiness anymore. I want you in a suit and out the door right this second."

"Mom—"

"I understand what you're going through," she snapped. "I do. But you can't just stop living your life. You know what…" She walked to my closet, flung the door open, grabbed my suit, and lobbed it at me. "Call Jaime. Tell him to get ready. I bet he's never gone to a dance before."

"He's barely moved off the couch since he got back from the hospital."

"Then give him a piggyback ride! You told me you wanted to add excitement to his life. Then do it."

"Okay. Okay," I mumbled.

She sucked in a triumphant breath. "And, honey, I know you don't want to hear this, but you need to start talking to your father again."

"I'm not ready yet."

"He's miserable."

"I said I wasn't ready, Mom. Now can you please leave?"

Stricken, she left. I phoned Cora as I donned my suit.

She wasn't enthusiastic about the dance—until I told her it was Jaime's one chance. She said she would be ready by the time I got there. And she was. In a strapless black dress that hugged her slight torso, but puffed out at the waist, making her hips appear less frail. She'd finished her outfit off with black combat boots. *And* she hadn't worn any makeup.

"You look beautiful," I told her.

"Shut up," she said. Her shiny black curls were fanned out over bare shoulders. "Jaime! Let's go."

"Thanks for making them attend the dance." Principal Matthews was adjusting his red-striped tie. "I'm late to pick up Maria. I'll see you in school."

He hurried to his car and swerved out of his driveway just as Jaime made it through the door. He was still dressed in sweatpants. Not that he had to wear a suit.

"I don't want to go," he said glumly.

"I don't either," I said. "And I'm willing to bet anything that your sister *definitely* doesn't want to go. But we're all going. And that's that."

His eyebrows bolted toward each other. "But my hair's so ugly."

I frowned, so he gestured to the back of his head.

"Is that why?" I asked.

He shrugged. "I know it's stupid, but—"

I walked past both of them.

"Where are you going?" she called after me.

I marched straight into the bathroom, located their father's razor in the mirrored cabinet over the sink, and shaved off a chunk of hair, approximately where Jaime's bald spot was. I chucked the razor blade into the garbage. Jaime and Cora were standing by the entrance of the bathroom, both wide eyed and speechless. "Tell your dad I owe him a new blade. Now let's go."

Neither talked during the drive over to the school. It was only after we'd parked and started toward the glowing school that Cora told me I was an idiot.

"But am I still pretty?" I asked her, waggling my brows.

She gazed at the glittering pavement—it looked as though all the stars in the sky had fallen into it.

"Pretty?" Jaime asked.

"The first time your sister talked to me, she told me I was a pretty boy."

"No, way," he said.

She quickened her pace. "I'm allowed my opinions." When she realized her brother couldn't keep up, she slowed down.

"So? Am I still pretty?" I teased her.

"*Pretty* annoying," she said.

Jaime and I both laughed. I held the door open for my dates, and together, we walked into the crazy-loud hallways of Francis Academy.

Chapter Fifty-Four

As soon as we materialized in the gym, people turned to stare. I swear, it was insane—they acted like a bunch of sunflowers gawping at the sun. In this case, the sun was Cora. Some glanced at Jaime, but his sister was the true center of attention. I could feel her anxiety grow as I carved a way through the crowd. I found an empty table drenched in glitter and covered with fake, flickering candles.

"I'll get us something to drink," I said. "Don't move."

"I don't think we could, even if we wanted to." She glared at the gawkers.

Gabe trotted over to me while I grabbed the pitcher of water. "I didn't recognize her!" he said above the music.

"Who?"

"Cora! She doesn't look like herself. She's ho—" He let the word dangle unfinished, dubious as to whether it would set me off.

"Hot?" I said. "I know."

His gaze darted to the pitcher. He seized it from me and set it back down. "You gotta try the punch."

The punch. Right. "I'm driving so I probably shouldn't be

drinking." But then I remembered it was spiked and poured some in a cup. I also poured out a glass of water.

Gabe trailed me back to the table where Cora was sitting cross-legged, foot tapping the shiny wooden floor. Next to her, Jaime gaped at the swinging crowd. I shoved the glass of water in her hand and the punch in his. He ogled it, and so did Gabe.

"Umm, Duke—" Gabe started.

I crouched down to Jaime's level. "You wanted to try beer," I told him. "Well, instead, it's rum punch. Or something-punch." I had no clue what Owen had mixed into the fruit juice.

His large eyes became broader. So did his sister's. At least she'd stopped tapping her foot. She tried to swipe the drink from her brother, but I caught her wrist.

"His list," I reminded her.

Those two words quieted her down. "One sip. Max."

Jaime beamed and took a long swallow of the drink. Gabe blinked a few times, whereas Cora fought my hold.

"That was way more than a sip!" she exclaimed.

Jaime ducked his face into the glass and took another gulp.

"Jaime! If Dad catches you—" she began.

"Gabe, take the glass. I'll take the girl."

"I don't want to dance," she snapped.

"Cora, be nice to Duke," Jaime said.

"I *am* nice. I came. I let you try the punch. I don't want to dance."

I leaned over and whispered in her ear. "I'm trading my last kiss for a first dance."

Smoke could've come out of her nose, and I wouldn't have been surprised. "Fine," she hissed.

The music didn't magically turn into a slow dance, yet I held her close to me and moved slow, as though it was. At first she was tense, but she didn't push me away. As the seconds turned into minutes, she burrowed in closer. I suspected it was because of all the unwanted attention and not the feel of my arms around her waist, but I savored the moment anyway. At the end of the song, I waited for her to step away from me.

"You can let go now." Her deep voice sounded raw.

"I don't want to."

She tilted her head up, black pupils pulsing. The urge to kiss her overwhelmed me completely, and I would've, had someone not cleared his throat right behind us.

Cora sprang out of my arms. Her father wasn't sure where to look, nor was I. Finally, our gazes converged on Jaime, who was talking animatedly with Gabe, and we set off toward them. Jaime was bright eyed, happy, perhaps even a little tipsy. Thankfully, he wasn't holding the incriminating cup of punch. It sat unfinished on all the glitter.

"Dad, could you take a picture of us?" she asked him.

"Of course." He took out his phone.

"I need to go find Liane before she replaces me," Gabe said. "Good to see you, Principal. And awesome talk, little man." He made a fist and held it in midair until Jaime responded, bumping his own against Gabe's. Before leaving, he asked me, "Meant to ask, what happened to your hair?"

"I was juggling ninja stars," I said.

Both Gabe and the principal blinked at first, but then they caught on that it was a joke. Gabe snorted whereas the principal's eyes got all glassy, because he understood what the shaved patch meant.

Once Gabe had left, Cora sat down, leaned toward her brother, and draped her arm around his shoulders. "Meyer? How long are you going to make us wait?" she asked.

"Huh?"

"Sit," she ordered.

Like a puppet, I sat on Jaime's other side. And I smiled. Wider than I'd smiled in a long, long time.

After the picture, we left. But I didn't take them home; I took them to the bluffs. I wanted to show Jaime the view. I didn't have a blanket with me, so we stretched out on the grass.

Between the stars and the rolling surf, I thought that if heaven existed on earth, this could be it.

"Do you think that's where I'll go?" he asked, pointing to the velvet sky. "You know, when I'm dead."

"I don't know," I said. "It'd be a nice place to end up."

"Yeah. I don't want worms to eat me," he said.

"They wouldn't dare, or I'll eat them," I said.

Jaime giggled. "*Eww.*"

"Come to think of it, you'll probably float around with other ghosts and make fun of us measly humans," I said.

"Maybe we'll play soccer."

"Or basketball."

"And my head won't hurt anymore. You can't hurt when you're a ghost because you're empty."

"Invisible maybe, but not empty."

"Why not empty?"

"I don't know. I just think you should at least get to keep your mind to remember and your heart to feel…even though hearts, according to your sister, are just organs."

He snorted. "Mom wouldn't have named her after an organ."

"Huh?" I lifted my body on a bent elbow.

She hadn't spoken a word since we'd gotten there, but her eyes were wide open, glimmering like the sky above—from the reflection of the stars or with tears, I did not know. "Is your real name Heart?"

Jaime tittered. "No, it's Corazon. Heart in Spanish."

"Corazon," I repeated. It sounded like a rush of twilight through a field of roses. It was beautiful.

She turned toward me, eyes narrowed. "If you tell anyone, I'll send you up there with Jaime." She pointed to the sky,

"We'd have so much fun," he said. "We'd get to fly around all day and all night."

I sat up and stared out over the bluffs…and had an idea.

Chapter Fifty-Five

"Ready, Jaime?" I asked as I adjusted his helmet.

"Who's Jaime?" He winked, tapping his T-shirt before zipping his parka over it.

I'd had it made in some grungy, pot-scented underground shop in Downtown Greenwich. The word Ghostboy was stenciled over it in such a way that the letters resembled apparitions. I'd worn an old basketball jersey with my first name printed in block letters, before which I'd scribbled the word *The* in indelible marker. Jaime had been stoked, but also disappointed that I hadn't made his sister a special shirt.

"Can you film everything…for Dad…for *after*?"

I winced at the mention of *after*, but got my camera phone ready. "On standby, Ghostboy."

"It's too bad we couldn't find a third teacher," he said.

I'd asked Cora last minute if she wanted to come and had only secured two pilots. Which was fine; I could go anytime. I was happy to give them this adventure. As one of the instructors made Jaime step into his harness, I walked over to Cora. She was gazing at the forest-filled horizon that looked, from our vantage point, like a field of broccoli.

"Usually we don't take kids up his age," her instructor told us.

We both glared at him.

"Usually kids his age have time to wait." My tone wasn't bitter, but definitely abrupt. We'd had to fill in health forms so he knew about Jaime's cancer.

He went back to securing himself to the glider.

"Can't believe I'm about to fly," Cora said. "Maybe you should go. Maybe—"

"No way am I dangling over five thousand feet."

A hesitant expression marred her sun-kissed face. "Thanks, Meyer. For this."

"Why don't you save your thanks for after?"

"I might not be so thankful after," she said. "I might be covered in vomit and possessed by a spirited will to kill you."

I chuckled.

Anyway, the real person to thank was Owen's brother. Eddy loved all air sports, from bungee jumping, to kite surfing, to skydiving. He loved velocity and void nearly as much as he liked microshorts and the girls wearing them. After I got home from the dance on Friday, I'd phoned him, and over the course of the weekend, he'd managed to find me a person willing to break a few rules to make an eight-year-old's dream come true.

I returned to Jaime, whose smile stretched all the way to the sides of his helmet. He was now sandwiched between the guy's back and the kite-shaped glider.

"Hold on to the bar at my waist during the entire ride," the instructor said.

"Okay." Jaime's voice was so lively it sounded as though it were jumping up and down in his throat.

"I'm meeting you down by that field, right?" I asked, gesturing toward the light green expanse. I didn't stare at it too long, already queasy from the high altitude.

"Correct. We'll be down in approximately an hour and a half. Ready?"

"Yes."

I pressed on the record button and began filming the tandem as they ran down the slope and jumped over the cliff. A faint *woo-hoo* drifted back to me. I imagined it was Jaime squealing with delight. I turned the camera over to Cora to capture her launch. Instead, I caught the most heartbreaking smile I'd ever seen. The dazzling sun overhead had nothing on this girl. When her eyes landed on the camera, her expression wavered. A second later, she ran down the slope, matching the pilot's footfalls, and soared through the air.

I stayed perched on the cliff overhanging the world, recording the two kites until they were white dots against the bright blue. Before I got into the Jeep and swung it around, I sent Eddy a still shot of the gliders floating, to which he responded with a, *Wish I was there.*

It took me nearly an hour to drive down to the clearing. During that hour, I called Gabe and Owen. Liane was planning an end of the year party at her place, and *everyone* was going. They made me promise not to bail. I wondered if Cora would go with me and decided to ask her after the flight—unless she truly was irritated.

The two kites were no larger than the seagulls that flew over the Sound, but I filmed them anyway. Another twenty minutes slid by in wind-rustling silence. They were close enough now that I could tell the difference between Cora and Jaime. I filmed the landing. Cora and the instructor sprinted past me, pulling the glider back to cut the wind.

I trotted over to her while Jaime circled above. "So?"

She was breathless. "Incredible." She was fighting off a smile. She tipped her head to the sky. "I wanted to see him land."

Her instructor whistled some tune as he unclipped himself, and then he started on her gear. I thought he was taking too long to free her of the harness, his hands slithering too slowly over her body. I wanted to push him away and do it myself, and

I would've, had Cora not startled me by grabbing my phone to aim it at her brother.

"You nearly missed it," she blustered, hitting stop and tossing it back over. "Send me the pictures. For the album."

Jaime was laughing. That was the first thing that struck me. Slowly, I turned away from Cora and the instructor who was still working on her gear. She didn't seem to notice, much too engrossed by the sight of her beaming brother.

"That was the coolest of all cool things I've ever done!" he said.

His enthusiasm was so contagious it obliterated my stupid jealousy. He must have repeated the word *cool* a thousand times during the long ride back to Greenwich. He probably would've uttered it more times had he not fallen into a deep sleep. I decreased the volume of the radio and watched as the green forest turned into gray buildings and the narrow dirt path became a wide cement road.

"Hey, Cora?" I said.

She was resting her elbow on the armrest and cradling her head with her open hand. "Uh-huh."

"There's this party to celebrate graduation. Wanna come with me?"

She glanced sideways at me. "I didn't finish the school year. Plus, I think Jaime's had his dose of partying."

"I wasn't planning on taking him." I glanced in the rearview mirror to make sure he was still under; I didn't want to hurt his feelings. "I want to take *you*."

Her elbow skidded off the armrest, and her hand fell onto her black leggings. She began toying with the material.

"As friends." I trapped her gaze. "We *are* friends, right?"

The tip of her tongue darted over the silver hoop in her lower lip. "I suppose we are. You know my real name. I have no more secrets."

I snorted. "Are you kidding? You're totally indecipherable."

She turned back to the shifting landscape. "But I don't want to go."

For a long moment, we were both silent. "Are you embarrassed about hanging out with me because I'm younger?" I finally asked.

She nipped her lip with her teeth. "Yeah."

Her answer made my ego swell with resentment. Not so much toward Cora as toward all of those people who said that age was just a number. It wasn't just a number; it was an airtight, boxed-in category.

We drove the rest of the way in silence. I would've gone over the speed limit to shorten our trip had I not been worried about being stopped by cops and verbalized for transporting other minors. When we arrived on Maplewood, the sun had dipped on the horizon, and the blue was replaced by violet and pink.

"Look at the sky," Jaime said. I hadn't realized he'd woken up. "It's so beautiful."

"You mean cool," I said lightly.

"It's *really* cool…Oh. You're making fun of me." I noticed him grinning in the mirror.

I chuckled.

"Do you think the air tastes different when it's a different color?" he mused. "Maybe when it's pink, it tastes like cotton candy. And when it's purple, it tastes like blueberries. And when it's—it's—"

"When it's orange, it tastes like carrots," Cora said.

"And when it's yellow, it tastes like bananas," I said.

"That would be neat," she said, pivoting in her seat toward her brother. "Jaime?" She tore her belt off and leaped into the backseat.

I twisted around, heart in my throat. *Not again….!* I spun the steering wheel and the car lurched into the fire lane. I jammed my foot on the break, flicked on my hazards, flung my seat belt off, and raced over to the backseat.

"Shit!" I yelled as Cora leaned him on his side and spoke to him softly, grazing his cheek with her knuckles. "Do you want me to drive to the hospital?"

"Let's wait until it's over," she said softly. "Hey, kiddo, I'm right here. It's going to be okay. I'm right here." The tips of her fingers traced his quivering, hunched frame. "Jaime, I'm here. Right here. Duke's here too. Everything's going to be fine."

But nothing would ever be fine.

Chapter Fifty-Six

After we'd driven to the hospital, Jaime was taken away from us again. They wanted to scan his brain, but his father didn't let them. I thought he wanted the doctors to leave his son alone, but Cora confided the true reason: the cost.

"What would it change anyway, Meyer?" she asked. "It's not magically going to shrink away. Not this time." Her irises appeared blacker against their bloodshot background. "You should go home. I'll call you in the morning."

"Cora?" I started. "Do you think it's because of this afternoon?"

She placed her palm over my arm, and my skin prickled. "No. It's because of the tumor." Lifting her hand away, she added, "You didn't do this to him."

I could only nod as I retreated into the parking lot. My pulse didn't drop until I made it home. I'd never been so happy to hear the sound of my mother and grandmother bickering in the kitchen. I kicked off my shoes and went straight toward them. The second they saw me, they stopped discussing the lumps in the gravy. They stopped talking altogether. Mom hugged me. I didn't know how she knew to do that—I wasn't crying or anything. Grandma grabbed my hand and squeezed it.

"Is it Jaime?" she asked.

"He had another seizure." My voice sounded as dry as the cracked earth of a desert.

"Oh, honey," Mom murmured, stroking my back.

Heavy footsteps resounded behind me. I knew they belonged to my father. I took a step away from Mom and was about to bolt upstairs when he trod out of the kitchen first. Seconds later, the front door slammed shut, and car tires skidded in the driveway.

The strain in Mom's eyes bled through to all her features. "Please forgive him, Duke. You're all he has." She rested both her palms on my cheeks like when I was small and she wanted to tell me how much she loved me. "What Jaime is going through…it should remind you of what's truly important in this life."

"Fine," I murmured. "I'll talk to him."

When he returned later that night, we filed into the living room in silence. I plopped down into the fat armchair while Dad poured himself a tumbler of whiskey from the rollaway bar in the corner. Slowly, he moved across the room and sat on the couch opposite me. We both stared at the cactus-like vase in the middle of the coffee table.

I took a deep breath. "I know it's not *your* fault."

The ice cubes clinked as Dad leaned over, placing his forearms on his thighs and knitting his fingers around the glass. "I still should've told you sooner, son."

"Wouldn't have changed anything."

"I told Mr. Matthews I wanted to help," he said.

I raised an eyebrow. "With what?"

"With the bills."

"Your company's giving them money?"

"No. I am. If the company gave money, it would be an admission of guilt. We can't—You understand, right?"

Something gnawed at my mind. "Was Cora there?"

"Cora?"

"The principal's daughter."

He took a sip of his drink. "She arrived at the end of our conversation."

"Does she know you're my father?"

"No. At least I didn't introduce myself. I didn't think you'd want me to."

I could sense a question dangling in the air between us, a question he was either too proud or too apprehensive to formulate. I gave him the answer. "I'm not ashamed of you, Dad."

His spine straightened, lifting his massive chest up, and his lips parted, but the doorbell rang before he could say anything.

"Are we expecting someone?" I asked.

"I'm not. Maybe it's one of your friends."

Doubtful. I checked the peephole before swinging the door wide.

"Hey," I said breathlessly.

Cora's lips quirked up in what resembled the rough draft of a smile. "My phone died, and I was on my way home."

I smirked. "My house isn't on your way home."

She glanced down at her scuffed combat boots. "Okay fine. You got me. I needed to walk. And I wanted to tell you something…"

The air suddenly felt thicker, nearly too dense to breathe in. "Is Jaime—?"

"He's stable."

"What is it then?" I asked, taking a step closer to her.

"I met—" She hesitated. "A man came by this evening."

My lungs emptied in a loud whoosh. She knew. There were no more secrets. "I heard."

She blinked. "You did? How?"

"What?"

"How did you hear?"

"He told me," I said.

"Dad told you?" she asked.

"Huh? No. *My* dad told me."

"Your dad?"

"The man you met. He's my father."

She scrambled backward. "No…" When she hit the curb, she stalled and her expression hardened. "I can't believe this! We trusted you, Meyer. *He* trusted you. And all along you were using us."

"Using you? How?"

"Becoming our friend, so we wouldn't sue."

I grunted indignantly. "*I* didn't even know until two weeks ago."

"Bullshit!"

I lurched away from my house and took long strides down the gravel driveway. I was barefoot, yet I couldn't feel the ground beneath my soles. "Is that really what you think of me, Cora? That I'm a pawn in some great, evil scheme to swindle your family?"

She retreated further down the dusk-cloaked street. "Stay away from me…from us!"

She hated me. I could see it. I could sense it. It crackled in the air between us as strong as an electrical current.

"I had nothing to do with it, Cora."

"You're his son! You have everything to do with it!"

That I felt guilt was one thing; that she made me feel guilty was another. My temper rose and with it my tone of voice. "I don't work at his company! I didn't make the fucking medication!"

A dog barked. Then a porch light came on in my neighbor's house.

"Go to hell!" she hissed. She spun on her heels and raced down the street.

I stood there throbbing, indignant, and outraged, staring at her fading figure until the entrenching obscurity swallowed her up whole. Only then did I head back in, slamming the front door closed, and barreling up to my room. Mom tried to talk to me, but I told her to leave me alone.

I didn't sleep that night, so I wrote until my shaky fingers ached from typing and my eyes were sore from the brightness of my computer screen. My anger had lessened, but the trembling persisted. Cora was no longer the cause of it though; Jaime was. I was scared he might hate me.

At five o'clock in the morning, I printed out the nearly finished book. I was still missing the ending. I wanted Jaime to dictate it to me, because it was his story to finish. Panic swished around in my empty stomach as I drove over to the hospital with the printout.

Yolanda—aka Hummer-nurse—was standing by the entrance, taking drags off a cigarette. "Came to see the li'l guy?"

"Yeah. What room is he in?"

"Three hundred fifty-six."

"How is he?" I asked.

Yolanda's eyes were lined with heavy blue circles. "Half his li'l body's numb."

"What does that mean?" I asked as the dull-gray sky above rumbled.

"It ain't good, that's what it means. He can't walk, and he's havin' trouble talkin'." She blotted her eyes with her knuckle. Her nails were superlong and psychedelic, with swirls of pink and gold and orange. It made me think of the sunset Jaime had liked.

Another roll of thunder shook the sky. It shook the earth too. It shook me. I clutched the pile of pages tighter as I finally slipped through the sliding glass doors. The rain began sometime before I reached his room. It pounded against the corridor windows, snaking down the glass like tears. When I arrived in front of the door, I lifted my fist, took a deep breath, and knocked softly.

Cora greeted me with an expression that made me jolt backward. Fury fired across her face like a bolt of lightning streaking complete darkness; it made her eyes glow and her jaw pulse as though her heart had deserted her chest to fill her face.

"I thought I asked you to stay away. Was I not clear, Meyer?"

"I came to see Jaime."

"No." She started closing the door, but I held it open with my fingertips.

"I wasn't asking," I said.

"Take one more step, and I'll call security." Her eyelids resembled marble from all the swollen vessels. She'd been crying.

I pushed on the door. "You're bluffing."

"I'll tell Jaime the truth. I'll tell him what you did!" The tendons in her forearms hardened as she pressed back.

"I didn't fucking do anything, Cora!" I growled. "It wasn't me! And for all anyone knows, it wasn't even the fucking medication!"

I wanted to hate her. And for a second, I did, but then tears began dripping down her cheeks, and I couldn't hate her.

The shaking in my bones finally stopped. "I'll go," I said, my voice hushed now. "For now. Just give him these." I thrust the papers at her. "And don't tell him. Please. I can live with your hatred, but not with his."

Wordlessly, she shoved her whole body against the door. I lifted my palm and let her shut me out.

Chapter Fifty-Seven

"You think she's on the Ferris wheel?" the Duke asked, slurping down a chocolate milkshake.

"I felt a signal, and it was coming from above," Ghostboy said. He tossed his cup into a bin. "The wheel's the only high point of the fair."

The Duke looked up, but the sun was blinding. He should've spray-painted himself a pair of wayfarers. When he turned back toward his sidekick, the little boy had already walked off in the direction of the big wheel. The Duke trotted to catch up. Soon, they were standing on the platform, waiting for Chameleon's passenger car to come down.

Ghostboy frowned. "She's still up there."

"Still?"

They both gazed up, shielding their eyes. They saw something flicker silver on one of the top metal rims. A body. Definitely Chameleon's.

"Cami!" Ghostboy called out, wiggling his arms to catch her attention.

She didn't move, so Ghostboy jumped into one of the pods. The Duke leaped in beside him. As they rose in the blue sky, Chameleon staggered like a tightrope walker on the hazardous structure.

"We're coming!" Ghostboy yelled. He waved to her and she waved back.

But then, the Duke caught someone staring at them from a passenger car above: evil Dr. Goor.

"Cami, watch out!" the Duke shouted.

She was about to spring into an empty car when Dr. Goor snatched her. Ghostboy tried to jump out and scale the railings, but the Duke held him back.

"You'll fall, Ghostboy," he said. "We'll get him. I promise."

But Dr. Goor had made off with Chameleon.

Again.

I groaned as I twisted my stiff neck to crack it. This was a load of crap. It was so freaking predictable. Still, I pushed on.

They ran through the fairgrounds, knocking over cracker-jack stands and small children licking ice creams. They squeezed through stables bursting with goats and cows and warm hay. They dashed into the parking lot, gasping. The hot air had seared their lungs, and their sides hurt.

Ghostboy was sweating, which had made him transparent in spots. Before anyone noticed, the Duke dragged him to the pickup and stuffed him into the passenger seat. He turned on the engine and blasted cold air.

"Where's she now?" the Duke asked, veering out of the parking spot.

Ghostboy furrowed his brow in concentration. "He took her down into a basement...somewhere on Commons Road."

That was only five miles away. The Duke careened through the streets like a madman. Of course, a siren sounded and a police car pulled him off the road. Annoyed, he punched his steering wheel and lowered his window.

"License and registration, please," the cop said, when he'd walked up to the truck. He peered past the Duke of Graffiti.

The latter gulped. He wasn't allowed to transport minors. He spun to face Ghostboy, but all that was left on the passenger seat was an empty bottle of water.

"License and registration," the policeman repeated, more sternly this time.

The Duke gripped his wallet and pulled out his license.

The cop held out his palm. "Truck's papers?"

The Duke glanced at the glovebox. It was a magical car, so he doubted it had magically appeared with documents. Still, he leaned over and checked the compartment. It was empty.

"I must've forgotten them at home," he told the cop.

The man took out his portable. "I need to run some license plates. Possible stolen vehicle on the corner of Commons and Thatcher."

As he circled the car to read the plates, the Duke whispered, "Ghostboy, the door! We gotta make a run for it."

"Right on." The door swung wide.

The Duke waited before he hopped over the gearshift. He didn't want to squash Ghostboy. He counted to five, jumped into the passenger seat and out onto the sidewalk. The cop saw him, but the Duke's legs were so long and the policeman's waist was so large that the man couldn't catch up.

After a minute, the Duke hissed, "Ghostboy?"

He heard him close by. "She's in here! I can feel her."

The Duke moved in the direction of the voice and found himself in an alley.

"Come on!" Ghostboy shouted.

The Duke spotted an open door and raced through it. It shut behind him. Outside, he could hear tires and sirens screeching. When the ruckus petered out, he exhaled a long breath.

"That was close," Ghostboy said, his voice still bodiless.

"Why aren't you reappearing? There was only a sip of water in that bottle."

"You can't see me?"

The Duke shook his head.

"I'm sure I'll materialize any minute," Ghostboy said, but the Duke wasn't so sure. He'd begun noticing his sidekick stayed invisible longer, and it bothered him. He wasn't jealous; he was worried. What if Ghostboy stayed a ghost?

"Did you feel that?" the little superhero asked.

"No. What?"

"I touched you."

"Try again," the Duke said.

After a second, Ghostboy asked, "So?"

"Nothing."

"What do you think that means?"

"That you're becoming more powerful," the Duke said, although another thought crowded his mind—one he refused to tell his friend.

I highlighted the last part and deleted it. I was tempted to delete the entire chapter. Ghostboy turning into a real ghost was just morbid. Jaime would think I was killing him off.

I checked my watch. It was one o'clock in the morning. In nine hours, I was graduating. I snapped my computer shut and left for the hospital. When I reached room three hundred and fifty-six, I didn't knock; I barged right in. Mr. Matthews jerked out of his chair like a foam dart from a Nerf gun. He rubbed the sleep out of his eyes before checking his wristwatch.

"It's the middle of the night, Duke."

"I know but I wanted to see him," I said.

Jaime's eyes were closed and the thin bed sheet covering his body lifted and fell rhythmically. It looked chillingly like a shroud.

"Are you mad at me, Mr. Matthews?" I whispered.

"At you? Why would I be mad at you?"

I hoped Jaime couldn't hear me. "Because of—because of my father."

"I'm not angry with you." Principal Matthews shook his head. "No. I'm angry with life, with God, with the doctors. I'm angry with myself for not being able to save my son. We don't even know why it happened. Maybe it was the medication. Maybe it wasn't. So, no, son, I'm not angry with you or your family."

I bit my lip as he walked toward me.

"If anything..." He squeezed my shoulder. His skin was cold yet his touch warmed me. "If anything, I owe your dad, for his generosity…for having educated you to be kind and caring. He raised a great kid. You're the kind of boy I would've wanted Jaime to become."

My eyes heated up. For a second, I thought I would cry, but then Jaime called out my name, and I forgot all about crying.

Chapter Fifty-Eight

"Did Cora give you the printout?" I asked him once we were alone.

Principal Matthews had gone home to get some sleep after making sure—for the twentieth time—that I really would spend the entire night with his son.

"Yeah. She gave it to me," he said in such a low voice that I scooted the chair closer to the bed.

"And?"

"I didn't read it," he murmured. "I…I can't focus my eyes."

His irises, usually dazzlingly blue, had this milky sheen to them. They reminded me of old people eyes. I lowered my gaze. "You should've asked Cora to read it to you."

"No." He gave his head a listless shake. "I wanted you to read it to me."

"Where are the papers?"

He pointed to the nightstand before letting his hand float back to the comforter. It barely creased the sheet that tented his small body.

I grabbed the pile, wondering if Cora had read them herself. What would it change? She wouldn't hate me less because I'd turned her brother into a superhero. She would probably hate me more because of the way I saw her: a lost, damaged soul.

"You changed…something…in the story?" Jaime's voice sounded like autumn, cold air rustling through withered leaves.

"We go to a fair. We ride the Ferris wheel and drink milkshakes."

A small smile drifted over his face. "Cool," he breathed.

I flipped through all the pages until I found the new chapter. As I read it to him, he closed his eyes.

At the end, his chest was rising and falling so evenly that I thought he was asleep, but then his lips parted, "Will you take me…?" He heaved a breath. "To ride…a big wheel…someday?"

A strange sound pitched out of me, like a sob. I clamped my lips shut before I could make it again.

"Don't you start too," he murmured, opening his foggy eyes. "Now…read me the end…"

"That's all I have," I told him, clearing my throat. But then, I added, "I was thinking Chameleon could be strapped to an old plaid couch—she'd be all green and chequered—and Dr. Goor could be threatening her with a knife. What do you think?"

"You're the writer," he said slowly. And it brought me back to our first conversation, not the one in the hospital, but the one we'd had that first day at his house. I wished we could go back in time.

"Me too," he whispered. "Then I could…have eight more years."

"I said it out loud?"

"Yeah." His chest puffed with a prolonged breath. It whistled through the gaps between his teeth. "I forgot to…thank you…for making Cora…pretty again…and—"

"She was always pretty," I said.

He gave me a miniature smile. "And…for this," he said, raising a heavy finger toward the windowsill, toward a blue velvet album.

"Can I?"

He nodded so I opened it delicately. It was filled with pictures; shots of Mr. Matthews and his wife, of Jaime as a skinny newborn, of Cora as a plump little girl with her curtain of dark hair, her hooded black eyes, and her gold skin. I flipped through more pages, stopping on a shot of Jaime bald. I changed the page quickly.

"Remember…that one?" he asked.

It was the picture of him at the swim meet, pointing at the fish with a conspiratorial grin. I'd taken it right before Shagdar had trundled in, ponytail swishing furiously. I wondered how Cora had gotten it. Probably the day she'd left for the hospital with my phone…the day of the seizure.

I glanced through the rest of the album, absorbing each and every image. I wasn't in many pictures, but I'd been there when they were taken. Jaime behind the wheel of my car, beaming; Jaime kneeling by Rita, arms wrapped around her neck; Jaime at the dance sandwiched between Cora and me; Jaime floating in the sky.

"Did your dad see it yet?" I asked him.

"Yeah."

"Was he mad about the hang gliding?"

"Nah."

As I shut the album, Jaime asked me for it. I placed it on his stomach. "It's not too heavy?"

He shook his head and caressed the velvet as though it were a stuffed animal. "Will you keep her safe?"

"Who?"

"My sister."

I was about to tell him she didn't want me too, but lied instead. "Always."

"She likes you a lot."

I snorted. I shouldn't have snorted, but the sound escaped me like the sob earlier.

"She does," he said.

"It's because I'm the Duke of Graffiti. Totally irresistible."

A faint giggle fluttered out of him.

"Now can we please get back to Dr. Goor and his knife?" I asked.

"Laser blade…not knife."

"Okay. Easy to change," I said.

Jaime had shut his eyes, but I could tell he was awake from the way his lids pinched and his forehead wrinkled.

"Does your head hurt a lot?" I asked him.

"Half of it does," he mumbled, opening his eyes. "I can't feel…the other half." When I stayed quiet for too long, he added, "I want you…to make him good."

"Huh?"

"Dr. Goor…I don't want him to…die. I want him…to become…a good guy."

As his words sunk in, my mind went into overdrive and my fingers flew over the keyboard. "Wow, Jaime, I would never have thought of that."

"That's because…you're the writer…Not the thinker."

"Hey," I chided him lightly.

As I smiled and plotted, as I captured each and every word Jaime uttered that night, my heart swelled with a crippling ache. Two months and yet I couldn't imagine one day without him anymore. It was so unfair. I fell asleep while thinking that. When I awoke, my neck smarted from being bent at an awkward angle and drool had snaked down my chin. I rubbed it off, and then jammed the heels of my hands inside my eyes, trying to force the blur out.

"Don't you have to be at school in half an hour?" Cora's voice made me jump.

I dropped my hands and blinked. She was sitting across from me, on the other side of her brother, staring at the piece of blue sky behind me.

"It's nine thirty," she added.

"Shit," I muttered. I checked my phone, but the battery had

died during the night. I read the clock dial on the small TV hanging from the ceiling. "Crap, crap, crap." I needed to change into my uniform and had no way of reaching my mother to ask her to bring it to the ceremony. I sprang out of the chair and picked up my computer, which had fallen on the floor sometime during the night. "Tell Jaime I'll be back as soon as it's over."

She gave a brisk nod.

I glanced back at him before stepping out. I didn't want to leave, but it was just for an hour, two max. I ran down the stairs because the elevator was taking too long and flew into my car. In ten minutes, I was home. I threw on my uniform, brushed my teeth and hair, splashed cold water over my face, darted down to my father's library to print the ending of *Ghostboy* so I could read it to Jaime, and then dashed back out to the Jeep. I made it to Francis Academy just as everyone was taking their seats on the metal bleachers in front of the makeshift podium they'd installed on the field.

I spotted my friends on the first bench and my parents five rows above. As I walked toward them, Grams waved to me and I waved back. Gabe scooted over to clear a spot just as Principal Matthews began speaking on the microphone. Even from a distance, I could see the worry lines around his mouth and eyes and the darkness underneath and inside his eyes.

As the freshmen collected their awards, Gabe leaned over. "Where were you? I called you six times."

"At the hospital."

"Jaime?"

I nodded.

His expression turned grim. "Bad?"

I nodded.

"On another note," he said, jutting his chin to the podium, "check out who came this year."

I looked in the direction he'd indicated and found myself staring straight at the Wolf. "Why is *he* here?"

"As an alum, a big donor, *and* his daughter's a freshman."

"I thought he lived in California."

"*He* does. But his kid and ex-wife live here." As the audience broke into applause, he added, "You should go talk to him after. Set a date."

I said *yes*, even though I wouldn't. Not today anyway.

Principal Matthews started the ceremony for our grade. Our school rewarded students at the end of each year in the belief that it created an incentive to study. Most of us perceived the event as an incentive to party.

When the principal called out my name, I rose and walked toward the stage. I received a first prize for English and history, second-prize for art, and a third prize for home ec—which Mrs. Gill gave me herself, commending me on my astronomical improvement. I smiled as I crushed my pile of books against my chest, and shook all the extended hands, including the Wolf's. I didn't think he would recognize me, but he stood up during our handshake and leaned toward me.

"I know why you postponed your induction," he whispered. "Take your time." He slipped something in my jacket pocket, and then sat back down.

Behind me, the air filled with whoops and hollers and a lot of applause. When I reached the principal, I extended my palm. Instead of shaking it, he gathered me in an abrupt hug. The applause increased in volume even though no one outside my family, Miss Brown, Gabe, and apparently the Wolf knew the true reason he'd embraced me. As I walked off the stage, I felt as if the earth beneath my feet had transformed into air.

Chapter Fifty-Nine

Two hours and twenty-eight minutes. That was the amount of time I'd been away from Jaime. It wasn't long, yet in those two hours and twenty-eight minutes, everything had changed. He hadn't woken up. A respirator covered his face and a tangle of tubes sprouted out of his small arm.

The euphoria I'd experienced when I'd hooked my new ruby cuff links into my shirt vanished, and I landed with a heavy thump back into reality.

"I was told you were the last person he spoke with. At what time did he stop responding?" a doctor I'd never seen before asked me.

I rubbed the back of my head with my left hand, lingering on the spot I'd shaved off. My other hand clutched the last chapters of *Ghostboy*. "I don't know. Around five. Five thirty."

As he scribbled the information in his chart, I strode over to Cora. She was staring out of the window, arms folded tightly, eyes lost on the bright blue. She seemed so tiny and fragile that if I blew on her, she would surely fall.

"I should've kept him awake. Kept him talking," I said.

I half-expected her not to respond, but she did. "It wouldn't have changed anything." Her voice sounded empty. "There's no more activity in his brain. Fucking tumor."

I wanted to touch her. "How—"

Her gaze hardened. "Tumor one, Jaime zero."

"Miss Matthews?" the doctor said.

I spun around in time with Cora.

"We can keep him on mechanical support to give your relatives time to arrive."

"Dad's on his way," she said.

The doctor sighed. "He's signed up for organ donation, but since the cancer spread—"

"Stop!" she yelled, sticking her palms against her ears.

He tapped his fountain pen against the chart, replaced the metal clipboard at the foot of Jaime's bed, and pocketed the pen. "Let me know when your father gets here." He left with the nurse and closed the door.

Cora turned toward Jaime, her hands balled up into fists at her side. Her dark eyes became as slippery as an ice rink at midnight. I inched closer, but she shifted away from me.

"He loved the album," I said.

"Don't speak about him in the past tense!"

I recoiled, but then squared my shoulders. "I wasn't. We looked at it last night. I can't use the present tense for something that happened last night!"

"He *loves* the album. He loves! Don't need to be an English buff to know verb tenses!"

Her outburst had nothing to do with grammar. I knew that. But I was still pissed she was acting out on me. "I don't want to fight with you," I said.

She had her back to me. "Then leave."

"No."

"Fine. I'll leave!" And with that, she stomped out of the hospital room and flung the door shut.

I was so stunned that I didn't move for several minutes. But then I erupted. I threw all the pages of our book on the floor and kicked them without reverence. Then I dragged a chair up to his bed and crumbled into it, resting my forehead on the sheet by Jaime's knee to muffle the sound of my frustration, of my anguish, of my despair, of my sadness. For the first time in years, my eyes created tears. They felt too large to stream out, but they did, and they soaked the sheet. I pounded my fists against the bed and cursed. The agony and anger lasted long after I'd shed my last tear, long after I'd leaned back and taken a deep breath.

"I finished the story," I said.

I willed him to wake up, but he didn't move. Only his chest rose and fell in a perfect, artificial rhythm.

"Jaime, please. Wake up. You didn't say goodbye. You can't leave without saying goodbye." My voice broke in many different places.

The heart monitor didn't spike, his breathing didn't quicken, his fingers didn't quiver. I hated this nothingness, this limbo. I reached out to close my hand over his just as the door flew open. Mr. Matthews hobbled forward, gray faced and red eyed. His entire jaw shook. Miss Brown stepped in after him and wound her arm around his waist for support. He would need more than an arm to keep him upright, so I rose from my privileged place next to his son and gestured toward the chair. Slowly, he walked toward it, sat, and laid his head where mine had been, adding his sorrow to mine.

Miss Brown bit her lip and swiped her eyes, all the while stroking Mr. Matthews's back.

"Where's Cora?" he suddenly asked.

I was about to hike up my shoulders when she walked in. "Right here, Dad."

The doctor filed in after her. I didn't like him, because he personified death. I debated whether to step between him and the respirator, but it wasn't my decision. And what would it change anyway? Jaime was already gone. Heart pounding, I turned toward the window and searched for him in the blinding sky.

The doctor began by saying how lucky Jaime was that it all happened so fast, that he hadn't gone through weeks of pain. Then he explained what he was about to do and I chose not to listen, filling my throbbing head with a melody instead.

A song about heroes.

About flying.

About bleeding.

About dying.

About fighting.

A song for Jaime.

"Ready?" The doctor's voice pierced the fog in my brain.

No.

"Bye, baby," Principal Matthews murmured.

I leaned my forehead against the windowpane and shut my eyes, and my mind, and every other sense I owned.

Epilogue

It has been three weeks since Jaime stopped existing. Three weeks during which I find myself driving toward his house on autopilot before I have to turn the car around. I haven't heard from Cora or Principal Matthews. My heart feels like it's made of lead, yet it keeps tearing as though it's made of paper. I don't know how long this feeling will last. Grams tells me it becomes easier. I want to believe her, but right now, it hasn't gotten easier.

Today is my birthday. I don't want to celebrate, but Owen, Gabe, and my parents are insisting I do. That's how I end up at the Modleys' mansion, the star of a party I didn't feel like attending. I stand alone in the middle of eighty people. I receive hugs for which I stay rigid. Even Amanda comes up to me to tell me how sorry she is about the rumor and the breakup. She doesn't know about Jaime. Or maybe she does. We don't speak about it.

God, it sucks, or rather, *God sucks*.

I stare at the cuff links the Wolf slipped inside my pocket during our award ceremony. They gleam back at me like rat eyes. "I think I'm going to head home," I tell my friends.

"No way!" Owen and Gabe say in unison.

Owen knows everything now.

"Mel's friend has the hots for you," he says.

Gabe slugs his shoulder and shoots him a look.

"What? The kid would've wanted Duke to have some fun."

Gabe keeps glaring.

"Owen's right," I say, my voice toneless. "It's just a little—" I'm about to say "soon," but the word dies in my throat when I spot the person standing by the entrance.

I blink. Cora can't be real. She would never come to a gathering like this. Yet she stands there, across the room from me, very real, wearing the T-shirt I gave Jaime. It's so short on her I can see her belly button. Something shines in it. I never knew she had a piercing there. It's the only one on her body tonight. Her skin's tanned again, her cheeks a tad fuller, her lips red.

I navigate through the warm bodies around me, accelerating when I spot how lost she seems. I press people away, step on feet, knock over drinks. Even though I'm getting closer, I feel like I'm getting farther. But I can smell the roses twirling in the air around me, filling the spaces in my chest that feel hollow. And then I'm there, standing in front of her, and she's tipped her head up. For slow, soundless seconds, we stare as though we've forgotten what the other looks like.

"Happy birthday," she says, and hands me a gift-wrapped box. Her nose wrinkles. "Was Owen's present beer-scented cologne?"

I hear laughter and realize it's mine. I want to ask her how she's been, but I don't want to cloud the moment, so I tenderly rip the stripy paper. My heart is catapulted against my ribcage when I discover that it's our story, bound like a real book. I think she made it herself because the cover resembles a ransom note, with letters cut out of magazines and stuck haphazardly together. I run my finger over the first word they form. *Ghostboy.*

"Did you read it?" I ask her.

"Had to." She shrugs and looks down at her beaten-up

Converses. "You left with the computer file, so I needed to type the whole damn thing."

I chuckle. "Did you like it?"

She raises her face back up to mine and nods. "It sounded like Jaime." A breath whistles past the thin divide of her mouth. "I never knew how worried he was about me."

"He loved you. We worry about the people we love." I want to tell her how worried I was about her these last few weeks, but that would be admitting I love her. I'm ready to say it, but is she ready to hear it?

"Flip to the next-to-last page," she says.

I turn my attention to the book. My chest constricts as I read that Ghostboy stays a ghost after his sister is saved, and floats up to the sky to find his mother—his last mission.

"Nice ending," I said.

She snorts softly. "I added *two* lines."

"They're good lines. It's exactly how Jaime would've finished it."

She beams and it shreds my heart into more pieces. "I hope Jaime found Mom," she says.

"I'm sure he did."

Her tongue moistens her lips. She seems nervous all of a sudden. "Turn the page, Meyer."

"There's more?"

"There's always more," she says.

As I read, the pieces of my heart swirl in a frenzy, as though blasted by a fan. They find the edges that linked them and bind again. "So the Duke and Chameleon end up together."

"It was Jaime's idea." She shifts from one foot to the other. "He wanted a happy ending. And apparently a kiss makes everyone happy."

I move closer. There's nearly no space between our bodies anymore. "Would it make you happy?"

"Don't make me say it," she says. "I'll never forgive you if you make me say it."

I grin. "Is it because I'm finally your age?"

"Yes."

"Will you break up with me each time you turn a year older?"

"Possibly," she says.

I chuckle, but then grow serious and close the book. "Does the real Duke get to kiss the real Chameleon now?"

She lifts her hands to my chest, gathers my T-shirt in her fingers, and rocks up onto her toes. Still clutching *Ghostboy*, I wrap my arms around Cora and meet her halfway for the sort of kiss that entire novels are written about.

Maybe I'll write our love story next.

For Jaime.

An aspiring teenage singer finds herself playing a different tune when she falls for a boy who could jeopardize her future dreams in Olivia Wildenstein's romantic YA novel, *Not Another Love Song*.

Angie has studied music her entire life, nurturing her talent as a singer. Now a high school senior, she has an opportunity to break into Nashville's music scene via a songwriting competition launched by her idol, Mona Stone. Discouraged by her mother, who wishes Angie would set more realistic life goals, she nonetheless pours her heart and soul into creating a song worthy of Mona.

But Angie's mother is the least of her concerns after she meets Reedwood High's newest transfer student, Ten. With his endless collection of graphic tees, his infuriating attitude, smoldering good looks, and endearing little sister, Ten toys with the rhythm of Angie's heart.

She's never desired anything but success until Ten entered her life. Now she wants to be with him *and* to be a songwriter for Mona Stone, but she can't have both.

And picking one means losing the other.

Available wherever books are sold.

Acknowledgments

There are many people I want to thank for helping me complete *Ghostboy*.

My older sister. For the hours, days, months she spent correcting and recorrecting my work. She pushed me when all I wanted was to give up. Without her encouragement and praise, I would never have dared share my story with others. Vee, I owe you so much more than an acknowledgement on the back of a book.

My beta readers—you know who you are. For the precious time they spent poring over my manuscript, and for the effort they put into untangling my plot points and sharpening my characters.

My writer friends. For helping me find and shape my voice, and invigorating me when my hope of becoming a true author faltered.

My family. For always believing in me and supporting me.

My children. For inspiring me.

My husband. For loving me.

YA PARANORMAL ROMANCE

The Lost Clan series

ROSE PETAL GRAVES

ROWAN WOOD LEGENDS

RISING SILVER MIST

RAGING RIVAL HEARTS

RECKLESS CRUEL HEIRS

A Pack of Blood and Lies series

A PACK OF BLOOD AND LIES

A PACK OF VOWS AND TEARS

A PACK OF LOVE AND HATE

Angels of Elysium series

FEATHER

CELESTIAL

YA CONTEMPORARY ROMANCE

GHOSTBOY, CHAMELEON & THE DUKE OF GRAFFITI

NOT ANOTHER LOVE SONG

YA ROMANTIC SUSPENSE

Masterful series

THE MASTERKEY

THE MASTERPIECERS

THE MASTERMINDS

About the Author

USA TODAY BESTSELLING author Olivia Wildenstein grew up in New York City, the daughter of a French father and a Swedish mother. She chose Brown University to complete her undergraduate studies and earned a bachelor's in comparative literature. After designing jewelry for a few years, Wildenstein traded in her tools for a laptop computer.

When she's not writing, she's psychoanalyzing everyone she meets (Yes. Everyone.), baking up a storm, and attempting to arrive on time at her children's school.

Wildenstein lives with her husband and three children in Geneva, Switzerland, where she's an active member of the writing community.

For more information
www.oliviawildenstein.com
press@oliviawildenstein.com